Between Two Worlds

Sandra Yohe

Contents

Chapter 1

I T HAPPENED JUST like that.

Being the type of person who never believed that "love at first sight" existed, I thought the well-known saying should have actually been "attraction at first sight".

Us girls—maybe some boys—all wished for our happily ever after's like the fairy tales. But, what do we get? That "love at first sight" just ended up being another heartbreak to tell.

However, this wasn't what this was about.

To explain my life in a succinct manner, it was average but satisfying. I was part of a happy family of four that happened to own a small, yet stuck in a busy street market. Lockhart's Pantry sold all your everyday necessities from fresh vegetables to tooth paste.

But, this particular day at the market changed everything.

Doing my usual routine, I was fixing up the snack and candy aisle, which usually sold out fast by the middle school students. Sadly, today wasn't our best day. The business has been slow for the past five hours, and I was stuck here until closing.

My younger brother, Mason, was waiting outside for another weekly delivery. Mason was on the verge of graduating high school. He was still at the crossroads on deciding what he wanted to do with his life. As much as I would encourage and love to see the boy in college, I wasn't exactly a poster image since college was the least of my worries, being at the tender age of twenty. I had no complaints though; I was content with what I had right now.

Yawning lazily, I glanced up at the store clock down the aisle, and it was 3pm. The time the delivery would arrive. As if its arrival were rehearsed, I heard the obnoxious noise of the truck outside.

Staying in my crouched position, I didn't bother to move because Mason could take care of it. Knowing him, he always took our market seriously.

However, I may have given him premature praise at the time.

Mason poked his head from the aisle I was in. A big, taunting grin grew on his face once he saw my bored expression.

"Maisie, get ready for more torture!" he snickered out.

Usually, I'd be up and running saying the words, "I'll get you, squirt!", but like I said, today was not the day.

So I thought.

Brushing off his taunt, I settled my focus back on the box of chocolate puffs I had to sort out. After a few minutes, I realized that Mason wasn't strutting his way here, carrying a bunch of rather lightweight boxes while calling himself "Mr. Macho Man". Growing curious, I walked towards the end of the aisle before noticing two figures. The one who had his back facing me was my brother. We shared the same dark brown hair and the way his short hair was tousled around explained it. The other one was the delivery guy.

Except, he wasn't your average delivery boy.

Not only did he appear my age, but when did delivery guys wear nice clothing and look like that?

The delivery boy was over-presentable wearing a nicely fit suit. He looked like something out of a fashion magazine, especially with his height. The delivery boy didn't notice my presence, and my eyes couldn't digest that he was actually captivating me.

His facial features were alluring from those sparkling, glacial blue eyes to his strong nose and chiseled jawline. The way his medium cut textured black hair complimented his eyes were simply gravitating.

Oh, the irony.

This was very unlike me. This was something my best friend, Vanessa Montgomery, would feel. It had to be because of her. Vanessa's "attraction" was rubbing onto me.

Unable to help myself, I was still peeking behind the aisle. Call it spying, but I considered it watching for business purposes. Something was definitely off though. The delivery boy looked completely lost with the clipboard he was holding. I assumed that it was his first day. He may want to drop the fancy suit and switch it out for some khaki button ups and cargo pants.

Mason's low-pitch voice projected loud enough for me to hear. He said, "The invoice... do you have it?"

After a moment, the delivery boy finally caught on and handed the paperwork to my younger brother. It appeared as though he was embarrassed because of the way he laughed. My eyes widened seeing the delivery boy's lips stretch into a charming smile. Mason let out a shrug, telling him that it was cool. The two began talking, but I had no clue what it was about.

When Mason turned towards my direction, he caught me. Mason was definitely going to say something about his older sister being a stalker.

Actually, I didn't care at the time — maybe.

It was a wave of relief knowing that the delivery boy was completely oblivious about me being here. Once Mason finished signing the invoice, the delivery boy waved a short goodbye. Before all of that, I was proven wrong, and the delivery boy's icy blue eyes jumped at mine momentarily.

He noticed, he saw!

I ducked down and paced to the end of the aisle, hoping that the delivery boy was long gone. As soon as a minute or two passed, I casually brought myself up the aisle, only to find my younger brother. Mason stood by the main counter, opening a packet of gummy candy. His round brown eyes caught sight of mine, and he popped some candy into his mouth.

"Maisie, what happened to you earlier?"

Playing with the sleeve of my red cardigan, I said, "I had to make room for the new delivery."

Mason, my sweet eighteen-year-old brother, scoffed in disbelief and said, "Really? I bet you had the hots for that guy, didn't you?"

I rolled my eyes. "Mason, just help me move the boxes please."

He shrugged, nodding his head. "Sure..." Then, his mocking eyes looked back up at mine. "I bet you want to know what his name is."

Damn it, I hated when he did that to me.

Gulping down, I tried my best to play it cool and focused on the packages. "No, I don't... okay, I might."

Mason made that "ah-ha!" kind of face soon after and pointed at me.

He guffawed, jumping slightly. "I knew it! Wait till Mom and Pops hear this! They will be so happy to know that Maisie finally caught her eyes on a boy!"

You may think that Mason sounded so adorable. Unfortunately, whenever he acted so, he was usually sarcastic and on the bridge of annoyance. Despite that, every single word Mason was saying was true. I made sure my expression was dull during his whole jumping spree.

Mason seemed to notice and cleared his throat. "What's wrong with you, Maisie? I bet you don't realize it, but he will come every week for the delivery."

He added emphasis on the word "delivery", making it sound more like "deliveryyy".

Running my fingers through my long hair, I pursed my lips and declared, "Stop talking nonsense. Now help me move these boxes!"

Mason clamped his mouth shut after.

As we carried the boxes to the middle aisle, I muttered under my breath, "So, do you know what his name is?"

Another chuckle came out of his mouth, and he made that "shush" sign with his index finger.

Mason gave me a mischievous look and said, "Why don't you find out next time?"

I gave him a little push to the side, enough to a point where it didn't look like I was hurting him. Regardless, it seemed like I finally had something to look forward to every delivery day.

Chapter 2

R EMEMBER HOW MASON said that the particular delivery boy would show up every week now?

Well, turned out he was wrong.

The delivery boy never returned to our market. It was just the same old, greasy looking man who would stare at me until he was finished with the delivery. The interaction was just plain creepy.

It was like this for the past month.

I couldn't believe how every Wednesday I would stand outside the market doors, anticipating for the delivery boy to come, and how I'd be able to finally talk to him. Mason was no help. He would always tease me into thinking that he knew what the delivery boy's name was. At first, I actually believed him. He made me do the dishes for nothing.

"Earth to Maisie!"

Glancing up, it was my ever-perky best friend, Vanessa Montgomery.

She angled her curious face as I stared dumbfounded by the cashier. We've been best of friends since the first grade because Vanessa wanted to share her beloved animal crackers with me.

Shaking my previous thoughts away, I smiled softly and said, "Hey, what brings you here?"

Vanessa's voice raised an octave from excitement as she pulled her honey brown hair behind her ear. "Maisie, you have a lot of explaining to do. I was calling you, but no answer! I even had to call Mason…"

Her voice trailed off in my mind as I giggled mentally to myself.

It was four years ago when Mason told me he had legit feelings for Vanessa. I laughed for a good ten minutes until I noticed how serious the kid actually was. It was a little secret I've kept from Vanessa because I knew how embarrassed Mason would get whenever she was around. The good thing was that Vanessa was completely oblivious to all of this.

"Did you hear me?" Vanessa asked, catching my absent-mind again.

I blinked. "What did you say?"

Her cheekbones lifted as she said, "It's me and Jason's three month anniversary today!"

Unlike me, Vanessa was currently with her thirteenth boyfriend. Out of all her boyfriends, not one had officially taken her first kiss.

Impossible, you might say?

When Vanessa was in a relationship, she had strict limits. Knowing guys these days, they broke up with her easily because to them, it wasn't all about holding hands—if you caught my drift. Nothing too extreme, she would tell me. Vanessa mentioned that she would know when the right boy came along to rightfully give her that perfect first kiss.

Jason was her most recent boyfriend. They met when they literally stumbled into each other the time Vanessa and I went to Love Light Café. Call it destiny, but I could rebuttal that. Jason was the type of person who was nice and humble at first, but after a while, he tended to get a little comfortable and evolved into this controlling monster.

I never told Vanessa that though. She was head over heels for him.

I forced a smile. "That's great. Do you two have any plans?"

Vanessa tapped her fingers against the counter and said happily, "Of course! He's taking me to Iridescent."

Of course, the bastard would take her to a fancy restaurant.

After ringing up a customer, who looked irritated hearing the two of us chat, I turned my attention back to Vanessa. She was deciding on what she should wear.

I placed the money into the cash register and said, "You have so much to choose from. Anything will look good."

Vanessa sighed out dramatically. "It's so hard to decide! Want to go shopping?"

This was an addiction we both shared, but I had to control the temptation at the moment.

Leaning against the counter, I smiled sadly. "I can't. I'm the only one here right now."

She nodded, understanding. Out of the blue, Vanessa's bright green eyes flashed back at me and asked, "Maisie, whatever happened to that delivery boy you were talking about?"

"I don't know, probably long gone."

"Don't say that. He never showed up? What if something happened to him?"

A sudden rush of worry ran across Vanessa's face making me laugh.

I shook my head and said, "Don't be silly, Vanessa. I'm sure he got promoted to a better job."

Vanessa looked at me in doubt. "No! That delivery boy will show up. I mean this is the first time you actually felt an attraction. That's like finding gold right there!"

Oh, the word "attraction".

When Mason gossiped to my parents about the delivery boy, they almost didn't believe Mason. They thought Mason was imagining things. Pops looked at me with shocked eyes and said these exact words, "A boy caught your attention today?".

However, Mom was beyond words. She was completely breathless about what came out of Mason's mouth. It reminded me of the time Mason first said the word "shit" when he was ten—I swear that he didn't get that from me. Anyway, Mom had been trying for ages to hook me up with the sons of mothers she usually spoke to at the market. Every attempt failed, which I was quite proud to say.

When I told Vanessa, she became delirious. During all the years we had been friends, I never really paid attention to the boys at our school. Yes, there were a couple cute boys here and there, but I just never found myself feeling that "attraction". Now, all of a sudden, I found a boy who gave me the "attraction". To make it all better, it turned out to be a delivery boy.

I finally replied, "Yeah, I guess. I think it's a once in a lifetime kind of thing."

Vanessa teased, "Tsk, you should believe in love!"

Love was too much of a word. I loved my family and friends, but that was all I could really love.

Vanessa took a glance at her phone before her green eyes widened in surprise. "Oh no! It's already five? I got to go, Maisie. I'll call you later, okay?"

Noticing her panicked reaction, I gave her a smile to ease up. "You don't have to. Just go and have a good time, okay? Tell me how it goes tomorrow."

Vanessa looked at me with a grateful smile and pinched my cheeks. "I'm so lucky to have a best friend like you!"

I gave her a pointed look, but she only laughed.

Once Vanessa left, it was lonely again. There were a few customers here and there. Most of the time, I was having endless staring contests with the wall. Unfortunately, the wall won every time. I wondered why. I spent the following hours organizing the market since Mason did such a bad job at it.

After finishing up the first and middle aisle, I was just about ready to walk towards the next one until I saw a familiar someone open the store door.

It was Vanessa's boyfriend, Jason. I glanced down at my watch, and it was nearing eight. Jason was already making his way towards me.

Confused, I asked, "What are you doing here?"

Jason wasn't in date attire—well, clothes that you would wear to a fancy place like Iridescent. It was just a simple tee and jeans, like he was going to do some grocery shopping.

Jason cleared his throat and said, "I need to tell you something."

Oh please, don't say something stupid. Please nothing stupid.

"Fine... what?"

He managed to jumble in one sentence. "Vanessa probably told you that it was our anniversary today... Well, I'm going to break up with her."

Blinking a few times, I raised my eyebrows and said, "You're going to... what! Why are you telling me this?"

Jason moved a step back from my sudden outburst as he stuttered out, "You're her best friend. It would be better if you told her instead of me."

This had to be some sick joke.

That jerk!

I knew something was up with him.

I massaged my temples, trying to control my uprising anger. "You know that's not how it's supposed to be, right?"

The idiot stared at me blankly and didn't know what to say.

Losing patience, I shouted through gritted teeth, "You know what, you really are a fucking jerk! I can't believe you right now. If you were a real man, you'd grow some and say it to her. You think doing this will make it all better? Well, you're wrong, you asshole!"

Jason continued to stand still, and nothing came out of his mouth. He was guilty, and we both knew it. What I didn't know was, when I turned around to what Jason was staring at the whole time, my stomach would twist at the sight.

It was Vanessa.

My best friend was all dressed up, just standing a few feet away from us. The distance was enough to hear everything. Vanessa's face grew pale.

Well, what a beautiful position to be in right now.

Chapter 3

THIS SURE ADDED the cherry to an ice cream sundae, didn't it?

Vanessa's boyfriend, Jason, did not tell me that he was going to break up with her—my own best friend.

To make matters worse, Vanessa was right here standing before us.

This was definitely something new.

Who in their right mind would tell their girlfriend's best friend to do the break up for him?

From what I saw, Vanessa inhaled deeply to take everything in. She must have heard from the very beginning. My palms started to get all sweaty due to the worry that Vanessa might burst into tears because of this idiot. Speaking of the idiot—I meant Jason—he was completely in shock. He thought he could get away from telling her.

Jason's voice shook as his blue eyes stared at Vanessa. "You... heard?"

Vanessa scoffed from disgust and said, "First, you blow me off. Then when I come to see my best friend, I find you here, telling her that you're breaking up with me?"

The idiot was keeping his voice sweet and gentle, saying how sorry he was for everything. Someone should give this guy the Worst Actor of the Universe award. Despite Vanessa fighting her tears, she pushed him away.

All of a sudden, Vanessa raged, "You're... Ugh! You even tried to tell Maisie to do the break up for you?" She frowned, the green in her eyes deepening. "You're hopeless, Jason. You're nothing but an asshole. I'll be the one to say that we're over. We're over."

The harsh words caused Jason's concerned facial expression to drop into distortion. He kept his chin up high and tried to shrug it off like it didn't matter. Jerk. He didn't even say anything in return as he tried walking out of the market coolly.

"Hey, Jason!" I yelled before he could fully step out of the market.

Jason turned, probably expecting me to say something, but no.

SPLAT!

Two fresh—yet wasted—eggs landed right onto Jason's face. The slimy egg whites and cracked yolk rushed down that cocky face. Jason transitioned into a tomato red color, growing infuriated. It was hilarious. Even Vanessa cracked a laugh despite the tears that were welling up in her eyes. Shoving Jason out of the market, he was still speechless.

I said, "The next time you mess with my best friend, it won't be just eggs. It'll be worse! Get out!"

Jason reached to wipe his face, and it sounded like he whimpered.

Being the tough guy he was though, Jason raised a clenched fist and said, "Maisie, I'll get you for this! You little-"

SPLAT!

Another egg was thrown at Jason.

This time, it was from Vanessa.

The egg landed perfectly into his large mouth. Vanessa always had great aim since Physical Education. This made Jason choke a bit. Well, when you had a whole egg in your mouth, you could only imagine. He spat the egg out.

Vanessa's eyes were dead on him, and her voice was sharp like needles. "Don't you ever think about insulting my best friend like that. Get out of here."

And finally, the egg-yolked jerk walked away miserably.

When I took a look at Vanessa, her once strong face was now tearing with emotion. Her lower lip started to quiver, and I quickly gave her a hug.

I said, "It's okay, Vanessa. Jason's an asshole. Forget about him."

Vanessa didn't reply but cried into my shoulder. Patting her back, I motioned her to sit down inside the market.

She muttered through her sobbing, "I don't know what I did wrong!"

Sitting beside her, I handed her a box of tissues and stroked her hair. Looking at her sincerely, I said, "You didn't do anything wrong. I'm sure of it."

"Why then... why couldn't he just tell me?" Vanessa cried out as she wiped her nose furiously.

Sighing, I grabbed a tissue to wipe the tears and said, "He was the one who made the mistake. You know why he couldn't just tell you? Because he's nothing but a coward."

Vanessa tried her best to stop her crying by taking deep inhales, but the poor girl was in so much pain. Glancing at her outfit, she was wearing a shimmery knee length silver dress. It suited her so well, and her honey brown hair was perfectly curled and bouncy. Jason was going to pay.

It took seven boxes of tissue and two bags of Vanessa's favorite orange-crème candy to calm her down a bit. Just seeing her in this state made me tear up. I never wanted to see my best friend hurt again.

Vanessa's reddened eyes blinked, and she softly laughed. "I'm stupid, aren't I? Maisie, tell me it's all my fault."

Shaking my head, I said, "No, you're Vanessa Montgomery. The only girl I know who can put up with anything."

We both giggled before Vanessa started to hiccup. She grabbed another tissue to wipe her shadowed green eyes.

Through a sigh, her shoulders dropped and said, "I think I'm done with boys."

Suddenly, Mason came walking into the store with his trusty guitar in hand. His "not so serious" band practice must have been over. My younger brother always had a strong passion for music. When he caught sight of the both of us, he stopped on the soles of his shoes.

Mason's brown eyes widened and said, "Whoa, what happened?"

"Well—" I was beginning to say something until Mason started shaking his head.

He walked over to Vanessa's side and clarified, "Not you. I'm talking to Vanessa."

He would say something like that.

Vanessa glanced up at Mason and smiled sadly. She tried keeping her voice leveled. "It's nothing."

Mason had his hands on his knees and examined her. His love for her was definitely showing.

He said toughly, making me suppress my laughter, "Did someone hurt you?"

Vanessa blinked away, not being able to answer. Mason gave me a long pleading look.

I sighed in defeat. "It's Jason. He... broke up with her."

The look on Mason's face dropped, and I could see his fists clenching together. "Vanessa, I swear to you, I will beat the crap out of Jason once I see him. He'll regret doing this to you!"

The determination that was coming off Mason made Vanessa brighten up a bit. A smile grew on her pale lips. We all started laughing after that. Soon after, Mason got his guitar and dedicated a heartwarming song to her. His soothing voice and addictive strumming definitely relaxed the once tensed atmosphere. I was grateful that Mason came at the right time.

Once Vanessa regained her stability, we all stood outside the store ready to part ways. The cool wind gently passed, making a chill run up my spine.

Vanessa said, "Thank you guys for everything. I don't know what would have happened if you guys weren't here."

Giving her a hug goodbye, I reassured her, "You know, I'll always be there for you."

Vanessa gave me a bigger smile and nodded her head in agreement. "Me too!"

My best friend pulled me into a tighter hug, reaching to a point where I couldn't breathe.

Before she headed to her car, Vanessa cupped her hands and said, "Maisie! I'm going on a boy break. No more boys for me!"

I gave her a thumbs-up but snickered at the side.

That wasn't going to happen.

Two weeks has passed since Vanessa's sudden break up with Jason. Things were a lot better. Our sales suddenly boomed. It was as if people finally decided to do some grocery shopping. The downside of all the goodness was the fact that the delivery boy never came back. The image of him in my mind was gradually blurring. Maybe he really wasn't the one.

False attraction was what I should call it.

Instead of being at Lockhart's Pantry, I was having lunch with Vanessa. She called me last minute because she had very important news to tell me. I quoted her on that. It must be important since she was offering to buy me food as well.

Pulling up to the nearest curb, I was meeting her at Brightside Café. I spotted her sitting in one of the tables by the window. It was our favorite seats. Her eyes were glancing around, probably in search of me. Getting out of my car, I ran inside the moment Vanessa started waving her hands around, motioning me to hurry in.

Taking a seat, regret started to overtake me. I grabbed a glass of water before chugging it down from exhaustion. I probably looked like a lunatic running inside but I was dead tired.

After catching my breath, I asked, "Hey, so what's the news?"

Vanessa seemed unsure and hesitated, "You'll listen to me all the way, right?"

Nodding my head, I hoped that it wasn't anything bad. My heart raced, wondering of all the possibilities. What if Vanessa had some type of disease or randomly got pregnant or something life changing at her age?

She finally explained, "Alright, so you know how I said I'm done with boys? Well, I am. I'm really not looking for anyone. But, this past week at school, I've been meeting up with this boy. He just, like, took me away! I never really knew about him, but it turns out his family owns this huge business. I mean, if he has such a big name, how come I never knew? Anyway, he's super sweet, and he's such a cutie. So as I was saying, he asked me to go out and have dinner with him."

Disappointed yet very relieved, I smiled. "I'm happy for you, Vanessa. But, are you ready to move on?"

She nodded surely and said, "I want to give him a shot. He seems different, but there's... something else."

Oh no. Please not some guy who has kids (or something along those lines).

"It's a double date. Me and him and his cousin. But, I sort of set you up with his cousin."

I nearly choked on the stolen glass of water from Vanessa. "You did what!"

Vanessa nodded again. "I know, I feel so bad for doing this, but it was kind of the only way it could happen. He told me that his cousin is really nice though! You'll love him."

This couldn't be happening. As far as dates went, especially blind dates, they never turned out right.

I repeat, never.

Giving Vanessa a terrified look, I said, "You can't be serious."

Vanessa clasped her hands together and pleaded, "Maisie, please do it for me! I owe you my life after this!"

I really did hope this guy she was so determined to go on a date with was worth it.

I sighed, nodding. "Yeah, of course I'll do it for you. But, I thought you were taking a boy break."

Her green eyes dropped momentarily until she exclaimed, "I know, but it's different this time. I'm reborn once again!"

Chapter 4

HOW DID I get into this situation again?

Here I was, getting ready for my blind date, which was prearranged by my best friend. Mason was excitedly knocking on my door, asking if I was ready. I swore that boy was more pumped for this date than I was.

Setting down the curling iron, I examined my loose waves. It matched well with the ivory three-fourths sleeve dress. Just a natural yet presentable make up was my kind of deal. Grabbing my black heels from my closet, I opened my bedroom door and found my family standing before me with eager eyes. Scared, I jumped from surprise.

Mom clapped her hands at the sight of me and said, "Our Maisie is going on a date tonight! Isn't this such good news, honey?"

Pops, who didn't mind what was going on, nodded his head. "Of course. Maisie, you look beautiful."

Mason smiled enthusiastically in agreement.

It was like they wanted me to get with someone, get married, and leave them already. To be completely honest, it did feel nice to dress up for an occasion. It has been a while since I did something like this. We all walked to the living room where I was just about ready to head out and meet with Vanessa and the boys.

My family watched me with such happy expressions that it caused me to stifle a laugh. Mom pulled me into a hug, and I soon felt Pops and Mason surround me. Was this really such good news to them? I smiled before giving my parents a kiss goodbye. As I made my way out, Mason was standing by the door, holding it open. He could be a sweetheart, I admit. Mason had such a wide smile on that even he knew it was goofy looking.

He winked and said, "Knock him dead, Maisie!"

I laughed, trying to reach up and ruffle his hair.

As I made my way out of our cozy one story home, I came to some sort of a conclusion. Maybe the reason why my family was so energetic about tonight was because they were actually going somewhere fun without me. That had to be it. Once I finished adjusting my heels, I glanced up and found something that I wasn't expecting.

A limousine.

Looking left to right, I wondered if that limousine was for me.

At that moment, a recognizable figure came out of the stretched vehicle. It was Vanessa. This had to be Vanessa's guy and cousin's ride.

You were probably wondering why I was classifying the two as "Vanessa's guy" and "cousin".

The thing was, I actually didn't know their names. Vanessa never told me, and I never really bothered to ask her. My mistake. My best friend soon came towards me. She was absolutely radiant, wearing a strapless gold knee-length dress. I smiled, giving her a small wave.

Vanessa said, "Maisie, look at you! You're gorgeous!"

A wave of embarrassment ran across my face, and I hesitantly walked next to her.

I complimented as well, "Vanessa, you look absolutely stunning yourself."

She looked at me with grateful eyes and said, "Thank you so much for coming. You don't know how much this means to me."

Telling her for the thousandth time that she didn't have to say her thanks, I followed her into the limousine. Once I went inside, I nearly collapsed. The inside was luxurious. The red velvet seats were aligned along the walls of the limo. There were two refrigerators in the front and back and mini flat screen TVs in every angle possible. There were buttons everywhere. Who knew what each one activated?

Something was wrong though. The limousine was empty except for the driver in the front.

I thought loudly, "Where are they?"

"Oh, they're already there," Vanessa said casually.

"So, wait. You're saying they're waiting for us?"

Vanessa sat on my left side and motioned at the driver, Mr. Johnson, to start driving. She pulled onto her seat belt. "I told them that you take a long time getting ready, so they said it'll be good to just meet at the restaurant."

I quickly flipped my head at her. "Vanessa! You're kidding me, right?"

Vanessa blinked and finally caught on. "Oh! You're worried about me telling them that? Don't worry about it. All guys know girls take a while when they are getting ready for dates."

Even though she apologized, I smiled and shrugged it off. Still, I hated having people wait for me. After a fifteen-minute ride, the limousine came to a stop while Vanessa and I were pressing all the buttons in the back. The car door opened, and it was Mr. Johnson. Vanessa stepped out, followed by me, and we both thanked him for a pleasant ride. I almost didn't want to leave.

As we fixed our dresses, I took a good look at the place. It was a hotel, called Legends.

Vanessa pulled onto my hand and said, "The restaurant is a couple floors up. David told me its family owned and absolutely delicious."

Before I could say anything, I found myself going inside Legends in a flash as I tried catching up to Vanessa. I wasn't even able to take in how it actually look liked. All I remember was bright—not neon bright, but white bright and open feeling. Then, I was in an elevator. The two of us stood there waiting for the elevator to hit the right floor.

"So, his name is David?"

Vanessa tilted her head at me as if I should have known. Her eyebrows rose.

She said, "I didn't tell you?"

I shook my head, and she gasped. Her green eyes widened.

"I can't believe I didn't tell you! Here you are going on a double date with me, and you don't even know their names! I'm horrible. Okay, so the guy I'm talking to is David Valentino, and his cousin is Logan."

Valentino?

That was an interesting last name and sounded oddly familiar.

The elevator door made a ding, and it rapidly opened. I was expecting something like us actually walking out and heading into a restaurant. Instead, the elevator automatically welcomed us to the interior of the restaurant. Vanessa motioned me to follow her, but it was hard to look where I was walking since the place was amazing. This whole entire floor was dedicated to the restaurant, Symphony's Fine Dining.

Symphony's was, in one word, fancy.

The people dining here were all high class—dressed up and ate so properly. I knew it was bad to stare, but this was my first time eating at such a restaurant. My typical place would be a nearby hamburger joint down the street of the market. When I snapped out of it, I looked straight ahead and noticed two boys right in front of me.

Both of them were tall, nicely postured, and well groomed. They wore nicely fitted suits. And, thank the heavens for decent hairstyles.

"This is my best friend, Maisie Lockhart," I heard Vanessa announce.

The boy, who was a bit taller, gave me a friendly look and took his hand out for a handshake. This had to be David. To be honest, he had the charm. I could understand why Vanessa took a liking in him. His facial structure was well defined, along with his ebony colored hair nicely styled up. Those midnight blue eyes stood out perfectly. Knowing Vanessa, she easily fell for boys with eyes worth looking at.

"Vanessa said a lot about you. I'm David Valentino. It's good to finally meet you."

Replying back with a smile, I told him the same thing as I shook his hand.

Vanessa then introduced, "Maisie, this is David's cousin, Logan Valentino."

Now putting my attention to my date, Logan almost gave me a blurry image of the delivery boy. It was peculiar, yet I had the same feeling when I saw David too.

Logan was just as good-looking, maybe even cuter—but I kept that to myself. He had those same dark blue eyes and jet-black hair, which probably ran in the family. He grinned at me, and I was shocked at how captivating his smile was. Logan revealed a row of shiny, white teeth. His voice was somewhat lighter than David's.

"Nice to meet you. I guess you know who I am already."

Through his grinning, I heard him chuckle. I couldn't help but laugh along. Soon, the circle of four laughed. We were then escorted to sit in probably the best seat of the house. It was its own room with a table large enough to feed triple our party of four. A large diamond chandelier hung right above it. The colors of Symphony's were splashes of dark reds and golds, giving off a warm feeling. Our waitress gave us a welcoming smile as she handed us the menus.

The elder lady slightly teased. "Well, I rarely see you boys here. But, I see what the occasion is."

My eyes made a sharp turn to see their reaction. David lowered his head. Was he nervous?

Logan grinned. "Dinner with new friends."

The waitress gave a pleased smile and left the table for us to decide on our orders. As we were glancing over the menus, I noticed that Vanessa was already bursting in conversation with David. I heard someone chuckle from across.

Logan caught my eyes and smiled. "Shall we get to know each other?"

Embarrassment ran through me, hoping that I didn't give the impression of a snob.

Logan placed his menu down and said, "The thing is, I'm not much of a topic starter."

That caused me to smile.

I laughed gently. "Okay. Well, I'm helping my family run our market. I—I..."

Trying my best to figure out what else to say, I was stumped.

Running my hands through the ends of my curls, I said, "I don't like talking about myself a lot. I'm sure you're more interesting than I am. I heard your family owns a big business."

Logan said, "I'm not interesting. Have you heard of Phoenix Empire, Maisie?"

Phoenix... Phoenix... The more I thought about it, I remembered.

Phoenix Empire was a huge company that was booming with popularity and revenue. They practically owned everything.

Wait a second.

No wonder the last name "Valentino" sounded familiar.

My eyes shot up at Logan, and he nodded. "This hotel right here is family owned. My dad and two uncles are all CEOs of Phoenix Empire. I'm currently in college right now getting into business. So, my life was set in stone since the day I was born."

For some reason, there was something gloomy about the sound of Logan's voice.

He sighed and joked, "See, not really that big, huh?"

Why didn't I say something?

"No, no. It's not like that."

"Oh, what's going on over there?" That was Vanessa's voice.

Looking over at her, Vanessa and David were both staring at the two of us.

Logan's voice was at ease as he explained, "We were joking around, right Maisie?"

Vanessa looked at me with a sly grin, and I shrugged happily. The waitress came back to get our orders, but I wasn't ready. Completely distracted from all the side talk, I saw that the prices in the menu weren't so friendly for the pocket. I gulped down, thinking of resorting to a bowl of soup. That was all I could afford.

"You know, you can order whatever you want. It's on us," someone whispered.

My eyes jumped to see where that was coming from. It was Logan.

Pops would always say to never let people pay because it puts shame to our family name. Sorry, Pops. I ended up ordering the chicken Italian pasta. Sounded very appetizing—and it was.

Once we got our entrees, we managed to squeeze some more talk while we ate. David and Logan were really nice. I could already hint that David had a thing for Vanessa. He was nervous, and it was like he'd always double check before saying something so he wouldn't appear stupid. I guess Vanessa could be right about him.

Before I knew it, our double date was over, and it was time to go. As we all stepped into the elevator, I sighed, calmly realizing that this date wasn't a complete disaster at all. Throughout the time, Vanessa was talking animatedly with David while Logan and I laughed at the sight. The limousine was already waiting for us in the front. I looked at Legends once last time since my next visit wouldn't be until a while—or ever.

Mr. Johnson had the door open already. Glancing over at David and Logan, I gave the two a grateful smile.

I said, "It was nice meeting you two. Thank you for the dinner. It was great."

David nodded and returned with a grin. "Nice meeting you too. I hope to see you around again."

Vanessa and David were bidding each other their farewells, and I gave Logan another smile before heading towards the limo.

"Maisie, wait."

Turning around, I raised my eyebrows. "What is it?"

Logan adjusted his suit and said, "Well... do you think we could see each other again?"

Instantly, there was a rush of blood I felt towards my head.

Don't blush!

It couldn't be helped though.

Flushed in the cheeks, I nodded, not trying to look overly excited. "Sure, just let me know when."

Logan was sweet, and I kind of wanted to know him more.

Delivery boy, who?

I noticed Logan was less tense now, and he smiled in response. Waving a final goodbye to the boys, I met back with Vanessa in the limousine. Shortly after, Mr. Johnson drove off, and Legends grew smaller from the distance.

Vanessa taunted as I buckled myself in, "Well, look what we have here. And you didn't want to go."

Laughing, I shook my head.

Even if that was the case, it looked like things were turning around for once.

Chapter 5

"OH MAISIE, DIDN'T I tell you that David is the one!" Vanessa sighed out as she was in her own little fantasy world.

It had only been a few days since our double date with the Valentino's, and Vanessa still couldn't help but talk about David. He was, so far, on my good list. My best friend took a step towards me as I was leaning against the counter of the market. Vanessa's green eyes glittered happily.

"But Maisie, you don't even know. Ever since that double date, David and I have been seeing each other more. It's so much fun on campus now," suddenly, she stuck her tongue out and said," but it would be much better if we went to school together."

Laughing, I would have been in my third year of college by now. But, there were too many complications.

"Enough about David and me, let's talk about Logan! Have you two been talking?" Vanessa questioned, batting her eyes with interest.

Shrugging, I greeted a customer who just walked in before I said, "Well, no. I haven't had a chance too. I don't know how."

Her jaw dropped as she wagged her index finger. "That's why I gave you his number, and I gave him yours, dummy! Wait, so he hasn't called you?"

It was careless of me to not give my number to Logan that night.

I shook my head and said, "No, he hasn't. He's probably busy with school."

Vanessa tapped her chin and murmured, "You may be right. I remember David saying that there's a huge project due in one of their classes."

Nodding my head, I easily believed that excuse, whether it may be true or not.

She then questioned, "Hold on! What did your parents say? You never told me!"

The sudden flashbacks of me returning home that night ran a chill up my spine. After the pleasant ride back, I entered the house and wasn't expecting to find the three of them wide awake, awaiting my return. I was nearly attacked by questions.

Clearing my throat, I said, "Uh, well, I told them it went great. My parents looked happy. Mom asked who my blind date was, and when I did, Mom looked surprised. Like, she said 'THE Valentino family?' It was kind of weird, but... they told me as long as I had a good time. It seems like Pops and Mom knew who they were."

Vanessa snorted, "Well yeah, they're practically celebrities."

Who knew that I would wind up knowing the next generation of Phoenix Empire?

That same night, Mason did some research about them and was hugely impressed. He even said the following words: "You scored big time, Maisie!"

All of a sudden, my phone started vibrating against the counter top. Checking, it read: Logan Valentino.

Stunned, I blurted out loud, "It's Logan!"

That caught Vanessa's attention. She shouted, "Go answer it!"

Several customers in the store looked at us oddly. My hands were getting all shaky.

I made up a lame excuse, "What... should I say?"

"Just answer it!"

In defeat, I picked up the phone, sounding completely normal with a common hello.

On the other line, Logan's gentle timbre welcomed my ears, "Hey Maisie, how are you? It's been a while. I was wondering if you're busy today? If you are, it's cool. But if not, may we meet up?"

My voice was ever so casual. "Hi Logan, I'm doing good. You? Oh... me, busy?"

My eyes then looked up at Vanessa who was shaking her head violently—it almost made me laugh.

Continuing on, I said, "Oh no, I'm not. Sure, where?"

On my peripheral vision, I could see Vanessa's lips lift into a smile.

Logan said, "That's great. How about whatever is near you? I'll meet you there."

Thinking of a place, I clicked my tongue until Vanessa nudged my side. She mouthed out Brightside Café.

Giving her a grateful look, I suggested, "There's this place called Brightside Café. Does that sound good?"

"Oh yeah, I've heard of it. I'll be heading over there soon, so I'll see you there?"

"Yeah, okay. I'll see you."

Clicking the end call button, I turned my attention back to Vanessa. There was a problem to consider now. How was I going to meet up with Logan if I was the only one here at Lockhart's

Pantry? I immediately noticed Vanessa talking to someone on her phone.

I heard Vanessa request, "Mason, I need you to do me a huge favor."

Of course, she'd ask Mason to watch the store. And of course, he'd do it for Vanessa.

"Thanks for meeting me here. It's great to see you. Anything new with you?"

Here I was, in Brightside Café with Logan Valentino.

It surprised me, knowing that he beat me here even though the café was a block away from the market. I felt a little self-conscious walking inside, noticing that he looked more decent than my market clothes get up. His simple gray shirt was paired with a stylish blazer that complimented his dark washed jeans. Logan had great fashion sense — not to mention his short tousled black hair that showcased his dark blue eyes well.

Getting comfortable with where I was sitting, I smiled and said, "Nothing much, I've just been taking care of the market. And, you?"

Logan let out a sigh. "I've just been with school, all these projects being thrown by the professors. It's stressful along with the family business. Other than that, it's nice to have a break."

I couldn't blame him. I wouldn't be able to juggle all of that either.

The waiter came by with two hot drinks and some really delicious looking pastries. Once the waiter explained what each pastry was and left, Logan slid me the mug.

He said, "I hope you like hazelnut coffee."

I beamed, "I absolutely love hazelnut coffee. It's what I get here."

Logan grinned to his surprise. "Really? It's my first time trying it here. Hopefully it delivers."

I promoted proudly, "Trust me, Brightside Café has the best hazelnut coffee."

We both took a sip, and I noticed a satisfied smile form on Logan's lips.

He nodded after taking in another gulp. "Mm, you're right. Guess this is my new place to get this now."

Letting out a laugh, I couldn't help but tell him that I told him so. Things weren't so awkward anymore. We both ate the famous pastries at Brightside's, and as always, their pastries were made for perfection.

Out of nowhere, Logan asked, "This may come out a little forward, but have you been looking for a job recently?"

Almost choking on a pistachio macaroon, I was lost on how Logan would know such facts.

Until, it hit me.

Vanessa.

After taking a quick gulp of my drink, my eyes gazed over at his direction as I said, "I did, but no luck. I've been busy with the market most of the time."

Logan had his lips pursed as if he was holding back from saying something. His dark blue eyes softened. "Oh, I see. Well, if you're in need of a job, I could help you."

My body almost lifted itself off the chair. I felt a big grin grow across my face and said, "Really, you could do that? That would be amazing!"

It made me wonder if this whole meet up was to help me, but I wasn't complaining. Mom and Pops would be so happy.

Logan smiled. "Remember the restaurant where we ate? I could get you a job there. The manager is looking for someone. I assure you the environment is great and nothing too—"

"Yes, that's fine with me!" I unexpectedly interrupted.

Mr. Handsome, I owe you everything!

His eyes slightly grew from my abrupt reaction, but Logan seemed pleased nonetheless. "Great, so I guess it all works out then. When you're ready, let me know okay?"

I said, "I can start as soon as possible."

Logan raised his left eyebrow and said, "You sure? You don't have to discuss this with your family?"

"No, this will be perfect to help my family out. So, I'm sure they won't mind," I said with a silly wink.

He grinned, nodding accordingly. "Alright, how does tomorrow sound? 11 a.m.?"

Not knowing how to thank Logan Valentino at the moment, I found myself giving him a hug as we both stood up from the chairs. I didn't care about what he was thinking right now.

Logan Valentino just didn't know how much I had to repay him.

If all of this—Vanessa executing the double date, meeting Logan, getting a job—never happened, I'd be stuck in the market expecting some cute delivery boy to show up.

Well, those days were gone.

Also, I wasn't going to see that greasy deliveryman any time soon, so you could just imagine how happy I was. Even though my parents were delighted to hear about my new job, Mom looked a little worried. Maybe it was because I wouldn't see them as much. I promised her that I wouldn't get myself into trouble, and I'd still be the same Maisie Lockhart.

Driving into the parking lot of Legends, I never thought I'd see this elegant hotel so soon. Now, I would have to see this place practically everyday. When I got out of my car, Logan was standing outside the entrance. He looked absolutely charming in that business suit as he waved.

Logan flashed me a grin and said, "You all set, Ms. Lockhart?"

It was like déjavu again, having to walk across the white and open hotel lobby and entering the elevator up the exclusive floor just for Symphony's Fine Dining. There was always a ton of people at Legends. This place must be popular.

Once the elevator rested at the designated floor, the doors slid open. There stood a middle-aged lady with her blonde hair fixed tightly into a bun. She startled me until I realized she must be the manager Logan was talking about.

Logan spoke, "Manager Gray, this is Maisie Lockhart."

Manager Gray presented a welcoming smile and said, "Well, Lockhart looks like you're our new addition to the family. Welcome aboard."

She continued informing me how things operate around Symphony's such as what exactly the waiters and waitresses should and should not do and all that jazz. Staying focused with Manager Gray's words, I felt something slid into my hands. It was a piece of paper. My eyes wandered around to see whom that was from until I realized that Logan wasn't by my side anymore.

Opening the note, it read: Good luck! I'll be back around 6:30. I have a request for you.

I smiled happily at this simple message yet curious for whatever this request was.

Luckily, it looked like I was getting a hang at being a waitress.

After some training and changing into a simple black and white uniform, I tied my brown hair into a ponytail. Manager Gray set me in the front to escort incoming guests and help them start off their meal. What made things a lot easier was how this new job was like working at the market. I saw it as helping a customer to find something that they needed. Manager Gray gave me a good slap in the back, telling me I was a natural at this.

Time quickly passed without my notice, and I found Logan stepping out from the elevator.

Glancing at the clock, I muttered, "It's already 6:30?"

Logan grinned. "So, how is it?"

I told him exactly how it felt. It wasn't bad at all. Manager Gray even complimented how I learned things quicker than others. Happy to hear that I adapted well, Logan then mumbled something close to Manager Gray's ear. In response, she slightly nodded.

Manager Gray glanced over at me and said, "I expect to see your constant hard work. I'll see you again, Lockhart."

After changing back to my comfortable blouse and dark jeans, I bid farewell to my supportive manager as I followed Logan back to the elevator. Once Logan pushed the elevator button, I supported myself against the handrail.

Tilting my head, I questioned, "So, what's this request about?"

There was a slight pause before Logan said, "I'm going to have dinner with my parents and family... and, I'd like you to be there with me."

DING!

The elevator doors slid open.

Before I could even have any reaction or respond to what Logan just said, I became paralyzed with whom I saw from the opened doors. How I hoped my eyes weren't deceiving me.

That particular day rewind and played of that particular person.

Standing there across from me was none other than the delivery boy.

No joke.

Chapter 6

I T WAS HIM.

My delivery boy!

My mind temporarily slipped from reality. That was him. It had to be.

Was I losing my mind?

Watching the delivery boy, it looked like he just came out of the other elevator from the other side and was making his way out. Just like before, he wasn't wearing your everyday delivery uniform. It was the same nicely fitted suit.

Should I go out and follow him?

Wait, what was I thinking? I couldn't just leave Logan.

After several struggles, I finally decided to let go of the delivery boy out in the world. My eyes reverted back to Logan.

Logan asked, concerned from my dazing, "Are you okay, Maisie?"

Finally absorbing what Logan said, I gulped down and realized that I would be meeting and dining with his family. Just the thought of it terrified me. I didn't even think that I was presentable enough for them.

Taking into consideration what Logan has done for me, I quickly nodded and smiled. "I'm fine. And of course, I'd love too."

There was an unexpected grin that flashed upon Logan's face that surprised me. He pointed out the elevator and said, "Thanks Maisie, I appreciate it. Just follow me."

Walking side by side, I carefully searched around the hotel lobby. The delivery boy was nowhere to be seen. I lost my chance.

The voice inside my head taunted, "You chose to stay in the elevator. Don't complain".

Go away, voice.

Taking another look at Legends, I got to see how glamorous it was. Chandeliers were equipped from place to place. The stone tile glittered against the light. Everything appeared so crisp and clean. All the neutral, earthy tones were scattered throughout the hotel, giving it that modern yet high-class feel.

We took another elevator after passing through a glass door with letters smacked in the middle that said "VIP". The elevator we were on had an open view of the entire city. The nightlife of the city glowed from our perspective. Almost pressing my face against the windows, I was in complete awe.

I praised the glowing lights, "Wow, this is beautiful. It's like we're on top of the world."

Logan said in agreement, "It's amazing, isn't it? Sometimes I take this elevator for no reason all the way to the top just to admire the view."

Seeing Logan absolutely mesmerized by the view had me hiding a smile.

This elevator was more technologically advanced than the others. Once we reached our destination, a voice announced, "you are on floor 52" before the doors slid open.

Fancy.

After some walking, Logan halted in front of French doors. As he turned the doorknobs, there was a group of people sitting around an elegant dining table with a magnificent view. The walls away from the French doors were glass windows, exposing the city once more. I couldn't have been more amazed.

Hold on. Was that Vanessa?

She was the first one I noticed. Once she spotted me, she waved with an amused grin on her face. The whole group then turned, and I assumed that must be the Valentino family. The only faces I recognized were Vanessa and David.

Getting closer to the table, I was being stared by dozens of eyes. I politely smiled at them along with Logan.

Logan introduced, "Mother, Father, this is Maisie Lockhart. She's a friend of mine."

Their names were Lucas and Cheryl. They gave me friendly smiles as I greeted them. Next were David's parents, Russell and Tricia, and they responded warmly to my greeting as well. There was another couple sitting to the far right.

The man nodded with a grin, saying his name was Curtis Valentino as I said hello. Unfortunately, his wife wasn't as welcoming. She simply shrugged. Well, that was awkward. I noticed that all the men had the same raven black hair and midnight blue eyes. The Valentino's were a very good-looking family. The ladies all looked like model women.

Taking a seat next to Vanessa, I whispered, "I didn't know you're going to be here."

She slipped in, "I know, me either. Totally last minute."

I couldn't agree more.

Logan's mother had chestnut brown hair that swiftly danced along her shoulders. Cheryl Valentino said as her hazel eyes reached the lady across from her, "Well, looks like we're ready to start. Oh wait, Monica we're missing—"

Monica Valentino was the one who shrugged me off. Her voice was like ice as she flipped her long, straight ebony colored hair aside. "He's always late, but we're in no rush, Cheryl."

David's father tended to lighten the mood up by starting a conversation. It managed to get rid of the awkward atmosphere Monica created. The entire time, Monica was staring at me directly. The way her piercing brown eyes darted made it appear like she recognized me. However, I didn't think that was the case. I have never met nor seen her before.

"Since when did we eat with the workers here?" A soothing male voice broke in.

Everyone's heads turned to find where the source came from. My jaw involuntarily dropped along with my fork once we discovered who that was.

Well shit, it was that delivery boy.

I quickly alerted Vanessa and mouthed out, "That's him!"

She had this confused expression on and grabbed a napkin next to her. "Napkin?"

Bryce's father garnered our attention and said, "Oh, was she the one who needed a job?"

I then heard David instruct, "Bryce, take a seat already."

So, the delivery boy was none other than Bryce Valentino—one of the heirs to Phoenix Empire. He was the son of Curtis and—ice cold—Monica Valentino.

Just my luck.

How could I have not known? I could blame Mason for doing horrible research on the Internet, but it was mostly my fault for not making a connection.

Bryce took a seat across from me, and there was a cunning grin planted across his face. Everything about him bought me back to that day. From his clean-cut textured black hair, to those sky blue eyes, to his masculine facial features.

Bryce's mother took a cold look at him and said, "Where have you been? We've been waiting."

Even though Bryce's father insisted that it was okay and we could finally start dinner, Monica was still not pleased. She abruptly scrunched her nose at me.

Dismissing her husband's words, she added, "Yes, this is something new. We never do these kind of things with workers at this hotel."

David's mother had beautiful wavy, reddish brown hair and a pair of blue-green eyes. She said lightly, "There's nothing wrong with something like that, Monica."

Like before, Monica brushed it off with a shrug. How strange was this turning out?

David's father let out a loose laugh and motioned the waiter to start serving the food. As we got our plates, I noticed the apologetic look Logan gave me. I smiled lightly to encourage him that I would be fine. However, the more I sat here, the more I felt like I shouldn't have came.

I felt Mrs. Monica Valentino's eyes stabbing through me during the dinner. When Bryce's mom finally decided to look back down at her food, Vanessa shot me a what-the-fuck-is-her-problem? look. I forced on another smile to indicate that it wasn't a big deal.

During the dinner, Logan and David's parents would begin talking, but it would shortly die out after Bryce's mother would speak. I was never judgmental towards people upon the first meeting, but I couldn't help it.

What a killjoy.

Luckily, Bryce's father was the complete opposite. I couldn't imagine how Bryce would manage if his father also carried the same attitude as his mother.

My mind couldn't focus on the food no matter how delicious it was. I wanted to look up and see Bryce. I couldn't believe that he was the delivery boy I was ogling about. Turned out he was nothing but rude. It was disappointing. Towards the end of our dinner, I finally glanced up to take in a glass of water.

Instead, I found Bryce staring at me.

His voice came out strong. "You know, you look familiar."

Logan entered in, puzzled, "You've met Maisie?"

Bryce said after he swallowed another bite, "Seems like it unless I'm mistaken."

Since he kind of recognized me, I thought it would do no harm to jog his memory and nodded. "Yeah, weren't you the one who delivered some produce to our market?"

Right after that, Bryce's mother suddenly choked on whatever she was eating. Our eyes went on her, and Bryce's father handed her a glass of water. Once she recovered, Monica Valentino wiped her lips with her napkin.

She roared, "Delivery? What's she talking about, Bryce?"

Bryce's eyes widened at his mother's question.

Oh no.

He shook his head and countered, "Don't know. Never mind, you aren't the same girl."

His mother was in disbelief and said, "Don't you lie to me. Was this during the time you said you'd work on the arrangements, but you didn't? Bryce Valentino—"

Bryce's father interrupted, "Honey, this isn't the right time to be talking about this especially with guests here."

Bryce then cleared his throat and said, "I need to be excused."

His eyes quickly met mine. I now remembered why I was attracted to those eyes. The blue in them were so light compared to the dark hues the other Valentino males had. Bryce used his head to point towards the door.

"You. Come with me."

As I gave an apologetic look to Logan and the Valentino's for the sudden departure, I followed him out the door. Even Vanessa appeared worried for me. A shiver ran up my spine hearing Bryce's mother demand her son to come back as he shut the doors. Her voice was still bouncing off the walls.

In the midst of all of this, Bryce suddenly surrounded me. My back was against the wall as the palms of his hands were pushing the wall. He was so close, causing my heart thumped.

Bryce shook his head, his voice smooth to the ear. "You don't know how much trouble I'm in now. Thanks to you."

I quickly retorted even though I was becoming breathless from the sight of him, "Hey, it wasn't my fault. You're the one insisting that you've seen me before."

Sighing from the uncomfortable position, I then demanded, "So, could you please stop acting like you're about to jump me, and give me a little space?"

Bryce motioned an inch closer to mine. I gulped, taking in that captivating face. It was attraction all over again.

He smirked and taunted, "What if I don't want to?"

I was about to punch him until he finally backed away with a satisfied smile. Bryce's reaction was enough to verify that he knew that he managed to allure me with his annoying yet attractive face.

He took a good look at me and said, "I have to watch out for you. Wait no, you should watch out for me since I need to get back at you for getting me in trouble."

Folding my arms, I complained, "How the hell would I know that you'd get in trouble for being a delivery boy?"

"I don't know if you noticed, worker, but my family owns a big company here. It's unlikely to see their sons making deliver to little markets, you know."

Biting my tongue, I knew he was right. So why did he even do it in the first place? Before I could even ask, Logan stepped out from the room.

Logan raised his dark eyebrows and asked, "What's going on?"

Neither of us answered. I was still completely speechless from all of this.

After a long gap of silence, Bryce released a crooked grin at his cousin and cleared up the confusion, "Nothing, man."

Then, Bryce turned his attention back to me and said, "Pleased to meet you by the way. I'm Bryce Valentino. I'll be seeing you around."

"Vanessa, I can't believe that it's him!"

I was lying on my comfy bed, ranting on my phone. Vanessa, on the other line, couldn't believe everything either. Just knowing that the delivery boy was one of the Valentino's made me believe that this was truly a small world. Not only that, but he was a jerk with a devil mother.

Vanessa said, "That's impossible! He's so unlike David and Logan, but did you see his mom? No wonder, right?"

Her words made me stifle a laugh. It was true though.

I shivered and said, "She's so scary. I already know that she doesn't like me."

"It's because she's a bitch. I'm sure everyone there could agree, even her husband. Anyway, Bryce seems intense. The way he just took you away like that. His mom was going crazy. Oh, David told me some deets bout' your delivery boy, want to know?"

All I knew was that Bryce Valentino was a jerk personally. Maybe that was all I needed to know. However, I couldn't help but say yes.

"Okay, so Bryce is the last one to be born in the same year of the three. Apparently, he's most likely to become CEO first. David did say that Bryce could come off as blunt sometimes but, something like we'd have to understand his position with his parents. Bryce is always expected to do his absolute best, especially with his evil mom. But hear this, Bryce goes to the same school as me, but he rarely attends because of all the work that's put onto him."

I muttered, "He's like the perfect kid for the family."

Vanessa chuckled and said, "You could say that, but the amount of stress he's given is more than what David and Logan has to go through. From the way I see it, at least they get to experience life more."

As much as I didn't want to admit, Vanessa had a point.

I sighed. "I see what you mean, but he wasn't what I pictured. I was just expecting an everyday delivery boy, not a future CEO of a huge company."

Bryce Valentino surely knew the right time to push himself back into my life.

Gee, thanks jerk.

Chapter 7

WALKING TO THE kitchen, Mom was already making her mouth-watering home cooked meals. I inherited my mother's heart shaped face, pretty cheekbones, and soft pink lips. The only difference would be our eyes—which I shared with Pops—and our hair length. I couldn't forget the fact I was three inches taller than her 5 foot 3.

Mom lifted her attention from the chopping board once she noticed my presence. "Work again, dear? Be sure not to overwork yourself."

Laughing, I defended, "It isn't hard, Mom. Just simple escorting and ordering."

"Okay, remember to eat some lunch though. You're getting thinner by the day. Will you be home in time for dinner?"

"Thinner? You're joking. I'll be home around 6," before leaving the kitchen, I said, "mom, is everything okay? I've noticed whenever I talk about the Valentino family, something seems different. You and Pops aren't worried about me, right?"

There was a slight pause, and Mom's hazel eyes blinked away momentarily. She tucked her dark brown hair behind her ear and chuckled. "Oh honey, we're just worried because, you know, they're rich. We're just simple people, and I just don't want them to take advantage over you."

My parents were always so caring.

I gave her a smile in reply. "Mom, the Valentino's are a good family especially David and Logan."

Concerning Bryce and his parents, I wouldn't know what to say about them. I haven't even told my parents or Mason that Bryce was the delivery boy.

Mom nodded and said, "Okay, but the moment something happens, you better tell me, okay?"

Following her words, I gave her a kiss goodbye and headed out the door.

It wasn't long before I made my way up the hotel elevator and landed right in front of the Symphony's Fine Dining. Manager Gray was already standing by the front, waiting for guests to arrive and dine. Once she caught sight of me, we switched places and, just like any other day, I prepared myself for encountering the "fancy" people.

Because it was still the early in the afternoon, no one was really here yet. On the verge of closing my eyes, I was abruptly awaken by—

"Hey! Why are you sleeping on the job?"

Expecting it to be Manager Gray, I jumped from my slumber, ready to apologize my life away. My face fell finding that it wasn't Manager Gray who said that—well, the voice was deeper—but Bryce Valentino. Bryce stood there before me with a smug grin slapped onto his face.

Him again?

You'd think I'd be jumping for joy since he was the delivery boy I was looking for.

Bryce had his arms crossed over his usual business attire as he clicked his tongue in disapproval. "Well, well, looks like I caught you in the act. Should I tell the manager about this?"

"No!" Quickly changing the tone on my voice, I corrected, "I mean... please no. It won't happen again."

Bryce chuckled at my misery. "Here I was, just wanting to eat at this very restaurant, but instead, I find a worker sleeping on her job. What a sight."

This guy had to be kidding me. The nerve. I wanted to punch him right in the face, but I shamefully resisted just looking at him.

When I didn't respond, Bryce said, "Fine, fine. I'll let you go this time. Just hurry up and find me a table, worker."

Excuse me, this worker has a name.

Shaking my thoughts away, I could put up with him. This would be nothing but a simple challenge. As I escorted and attempted to set Bryce a table, it was the same kind of response every single time.

"No, this isn't good for me."

"Are you serious? This table out of all of them?"

"I want another one. This one isn't my calling."

"You know, this table just doesn't feel right."

If Bryce said something along those lines one more time, I swore I was ready to toss him out the window. I had to keep my cool though. I wouldn't let this nuisance get to me. Finally, after the tenth table he rejected, Bryce gave in to the table by the window.

Bryce took a seat and sighed. "See, was that so hard?"

Biting my tongue, I forced a smile as I handed him a menu. "Just call me over when you're ready."

However, he held his hand up and insisted, "Hold on, you can just stay right here."

After five minutes of standing there, I impatiently asked, "So, you ready?"

Bryce turned his attention to me as his light blue eyes lifted from the menu. He nodded with sarcasm written all over him.

"Yes, I am. Thanks for rushing me," he then cleared his throat and said, "anyway, I'd like to have—no, wait scratch that—make that a double—change that order with this one—wow, this one sounds better actually—did you get that? Hey, are you even listening?"

It went on like this for another five minutes. My order form was completely scratched black from the pen, nearly making a hole through it.

That was it.

Gritting my teeth, I said, "Listen Mr. Valentino, you may be having fun tormenting me like this, but let me tell you something—"

Bryce interrupted with a teasing grin, "It's working, huh?"

See, that was where he got me. I ended up glaring at him, but he stared back. Through his staring, I felt myself gradually surrender after locking eyes with him for too long.

What has gotten into me?

He laughed gently. "Yeah, I knew it. Just get me that one."

At last, I was finally away from his presence. When I walked back to the front, I found a line of people waiting to be seated. Manager Gray gave me that where-in-the-world-have-you-been? look. If she only knew. Once I placed the last group to their table,

I staggered back to the front. Completely exhausted by the rush, I let out a long sigh.

"When's your break?" a voice entered my tired mind.

Looking up from my palms, I found Bryce standing in front of me again.

Raising my eyebrow, I hesitated, "Not until another hour, why?"

"Meet me in the lobby."

Before I could say another word to him, he turned away, walking towards the elevator.

"Mr. Valentino was quite impressed by our restaurant, Lockhart."

Looking over to my right, it was Manager Gray holding a content smile. Giving her a confused response in return, she let out a laugh.

Manager Gray said, "Yes, Mr. Valentino apologized for causing a rush. But, he said he enjoyed dining here. Great job, Lockhart."

What was that all about?

After that experience, I'd expect myself to get as far away as possible from a person like Bryce Valentino. However, what he said to Manager Gray had me all curious. I just had to see why Bryce would want me to meet him at the lobby. Just like he mentioned earlier, Bryce was waiting in one of the lobby's sleek white leather chairs.

Approaching him, I said, "Why'd you call me down here?"

Bryce stood up from the chair, and that was when realization hit me on how tall he was.

"Worker, you work here, but I bet you don't even know how this hotel looks like. Am I right?"

Nodding my head, I wondered what his point was.

"Allow me to show you around."

Taking this as a joke, I started laughing. He was offering a tour of the hotel after all that crap he gave me earlier?

I scoffed. "I'm not stupid. If this is your way of making up for what you did earlier, you can forget it. Besides, tell me why I should go with you."

Bryce settled his pale blue eyes at me, which glittered beautifully in the bright lobby. "Because who else would know the hotel any better than the CEO's son himself? You know, you say you're not stupid, but with the way you're asking these questions make it quite doubtful. When someone wants to do something nice for you, it's usually good to let them."

Damn it.

Taking back what I said, I mumbled, "You're right. I'm sorry."

Did I regret saying those words?

Hell yes.

Bryce teased, "You're such an easy target. Say no more, come with me."

Pathetic, I walked a step back from Bryce as he showed me the wonders of Legends. My mood changed after going through the different places and activities the hotel offered. To be honest, I never expected a hotel to be so grand. Even if it was a skyscraper, I was surprised to see how many of the floors weren't just hotel rooms.

Most of the floors were recreational places for the guests. There were at least five floors dedicated for gym equipment, and there had to be at least three indoor pools we passed by on separate floors. Not only that, but there were various floors where people were able to engage in sports indoors. Things like this I could only dream, but Legends made it reality.

Heading to another floor, this would be Mom's haven. Bryce showed me some of the spas their hotel had. He mentioned that there was a good fifteen spas scattered throughout the hotel. Legends wasn't only for the adults, but it appealed to the younger guests too. I felt the inner kid in me rush out, seeing the three floor bowling alley and arcade.

Bryce shrugged casually as we walked out of the arcade. "It's not too much, just enough to please the people staying."

Giving him a bewildered look, I blurted, "Are you kidding me? I bet you not one person wouldn't want to live here."

"Actually that one person would be me."

"Why's that?"

"Nothing. I guess it's probably just me," Bryce said as he continued walking.

Letting the subject go, I noticed that we were just midway in the hotel, until something caught my interest.

My mouth dropped as I looked out of the window. "What is that?"

Bryce followed to what I was staring at and expressed amusement. "By that, did you mean the water park being built?"

My eyes scanned the colorful slides and rides being placed around the perimeter. Pools were being filled with tons of water.

His voice was dull. "Don't be too surprised. The water park will be done when summer hits. You can bring your family if you want."

Something I noticed throughout this tour was whenever I complimented the hotel Bryce's mood would drop oddly. There had to be something bothering him, but I knew he would never want to talk about it.

Especially with some worker like me.

As soon as we were done covering the inside of the hotel, Bryce presented me the outdoors. The Legends Garden had to be my favorite spot. Even if the idea of a garden seemed so simple, I always loved flowers. Legends Garden was simply breathtaking. Different bursts of colors and scents were scattered throughout the outdoors. The air smelled so fresh unlike the smoggy atmosphere of the city. From afar, I noticed a huge garden maze with people walking in and out of it.

I couldn't help but say, "This is so beautiful. It's like a whole new place."

Expecting Bryce to counter, I was caught by surprise when he actually agreed with me. Shifting my body to face Bryce, he seemed renewed as his eyelids were shut.

He was at ease as he said, "You know, this hotel may have the luxuries, but this garden has something the hotel doesn't. A reason for being here."

It shocked me to hear that.

"Mr. Valentino," a voice broke the calm atmosphere.

Bryce's eyes rapidly opened as we both followed that voice. It turned out to be an elder man dressed in a suit as well.

The man said respectfully, "Your mother awaits your arrival."

Bryce nodded and mumbled low enough that I heard, "Back to the dungeon tower."

Or maybe I was just hearing that.

Bryce then turned to face me. "So worker, I hope you enjoyed Bryce Valentino's exclusive tour."

Ignoring the worker classification, I thanked him anyway, "It was an interesting experience."

There was something in the smile that grew on Bryce's lips that almost made my heart skip a beat.

Chapter 8

I T WAS ANOTHER tiring day.

Walking out of the elevator, I released an exhausted sigh. It seemed like all the guests wanted to try out Symphony's Fine Dining today. Rubbing my eyes, I was just about ready to head out the lobby doors until Logan was walking my direction. His attention was stuck on the manila folder he tightly held onto. Serious stuff, I assumed. I smiled involuntarily because I haven't had the chance to talk to him.

Yet, I found myself spending more time with Bryce.

Go figure.

Once Logan glanced up, he caught my eyes. I swiftly looked away before waving him a hello.

Logan approached me, his dark blue eyes looking slightly tired. "Maisie! I haven't seen you around. How are you?"

I smiled and said, "I'm doing great. Just tired because of work today. And you?"

"I could say the same. Finals are coming up soon, deadlines need to be met, a little too much to handle."

"You can do it! You're Logan Valentino."

Logan let out a short laugh. "Thanks to you, I think I can now."

The way his midnight blue eyes lifted as he smiled was really cute, but I tried my best to not let it get to me.

When I was ready to leave, Logan quickly stopped me. "Bryce... he hasn't been bothering you, right?"

Thinking about it, I didn't want to bring up Bryce's fun filled experience he made me go through at the restaurant a few days go. This was his cousin we were talking about—flesh and blood.

Shaking my head, I said, "No, he actually showed me around the hotel when I got off work."

His blue eyes widened, taken back. "He did? Oh okay. When summer vacation comes, we should go out sometime, yeah?"

Assuming Logan meant it as a friends kind of deal, I nodded happily before watching him head to the main elevators. Logan's expression when I told him about Bryce giving me an exclusive tour was kind of questionable. It looked as though Logan was in disbelief. Well, I couldn't blame him.

Now that Logan mentioned it, everyone's school year was closing to an end. My younger brother's graduation was in two weeks.

"Hey, worker. Stop spacing out, you're blocking the way," a voice poked my thoughts away.

Just as I expected.

Bryce Valentino.

Once again, Bryce had his arms folded across his tailored suit in a mocking manner as if he was the big boss.

Wait, scratch that, he was going to be one eventually.

Clearing my throat, I replied dryly, "Sorry, Mr. Valentino, I was about ready to leave."

"Don't talk to me like that. I'm not my father," Bryce said, slightly disturbed.

"Well, Mr. Valentino, you don't like it when I call you Mr. Valentino? But Mr. Valentino, you don't even know my name. So Mr. Valentino, I should continue calling you Mr. Valentino. How does that sound, Mr. Valentino?"

Those icy blue eyes were glaring darts at me every time I emphasized "Mr. Valentino". Allow me to cash in my victory.

Bryce's jaw clenched before he said, "Fine. Daisie, stop standing there. You're blocking my way."

Raising my eyebrow, I said, "My name is not Daisie."

Bryce appeared to be surprised as he replied slowly, "It's not? But, your work name tag said Daisie."

Laughing, I shook my head. "Are you blind? My name is Maisie, not Daisie."

"Well, you never told me your name anyway, Daisie."

The more I thought about it, I asked, "Hold on, can you read that sign over there?"

Puzzled, Bryce followed to where I was pointing. It was only inches away. Bryce squinted his eyes. In the midst of this, I noticed how his nice dark eyelashes were being showcased. I needed to stop staring.

After a long pause, Bryce murmured, "Yeah."

"What does it say?" I asked with a content grin.

"... Do I have to tell you?"

"Come on. What does it say, Mr. Valentino?"

Bryce sighed in defeat. "Daisie, I can't read it. You happy?"

Just what I thought. And then, a rush of thoughts crashed in like a tidal wave. How could the heir of Phoenix Empire not have glasses or at least contacts if his eyesight was that bad? What would happen if Bryce couldn't read a slide show presentation or an offer, and he made a mistake because he couldn't see?

More importantly, why was I worrying about Bryce Valentino?

Shaking my head, I said, "You should go to the optometrist, and get some glasses or contacts if you want."

"Take me," Bryce abruptly demanded.

"You can do it yourself! You're capable of going there."

"What if I can't find the place because I can't see?"

"That's not my problem," I said bluntly, ready to walk away and head home.

"Because of you, Daisie, my secret has been revealed. So, you must help me. If not, you'll lose your job."

A cunning grin formed on Bryce's lips, knowing he got me tied. He was pulling the blackmail card.

Stupid delivery boy.

As much as I knew I was going to regret my decision, I hopelessly agreed and told him to follow me. It seemed like Bryce always had the free time. Why was he never busy when I was around? When we walked to my car, Bryce complained that my car was too small for his taste even though he was laughing to his amusement. In the end, I plastered on a smile because he was the son of my boss.

Once we got in, Bryce said with a grin, "The best optometrist, you got that, Daisie?"

"It's Maisie. And, don't you have an optometrist? A family one at least?" I mumbled, turning on the engine.

He was a Valentino, for crying out loud.

"Daisie, if we did, then we wouldn't be in this situation. Am I right?" he answered in a clever tone.

Stupid, stupid delivery boy.

Taking a deep sigh, I pulled out of the parking lot, and off we went. How was I going to find the "best" optometrist?

Clicking my tongue as I searched from place to place, there was no optometry in sight. Well, this wasn't going in our favor or more towards my favor. When I glanced over to the passenger seat, Bryce was minding his own business on his cellphone. Not going to lie, I felt pity over him because it really did look like he was struggling to read whatever was on his screen.

Settling my attention back on the road, I ended up choosing whatever optometry we ran into. Bryce had no say in what was the "best" or not. He better deal with it. Spotting a sign that said The Looking Glass, this would be the lucky optometry that would have to deal with Bryce Valentino.

When Bryce noticed that I was parking, he lifted his head. His blue eyes scanned the place.

He teasingly remarked, "If they ruin my eyes, it's all your fault, Daisie."

Giving up on correcting him, I unbuckled my seat belt. "Stop whining, and let's go."

We both walked inside, and the receptionist immediately greeted us, standing up from her chair. As I looked over the counter, she had been reading a magazine. And, guess what? The Valentino family happened to be on the front page. That was no surprise.

The receptionist balanced her thick-rimmed glasses against her sharp nose bridge and seemed hesitant. "Mr. V-Valentino?"

Bryce said casually, "Call me Bryce. Anyway, something's wrong with my eyes. Daisie, over here, is telling me that I need glasses or something."

The receptionist never looked so nervous. Her leaf green eyes shook as she was fixing her bob-cut red hair to appear presentable. Trust me, Bryce Valentino was nothing to be nervous over.

If only I could tell her and myself that.

She quickly nodded as she shuffled through some papers. "You'll meet with Dr. Henderson, and she'll assist you on what needs to be done. If you'd just take a seat over there and fill out the paperwork on the meantime."

As Bryce was going through the questionnaire, I couldn't help but notice how much he struggled to read it. I offered to help, but the delivery boy waved me away. Giving up, I decided to let him be independent and suffer.

Through my waiting, I finally found this the perfect opportunity to ask, "Bryce, why did you make deliveries that one day?"

Bryce's attention was still on the papers as he said nonchalantly, "I wanted to ditch work. Your market just happened to be on the route. Hey, what's this say?"

"It's asking if you have any allergies. Um, how did you become a delivery person?"

"Gave the guy some money. Easy stuff. Why? You actually thought I was some delivery guy?"

"Of course not! I was just wondering."

Bryce scoffed in return, probably not believing my horrible lie. "I'm quite offended that you didn't recognize me as the incredible Bryce Valentino."

Could this guy get any more conceited or what?

Still, his confidence was starting to divert me.

Once Bryce was finished, we both waited. It wasn't long before the optometrist quickly came out of the opposite doors and called for Bryce's attention. Dr. Henderson had her blonde hair tied in a perfect ponytail and showcased naturally large green eyes. She revealed a friendly smile and motioned Bryce to follow her.

Checking the time, I wondered why my parents never called me. They knew I got off an hour ago. Because I was so tired and it seemed like Bryce was taking forever, I was starting to get sleepy. Folding my arms across my chest, my eyes fluttered. I felt my head bop up and down, trying to regain conscience.

"Daisie, wake up," a gentle voice bought me back.

"Huh?" I rubbed my eyes, and Bryce was standing in front of me.

This wasn't the first time, right?

Fixing my position, I cleared my throat and asked, "So, what's the result?"

Bryce gritted his teeth and said, "I need some reading glasses. Choose one for me."

Must I do everything for him?

As I was about to decline, Bryce quickly mentioned about firing me if I didn't. Grunting, I stood up and found a smile of satisfaction on his lips.

Keep smiling, delivery boy.

Glancing around the racks of multiple glasses, I found the perfect one for him.

"What the fuck is that? You think I'm some grandpa?" Bryce's face dropped in disgust as I handed it to him.

Holding in my laughter, I couldn't help but grin broadly watching Bryce's expression. I gave him those glasses with humongous lenses, and it was clear plastic. In my thoughts, Bryce would look like a dorky professor. Thinking Bryce would put it back, he ended up trying it on anyway.

Why did he still look good in those ugly glasses?

Bryce nodded, glancing in the mirror. "Not bad, but I don't think I'll be taken seriously with these on. Next."

Frame by frame, all of them managed to surprisingly fit Bryce. Yet, the word "next" would always escape from his mouth. Honestly, I did like the black framed glasses on him, but I didn't like the fact how almost every pair glasses took away his beautiful, blue eyes. After the thirteenth one, we were still nowhere.

Exhausted from choosing, I suggested impatiently, "What about contacts?"

And that way, his eyes would be perfectly visible.

Placing a failed choice back onto the shelf, Bryce turned to look at me. "You want me to poke my eyes out?"

Shaking my head, I explained the benefits of having contacts. Sure, it may be hassle to put on and take off, but that way, Bryce wouldn't have to worry about revealing his so called secret. To my amazement, he went with it.

Bryce Valentino actually listened to me?

Usually, it would take a day or two to prepare the contacts, but it seemed like this certain optometry wanted to show its best for a Valentino and had them already prepared just in case while we were glasses shopping. Dr. Henderson was guiding Bryce step by step on how to put them on, and I never found such entertainment like this before.

Bryce would flinch every now and then when placing the lens into his eyes. It was hilarious, but I did everything I could to not laugh because the action was too risky. I even resorted to cheering for him. A jerk should be thankful. After a couple tries, Bryce managed to perfect it.

The receptionist and Dr. Henderson happily exclaimed, "You did such a good job!"

Look, he already has a fan club.

Chuckling at the sight, I ended up clapping along. As we were about to leave, Dr. Henderson stopped me.

She gave me a kind smile. "It was so sweet of you to support your boyfriend."

I coughed from doubt, "Him? Oh no, he's not—"

"Daisie, let's go!" Bryce said after speaking with the receptionist.

Before I could even explain myself, I followed Bryce out of the optometry. Last time I checked, he was not my boyfriend.

After closing the store doors, I asked with a small frown, "Why does Dr. Henderson think I'm your girlfriend?"

Bryce was standing by my car door and was suddenly occupied with his phone. He shrugged, bringing his attention to me. There was a taunting smile growing on his face.

He said, "Don't look at me. I should have told her that you're my personal servant."

Rolling my eyes, I unlocked my car, and the two of us headed back in.

As he took his seat, Bryce's face actually showed sincerity. "Thanks, by the way."

I replied with a sly smile, "So Mr. Valentino, now that you have a pair of eyes, you'll call me by my real name, right?"

Despite his phone ringing non-stop, Bryce pressed the ignore button before shutting it off. Those alluring, sky blue eyes then jumped at mine.

Bryce returned back the grin and said, "You'll always be Daisie in my eyes."

Chapter 9

I was stuck taking Mason to five university tours on this fine Wednesday. He kept begging me over and over to come with him. Since this had to do with his future and I didn't want to see my little brother ride the bus, I agreed.

Plus, he was doing the dishes for two whole months. It was a good deal, if you ask me.

"Last one on the list."

Mason's eyes had been scanning the brochure for a good five minutes.

One — and the last — of Mason's choices was the same university Vanessa and the Valentino's were attending. Some part of me was thinking that he just wanted to go there to see Vanessa. But, this school had a very notable music program, if Mason wanted to do something like that.

Come to think of it, it has been three years since I walked foot on educational grounds. I was surprised I didn't get a rash or an allergic reaction of some sort!

Walking beside my younger brother, I glanced at every direction of the university. The campus was beautiful, remembering the pictures I saw online or the ones Vanessa would take every now and then. Mason nodded his head, taking in the school's old yet charming brick buildings and peaceful landscaping.

"Pretty cool, don't you think?"

"If that's really the reason why you want to go here," I muttered under my breath, joking.

He caught that but ignored it, "Anyway, I'm going to meet with the tour guide. You should meet with Vanessa."

"You sure you don't want to see her?" I teased.

Not even bothering to reply, Mason walked off as he waved goodbye. Laughing quietly to myself, I soon whipped out my phone to call Vanessa. Fortunately, she has no class at this time.

Vanessa beamed on the other line, "I'm so excited! Go to the Student Center, okay? It won't be hard to find!"

Telling her I would, I hung up and took a deep breath. Really Vanessa? This campus was huge. How was I supposed to find it?

"I can't believe you're here. You'll love these!" Vanessa chimed and was happily tossing desserts onto a ceramic plate.

The Student Center wasn't so hard to find. In fact, it was its own building. This place was where all the students attending could dine, study, even relax. It was very spacious with four floors. The first floor being the not-so-typical cafeteria, the second and third floor being a casual "talk or study" place, and the fourth designated for quiet and serious studying.

Instead of going to class, I'd rather be here.

"Van, this is the only college experience I'm missing out on," I praised.

Vanessa giggled as she paid the cashier.

"Typical Maisie."

We both sat down in one of the square, dark wood table and chairs. As I surveyed the open space, there were various seating areas with leather sectionals and the same dark wood coffee tables scattered around. Many students occupied these spaces to relax from their stressful classes or even just to catch up with friends.

Popping a bite-sized cheesecake into my mouth, I commented, "You never told me you eat food like this everyday. You should bring me some!"

Vanessa shook her head, grinning.

"All you think about is food, Maisie. Where does it all go? So, how's the university search going?"

Shrugging, I replied, "Mason got his eyes on a school, and I have a feeling this one too."

She answered, pleased, "Really? That's great! He'll love it here."

Oh Vanessa, if you only knew. I was sure Mason will.

"Is it me, or do I see two familiar girls?"

As we both looked over to the voice's direction, it turned out to be David. Alongside David was Logan. They both grinned, wearing their casual yet fashionable attire that opposed their usual professional get up. Vanessa managed to yelp out David's name and instantly hopped out of her seat.

Following behind her, I smiled.

"It's nice seeing you two here."

David had his attention on Vanessa, but managed to slipped in, "What brings Ms. Maisie Lockhart here?"

I explained through my grinning, "My younger brother needed to look at some universities. One of them ended up being here."

Logan chuckled, "For a moment, I thought you were actually going to school with us."

Vanessa sighed happily.

"Wouldn't that be great?"

The four of us laughed, bringing me back to the night of our double date. For the most part, we all managed to catch up. It wasn't a surprise when David and Logan jokingly complained how hectic their lives were. It was all fun and joy until Logan and David were approached by some guy.

He was shorter than me and Vanessa's equivalent height. The guy had pale skin and a round face — make that round blue eyes too — and sported a buzz cut hairstyle.

He rejoiced, giving them the "dude" handshake, "What's up, bros! So, I hear Bryce is finally back. Haven't seen him in forever! Let's all party, yeah?"

Bryce was back in school?

Vanessa flashed me a 'did you hear that?' look, but I pretended I didn't catch anything.

From what I heard, Logan replied back with a, "Hey man, yeah, it's sure looks like it. Oh, you know that's something Bryce would do."

Round Face oddly gazed at me before his eyes jumped back to Logan.

"Alright, but when you guys are free, you know who to call."

Before leaving, he just had to say something totally uncalled for. Round face flushed out red.

"And bring your friend here too."

Wonderful — I think the cheesecake is rushing upstream. When Round Face finally left, Logan and David turned around to see my expression while Vanessa was laughing her head off. David joined in as Logan chuckled to the side.

Wasn't this just humiliating?

Vanessa joked, "Wow Maisie, you don't even go here, but you're scoring guys."

Before I could defend myself, a sudden outburst stole everyone's attention.

"Yo, Bryce! I missed you, bro!"

We all turned around, finding Bryce entering the premises with a group of giggling girls swarming him.

Round Face approached Bryce and gave him the same handshake.

David lightly commented, "Looks like the prince has officially returned."

Sudden groups of people got up from their seats and greeted him. This was blowing things way out of proportion. You have two other Valentino's over here — why weren't the people going gaga for them?

From the looks of it, Bryce was truly missed. Everyone was telling him how he missed all those bad-ass college parties and asking how in the world he "rose from the dead". I was just surprised Bryce wasn't kicked out yet for missing classes.

Vanessa exclaimed through her amazement, "Might as well throw a parade while they're at it."

Along with that, Logan replied half-serious, "Don't say that too loud. It might actually happen."

What made me cringe was seeing the group of girls craze over Bryce.

If they only knew that delivery boy is actually a jerk — at some points. Bryce appeared to be tuning everyone out once he approached us. I quickly looked away, hoping he wouldn't spot me. Peeking through my eyelashes, I saw Bryce handshake his cousins while adding in some side talk and laughs.

Once he greeted Vanessa, his eyes immediately bounced over to mine and that mocking smirk grew. Giving Bryce a short wave, I tried to walk away to get more food as an excuse.

"Daisie, is that how you're going to treat me? What are you even doing here?"

Of course, he'd follow me.

Flipping my hair around to face him, I explained a matter of fact, "Don't get any ideas. I'm just here for my younger brother."

Bryce nodded, but he chimed, "Why are you acting like you don't even know me? Can't you see how missed I was?"

Playing along with his ego, I smiled.

"Of course. I mean, I totally wanted to be one of those stupid girls tagging behind you. It's an opportunity I wouldn't ever want to miss. Poor me."

Bryce gave me a look as he gritted his teeth together. The word "whatever" slipped through his mouth.

Chuckling softly, I asked to make our conversation more decent, "How are you finding your renewed eyes anyway?"

"Oh. Look. What. We. Got. Here."

This interruption wasn't anything pleasant at all.

I felt my fists tighten, immediately recognizing that it was Jason. I completely forgot the bastard goes here. Bryce promptly acknowledged Jason's presence with a scowl. Jason was oblivious to the fact I was talking to someone and stepped closer to me. Behind him, were three of his friends.

Jason's cocky expression jeered right at me, "You don't belong here. Did a cat drag you in, Maisie Lockhart?"

How I hated the way he said my name. He wanted to pick a fight in front of everyone — in the university he was attending? How stupid could a guy get? Whatever, it would be his lost. I scoffed a laugh, forgetting that Bryce was beside me.

Right now, it was time to finish off this stubborn mind. Shaking my head, I crossed my arms.

"That's none of your damn business. After all of this, what good will it do?"

Jason's brown eyes darkened, causing a few heads to turn.

"Shut up, bitch! You still have to pay for what you did!"

I retorted, "At least I'm not an asshole like you. Grow up, you know so well that you deserved what you got."

Jason motioned his fellow losers to come forward.

"No! This is what you deserve!"

From the corner of my eyes, I spotted Vanessa with a shocked expression. She looked like she was ready to jump in as well. When I looked back to react, I found Jason collapsed on the floor.

What just happened?

"You should know when not to make a fool of yourself. Oh, I forgot. You're already an asshole, why not be a dumb ass as well?" Bryce spat out with disgust.

It was Bryce. He knocked the bastard to the floor.

Vanessa pushed her way through the crowd. Logan and David followed behind yet were holding puzzled looks, not knowing what was happening. I've never seen Vanessa so angry — well, except the time Fiona Hughes called Vanessa "ugly" for demolishing her at tennis during the sixth grade.

Vanessa glared at Jason as he got up.

"What the hell is wrong with you? See, this is why I couldn't stand you. You pick fights, and you can't even stand your own ground."

Literally.

The mob of spectators all instigated everything by adding "Ooo..." to what Vanessa just said. However, like last time, Jason tried brushing off all the embarrassment with the help of his hopeless minions.

Jason shouted, not to Vanessa or me, but at Bryce, "Who the fuck do you think you are just pushing your way into my business?"

Of course, Jason wouldn't think about messing with a Valentino because, watch out, the monster I've been talking about was finally unleashed. As Jason was on a rampage, he practically tossed me aside to make way towards Bryce.

The two were nearly face to face — Jason might want to give some breathing space — when he shoved Bryce and threatened, "Let's take this outside. Forget these bitches, it's time I teach you a lesson."

Even through Jason's shoving, Bryce didn't appear affected at all. There wasn't the slightest sign of fear in Bryce's face. Bryce sighed, those icy blues leveled darkly.

"This isn't elementary school anymore. You know, you really are an asshole."

Right away, Bryce landed another punch sending Jason flying backwards. His "back up" were a lot smarter than Jason and didn't bother to fight Bryce. The three scurried beside their fallen bastard.

That was when David and Logan jolted in before Bryce continued with what he has done. Everyone was completely stunned, holding wide-eyed expressions. My heart nearly stopped.

Vanessa was suddenly beside me, her voice fluttered with worry.

"Maisie, Maisie! Are you okay? Talk to me!"

Why on earth was she freaking out like that? It wasn't long before I found my state of mind and noticed traces of blood flowing beside me.

Was that... my blood?

As if reality finally hit me, it all made sense. Jason had shoved me towards the table with ceramic plates and fragile glasses. The broken pieces had penetrated my right arm.

Trying to look away, the blood was already too much to handle especially since I was the person to absolutely hate the sight of blood. The last thing I saw was Logan — if that was him — rushing towards me before collapsing to darkness.

I didn't even go here, and this was what happened to me.

Just imagine my university life if I actually did.

Chapter 10

Never in my life had I felt like this before.

My eyes rapidly open, trying to figure out where in the world I was. There were bright white lights that lingered, causing me to cringe. Putting everything together, it was no surprise that I was in a hospital bed.

"Maisie, you're alive!"

Was that Mason I heard?

Shifting my head towards the sound, I found Mason a foot away on my left. His eyes glistened with concern.

I managed to laugh out, "Of course I'm alive. What happened?"

"Shit, you have amnesia! I'm going to call the doctor right now!"

There were many things that Mason didn't understand.

Shaking my head, I explained thoroughly, "Mason, no. I remember what jackass Jason did to me. What I'm asking is, do you know what happened after I passed out?"

A look of relief spread across my brother's face. He soon nodded his head, looking angry.

"You scared the hell out of me. I'm going to rip jackass Jason's spinal cord out! Man, I gotta give it to Bryce. If it were me though, Jason wouldn't have made it out alive," not even letting me speak, Mason continued to rant out, "you didn't even tell me that Bryce was the delivery boy? And that he's a Valentino? Then again, it's so typical of you to keep secrets from me. Don't worry. Since I found out, I already told Bryce how you had the hots for him."

Could I just strangle Mason right now?

Reaching out to punch him, I soon found silverware on my upper arm. I wasn't a robot. Where did this come from? Turned out, that was how much damage was done. Stitches, about ten or fifteen. Disgusted at the sight, I quickly dropped what Mason said and stared at my injury.

"I'm going to kill Jason."

Mason spoke up, "Not if I do first! Jackass Jason is long gone from the university, and I think the Valentino's got some restraining order on him..."

Blinking, I requested, "Tell me everything, Mason."

Tapping his chin, Mason replied, "Okay. So Bryce could have been in huge trouble since he punched Jason first, but Mom and Pops were complaining to the dean about what Jason did to you. Also, you know the Valentino family — they're stinking rich. The guys were here, but they left a while ago. You were sleeping for five hours!"

Mason then lowered his eyes and continued, "You know what? I kind of overheard Bryce and Logan arguing outside earlier."

This was a lot for me to take in after passing out. I gulped.

"Arguing? About what?"

"Logan was pissed about what happened to you. He was telling Bryce that if he didn't provoke jackass Jason, you wouldn't have gotten hurt. Bryce was saying how he had to shut jackass Jason up. After that, I think their parents called, and they left. Maisie, you got two Valentino's caring about you!"

Even if that did happen, I still needed to thank Bryce.

Shaking my head, I murmured, "What a mess. Hold on, did you really tell Bryce that?"

"That you had and still have the hots for him? Hell yeah."

"Mason, I'm going to kill you first!"

Mason shook his hands out with glee.

"I'm kidding! When I came to the student center, Vanessa looked vicious — shit, people had to hold me back too — I've never seen Pops and Mom so angry. They also met the Valentino's you've been hiding, I can tell they like them."

For some reason, it felt like Mason was some kind of reporter. Still, I was glad he was aware of all of this.

Thanking him, I asked "So, everything's okay, right? Where's Pops and Mom?"

Mason replied, nodding his head, "They went out to grab some food. Do you need anything?"

I couldn't put my finger to it, but there was something different about Mason's actions. He was very — how could I put this? — unusually nice. Shaking my head, I glanced over to my right, finding my best friend sleeping peacefully in the hospital chair.

I knew it!

Flicking my attention back at Mason, I teased, "You don't have to act like an angel just because Vanessa's around."

Mason, despite being really informative, was caught in the act. He shook his head, keeping his voice low.

"Maisie, don't talk so loud!"

I just gave my younger brother a sly grin until Mason pulled the Bryce card on me again. When I was about to raise my voice again,

Mason quickly cut me off, and we both agreed to keep our mouths shut.

Mason then quietly confessed, "I really don't like that David guy, Maisie. He's always with Vanessa."

Stifling a laugh, I defended the kind Valentino, "Come on now, no need to be bitter. David's a really good guy."

That was when Mason rolled his eyes.

"Right. That's what you said about jackass Jason."

"Uh no. I always knew that jerk was a jerk. Trust me on this, okay?"

Mason shrugged his shoulders.

"Fine. But, I'm still the best, right?"

I wasn't going to lie; Mason was a really good kid. I wouldn't have asked for a better brother. Smiling warmly, I nodded.

"Of course, no one can ever beat my little brother."

Because of the accident jackass Jason caused, I was given three days off from work despite the fact I was up and ready to go.

Manager Gray would tease that I would make the guests lose their appetites if they saw my exposed stitches. If that bastard — I mean, Jason — hadn't been such an ass — I mean, bother — then this wouldn't have happened.

During the past three days, I wasn't able to thank Bryce. Vanessa told me he never came back to school. As much as I didn't want to, I was worried that Bryce might have gotten into trouble. If not by the school, but by his mother.

Now that I was back to work, I wanted to test my luck and see if I'd run into that delivery boy. As I ended my shift, I bid my goodbyes to Manager Gray and coworkers who all told me to get better. Taking the elevator down, I jumped when I saw David walking towards me. He was the first Valentino I've seen in days. David didn't notice at first, but when he did, he gave me a friendly wave.

David grinned and greeted, "Maisie, good to see you! How's your arm?"

Giving him a smile back, I replied, "Same to you. My arm's doing better, thanks for asking. It's been a while since we've seen each other."

"It has, hasn't it? The last time was when you were in the hospital."

After moments of chatter, I realized out of the three, David bought that cool, down to earth vibe — well, I guess it comes naturally being the oldest. He was very easy to talk to. No wonder Vanessa liked him so much.

David then asked, "Is Vanessa doing okay?"

Did he knew that I was thinking about Vanessa?

I revealed through a laugh, "Yeah, of course. She told me how nice it was of you juggling your time with her and everything."

David's face lit with delight afterwards and mentioned how special Vanessa was to him. Usually, I never fell for that cheesy stuff, but hearing David say that he never met someone like Vanessa and how joyful he felt whenever he was around her made me want to give him a hug.

Out of all the guys' Vanessa has talked to, David was definitely the most sincere.

I teased, "David, you are such a romantic."

Vanessa would probably strangle me with happiness when I told her this.

Tilting my head, I inquired, "If you don't mind me asking, where's Bryce? I never got to thank him."

"Bryce is in New York attending a convention. He's usually the one sent out to do it. I think he's coming back in a day or two though," David eventually added, "I'm really sorry about what happened, by the way. If Bryce hadn't punched that guy, you probably wouldn't have gotten hurt."

Shaking my head, I indicated it was fine. What I was more focused on was the fact Bryce had to take care of all that himself. The Valentino's were my age yet their lives were so complicated.

I asked again, "Bryce doesn't have to worry about missing school? I mean, he just came back, right?"

David shrugged.

"Missing school is nothing new for Bryce. He doesn't even really need to go to school. I guess the diploma will show that he's 'eligible'. The thing is, almost all our investors, agents, stockholders and what not, know who he is because he's been doing this since high school."

I wouldn't deny it, besides being a jerk — sometimes — Bryce really has his work cut in front of him.

Messing with the ends of my hair, I commented, "Well, he'll make it through. He is Bryce Valentino."

"You're actually right. Bryce is the only person I know who can work and party at the same time. I feel bad for him though because he's always busy with the family business. I guess now, Bryce can't tolerate Aunt Monica anymore," David mentioned as he laughed.

As I followed his laughter, David suddenly smirked.

"I don't know about you, but it's kind of weird to be talking about Bryce right now."

Exactly.

Agreeing, I switched the topic, "Yeah. Hey, I'm sorry if I took up your time. You probably have some place to go?"

Soon after, David pulled up the sleeve of his white dress shirt to check his watch. His lips pursed before mentioning he had a meeting to catch. David's dark blue eyes momentarily met up with mine before picking up his briefcase.

"Don't worry about it, Maisie. Feel better, okay? I'll see you around, and let's talk about Bryce more."

He let out a smile, implying it was a joke.

Playing along, I nodded.

"I'm sure you like talking about him, that's why."

If I remembered well enough, I headed back to the market to see my family after work. Surprisingly, Vanessa was there too. Perfect timing, right?

As I told her about my conversation with David that day, her green eyes glittered with joy, and she hugged me until I couldn't breathe. The good thing was, Mason wasn't there. He would have been thinking of ways to get rid of David in the back of his mind. But, it was nice to see Vanessa with a guy that genuinely made her happy, and to know that he was happy when he was with her too.

"I'm thirsty," I complained quietly as I dragged my tired feet through the hotel lobby.

Once again, my shift ended, and realization hit me that I didn't take any breaks. My throat was yearning for some hydration, especially since I dealt with a lot of talking with the guests at the restaurant. Scanning around the lobby, I tried to find the nearest store, soda machine, whatever, just something to quench my thirst.

Instead of finding any of that, I spotted Bryce!

He was back?

Bryce came walking in the lobby through the revolving glass doors. He was looking very spiffy with his nicely fitted attire. The way his black hair perfectly crowned his masculine face and bright blue eyes was very attractive.

Snap out of it.

It has been a week or so since I last saw him. Still owing Bryce a thank you for what he did, my eyes only landed on the drink he was holding. Usually, my pride wouldn't allow me to do such things, but right now was a matter of life or death. I just didn't know if I could forgive myself after this.

Heading towards him, I called out, "Bryce!"

Catching sight of me, he absolutely wasn't expecting me to be there. Bryce gave me this "what the hell" expression. Maybe I just needed to back away and pretend that none of this happened. Bryce raised his left eyebrow when I came close by.

"You're unusual today. Wait, I forgot, you're always unusual."

Shaking my head, I pointed to the cup.

"Never mind that. Can I have some? I'm dying."

"You know, you shouldn't tell others you're dying when you're not. That's lying, Daisie," Bryce informed, handing me the cup any-way.

Hearing him call me "Daisie" was surprisingly relieving to my ears. These odd feelings, had to get out. Taking a gulp of the unknown liquid, not only did it burn my tongue to hell, a familiar taste tickled my taste buds.

"Ow, that burns," I winced before taking another gulp.

Bryce's voice cut in, "Obviously, it's a hot drink. Hey, don't take all of it!"

The familiar taste was hazelnut coffee — my favorite drink in the whole world.

The sudden memory jogged when Logan and I met up at Bright-side Café. Was this a family thing? Handing it back to him, I thanked him before adding in another thank you for having my back during the time with jackass Jason.

He shrugged casually.

"That asshole deserves it. I see your arm is doing better."

I nodded my head, giving him a small content smile. Bryce then looked down at his cup.

"Now, I don't even know if I want to drink it anymore. You probably contaminated it."

How our conversations changed so quickly.

Scoffing, I retorted, "No, I didn't! I should be the one worried. If something happens to me, it'll be your fault."

Bryce laughed before mentioning, "Wow, you really know how to make my day bearable. Maybe I should have let that asshole pounce on you and walked away from your poor beggar self."

Biting my tongue, I eyed him darkly, making him laugh even more. He then grinned.

"Daisie, I'm kidding."

Moving that aside, I unintentionally blurted out my observation, "You and Logan both like hazelnut coffee. Guess it's a Valentino thing?"

During the time I asked, Bryce was taking a sip of his drink, and it seem to have made him choke. His voice grew up a notch.

"Are you fucking joking?"

Several people passing by turned to look at the commotion, and Bryce immediately straightened himself out from his sudden outburst. Giving him a surprised look, it didn't make sense why Bryce got all worked up. The delivery boy lowered his voice.

"Daisie, what are you talking about? Logan hates hazelnut coffee with a passion."

Before I could even reply, Bryce began declaring how Logan lied and probably forced himself to drink it. For something so simple, it wasn't a big deal. I was sure Logan had his reasons for a silly lie.

Bryce muttered out, "This is some welcome party. Anyway, I got to go. Ask Logan for the truth, and you'll see."

Give it to Bryce to make hazelnut coffee a drink only he can enjoy.

As Bryce was walking ahead, he looked over his shoulder.

"I don't regret what I did to Jason. Logan may have blamed me, but I wasn't going to let him treat you like that. If they hadn't stop me, Jason wouldn't just have a broken nose."

Stunned, there were so many things happening upon Bryce's return. Those words actually struck me. Mason did hear right; Bryce and Logan did actually have an argument. Did Bryce actually care? No, he was just being nice — probably in return for taking him to the optometrist.

Shaking my head from those thoughts, I put my mind back to Logan. Once I saw him, I' would definitely ask about that.

It made me wonder why Logan would pretend to like something as insignificant as hazelnut coffee.

Chapter 11

Since I was so curious about Logan's hazelnut coffee mystery, I gave him a text if it was okay to meet up once I finished helping out in the market. I knew wasn't a serious topic, but seeing the way Bryce reacted made me think. What made me feel guilty was when Logan replied back, saying that he wouldn't mind driving over to the market instead. It has been a while since Logan had time to spare.

Taking care of Lockhart's Pantry by myself today, a rush of nervousness ceased over me once I saw Logan walk through our market doors. I haven't had an actual conversation with Logan since who knew when. Sure, we would wave to one another at the hotel for a millisecond when we happened to pass by each other. Most of the time, Logan had to keep his mind on Phoenix Empire.

As Logan approached me in his usual business attire, he gave me a smile.

"Hey, how are you? Is your arm doing better?"

Nodding my head, I pointed at my somewhat healing stitches.

"I'm great! It's become more of an accessory, if you ask me. Thanks for coming here, Logan."

Logan laughed at my enthusiasm. He looked so carefree as his eyes crinkled through his chuckling.

"That's some jewelry you got there. Don't worry about it, I needed to get out of the hotel. So, what's the thing you wanted to ask me about?"

Were the Valentino boys really under that much stress?

Chuckling hesitantly, I asked as I messed with the ends of hair, "This might come out weird — don't think of it like that though — but, do you like hazelnut coffee?"

Great, with the way I said it, I just made it even more awkward.

Logan's dark eyebrows knitted in confusion and replied, "Sorry, but what makes you ask that?"

I couldn't even look at Logan in the eye anymore.

"It's kind of a long story. When I saw Bryce the other day, I took a sip of his drink, and it was hazelnut coffee. I told him you both liked it, but he didn't believe me. Bryce said that you hated it and to ask you to prove it."

As Logan listened, he didn't reply, but instead, his jaw clenched noticeably with sudden hesitation. Apologizing soon after, never did I want to make a situation awkward.

"It's okay, sorry if I made things... uncomfortable."

After a pause, Logan finally spoke, "It's not like that. I'll be honest with you, I really don't."

My mind went back to that day at Brightside Café. Logan seemed pleased with the drink. Why fake something like that?

Raising an eyebrow, I murmured out of curiosity, "You didn't have to pretend to like it. It's okay to drink what you like."

The Valentino seemed half attentive, like his thoughts were on something else.

Logan eventually nodded his head and revealed, "I... well, I actually asked Vanessa earlier that day what drink you liked just so I would be prepared when we met up. When I drank it with you though, it tasted decent. But Maisie, I can't tell you the reason why right now."

I nodded back, understanding. No big deal, right? Letting the awkward atmosphere lighten, I smiled jokingly.

"Don't worry about something like that. I forgive you for your horrible lie."

Logan's posture became less tense, and he grinned in gratitude for ridding away the tension.

"It would have worked if Bryce didn't reveal my dark secret."

"Whoa, surprised to see you here, Logan."

It was Mason.

Our interaction broke off as we glanced over to Mason approaching us. Mason was wearing his usual simple black tee and jeans, carrying his trusty acoustic guitar with that signature grin on his face. The kid was graduating in two weeks. I had to say, I was very proud of him.

Last night, Mason showed me his yearbook and how he was given the title "most talented" out of the whole senior class.

Logan soon greeted Mason with a handshake. The two got along so well, but I wasn't surprised — Logan was a great guy. He soon took a look at Mason's guitar, complimenting it.

Mason smirked.

"Thanks man. You play?"

To my amazement, Logan nodded with a small grin. As a response, Mason offered his guitar for Logan to showcase his ability. My younger brother would always try to find someone to compete with.

Logan gave out a soft chuckle as he lightly warned, "I haven't played in a while... You're graduating soon, aren't you?"

As Mason nodded his head, Logan grew a charming smile.

"Okay then, so I'll dedicate this song to the Lockhart family. For congratulating Mason... and for the need of forgiveness from Maisie."

That caused a giggle to escape from my mouth.

As Logan strummed the guitar, Mason tossed me a confused expression, but my attention was stuck on Logan. His playing was absolutely mesmerizing. There was always that special something about a guy who could play guitar. Even Mason seemed impressed which was — mark my words — highly rare.

Several people, who were doing some grocery shopping, stopped to find where that sound was coming from. The few females who recognized him as Logan Valentino all broke out into sheepish grins and giggled amongst one another. I couldn't blame them. Was there anything these Valentino's were bad at? Once Logan was done playing, I gave him a cheerful applause, and Mason nodded his head in approval.

Taking the guitar back into his hands, Mason complimented with a sideways grin, "Not bad, Valentino."

Logan smiled warmly at the two of us and mentioned, "I don't normally play in front of people, so this is a secret between us three."

It was finally Mason's graduation.

No words could express the joy and love he received that day. I couldn't help but grin proudly when they called his name. Okay, I didn't just grin proudly — I stood up from the cold metal benches of my old high school football stadium and shouted to my heart's content.

To make Mason's day even better, I bought Vanessa along to his graduation. When the two hugged, he caught eye contact with me and mouthed the words, thank you.

No matter what, Mason was always going to be my silly younger brother.

While we were all crowding around Mason, I felt Pops place his broad hand across my shoulder.

His soft eyes were glassy as he told me, "It seems like only yesterday you were the one graduating. I'm so proud of you two."

Gosh Pops, you didn't have to make me cry. That was a very memorable day.

To add the cherry to this wonderful ice cream sundae, a few days after Mason's graduation, I had my usual check up with the doctor. I was finally able to get my stitches removed.

It would still take time to fully heal, but at least the cut finally closed up. Now, I didn't have to be so disgusted looking at my arm.

Today, my family were all at Lockhart's Pantry — family bonding to start the summer! We were doing our routine stock and inventory.

Throughout the whole afternoon, Pops and Mason were jokingly complaining at me for not treating them at Symphony's for Mason's graduation. It wasn't like I didn't want my family colliding with Legends at all cost. I was because I overheard my coworkers talking that Bryce's mom was having a group conference there the same day. I didn't want to cause an uprising if they saw how cold Bryce's mom treated me.

My mood always dropped whenever I happened to stumble across Bryce's mom. She would always smile courteously to those who passed by her, from guests to a few workers. However, when she caught sight of me, her lips fell tremendously into a frown. Her scowling expression would stay etched onto her face until I lost eye contact with her. I guess you could say I was already used to it.

Not only was she resentful towards me because of the Valentino dinner event, but the fact her son almost got into trouble at school because of me added more fuel to the flame.

Carrying a box of shipment, I said in my defense, "I took you guys to Iridescent. That place is so good — even better. Right Mom?"

Mom nodded in agreement. Good thing she was on my side. I didn't think I'd be able to handle three against one. Mason chortled as he rolled his eyes.

"Last time I heard, you said that you loved the food at Symphony's," he then cleared his throat, changing his voice as if he was mimicking me, "I'll even quote your words 'it filled my stomach will utter happiness'."

Soon after, my parents were laughing at Mason's entertainment. My lies were getting caught by this punk. Before I could counter back, our attention was taken away when a customer came walking through the store doors.

This wasn't your average customer though. It was Bryce Valentino.

He was wearing a white v-neck shirt paired with a trendy leather jacket and dark washed jeans. His black shoes complimented his outfit as a whole — this delivery boy had style.

Back to the point.

What kind of business would Bryce be having here?

My eyes widened, and I quickly glanced over to see my family's reaction. Mason grinned slightly, seeing Bryce stroll in. Pops and Mom greeted him, and Bryce gave them both a captivating smile. Once Bryce caught sight of me, he smirked as usual.

Placing the box on the floor, I asked not too harsh, "Bryce, what are you doing here?"

Pops coughed a reminder, "Maisie, you shouldn't treat a customer, especially a friend of yours like that."

Bryce looked at my parents and in reply, he shook his head saying that it was fine. He appeared to be the perfect guy at the moment.

"No, it's my fault for coming here without notice. I actually came here to ask you two something. It's concerning your daughter."

What on earth was this delivery boy planning?

My parents nodded their heads in unison, waiting for Bryce to continue. Bryce had this enchanting smile on which I knew Mom would fall for — it was kind of rubbing onto me.

Bryce's icy blue eyes reached my parents, and he announced confidently, "It's my birthday coming up this June. Since there's a party being thrown for me becoming twenty-one. it would be nice if your daughter could attend."

Who did this guy think he was? He thought playing the "asking the girl's parents first" card would work?

Well, let me tell him, that was not —

"Sure, that's fine with us," Mom replied with a pleased smile.

Not the answer I was looking for!

Pops appeared quite impressed with the manners Bryce was showing. Looking over at me, Pops grinned.

"That's really nice of you, Bryce. Did you hear that, Maisie? He wants you to be there."

I smiled bitterly and noticed the grin gradually growing on Bryce's lips. He knew this was killing me inside. I just knew it.

Shouldn't I be happy that he wanted me to go though?

Bryce soon gave my parents a sincere look.

"That means a lot to me. I apologize for bothering you all. I'll be heading out now. So, I'll see you there, Maisie?"

Hopeless, I simply nodded my head even though in the back of my mind I was screaming with mixed emotions. Before his departure, Bryce looked over at Mason and congratulated him for graduating.

Bryce suggested with a friendly grin, "You should invite your friends over to Legends. I could rent out the bowling space and arcade if you'd like."

Mason's brown eyes illuminated happily as he chimed, "For real? That would be awesome! Thanks, man."

I couldn't believe my family was falling for this act — or was it real? Bryce waved a goodbye to everyone before he smiled cunningly at me and walked out. Pursing my lips, my ears were soon being flooded with praise for Bryce Valentino.

Mason stated to Pops, "I think I'm staring to like Bryce more."

Coughing, I joked, "Make up your mind, Mason. You're always stuck between Logan and Bryce."

My parents chuckled as Mason stuck his tongue out, mocking me once more.

Through it all, I heard Mom say to herself, "He looks exactly like him..."

"What did you say, Mom?" I asked, tilting my head with curiosity.

"Oh, nothing dear. You know, I'm happy for you, right?"

Her eyes were suddenly filled with joy before returning her attention to the boxes of crackers that needed some sorting. That was weird. She probably thought no one caught that, or maybe I was just hearing things.

Still, I couldn't believe Bryce did that. This delivery boy always seemed unpredictable.

Chapter 12

"**B**efore our semester ended, people were all talking about how Bryce's party is the start of an amazing summer," Vanessa beamed as she was busy reading her monthly sent fashion magazine on the market counter.

I remembered her always telling me reading magazines was homework being a fashion major, but I knew the girl just wanted to procrastinate on writing her English essays.

Throwinging out all the old and not-so-presentable vegetables, I complained with a laugh, "Wow, people are definitely going crazy."

Vanessa giggled, turning the page of the magazine. Ever since Bryce did his gentlemen move, it made me wonder why he would go through all that. It seemed very unlike him. Especially since he had been throwing threats of firing me if I didn't do what he said a month or so ago.

Then again, it was Bryce.

Breaking my thoughts, Vanessa exclaimed, "Time flies, you know? His party is already this weekend! You shouldn't be sad, Maisie. You got invited... personally."

There was a joking tone in her voice as she winked. This was definitely not a laughing matter. Shaking my head in return, Vanessa simply threw on a goofy smile and continued reading.

Sighing, I explained, "It's not that, besides, I never even said yes. That delivery boy just asked my parents."

"Did they say yes?" Vanessa inquired.

"Yeah..."

I tossed a tomato into the trash can.

"What the hell, Maisie. Just go!"

"How are you and David doing, by the way?" I asked with a curious smile, hoping the change in our conversation would get Vanessa off my back about going.

Vanessa gave me an amused look as her green eyes brightened.

"Let's just say, I couldn't be any happier. Now unlike me, someone over here is obviously hiding her true feelings."

Great. So much for a topic switch.

Before throwing another bruised tomato, I pursed my lips.

"I am not hiding anything, Vanessa. And, what if I don't want to go?"

Closing her magazine, Vanessa wagged her finger, and she reminded firmly, "Don't you try fooling me. In case you forgot, Bryce was the one you were gawking about when he went to your market. He caught your eyes, remember? You should be happy you found him again. How come you're acting like he's a complete weirdo?"

For some reason, this made me burst into laughter. Vanessa seemed a little taken back from my little outburst. I hate to admit — as delusional I was back then — it was indeed Bryce Valentino who I felt this "attraction" to. Even up until now, the things he says and does surprised me. Never did I expect my delivery boy to be one of the heirs of the almighty company, Phoenix Empire.

Shuddering at my thoughts, I noticed Vanessa had been staring at me, waiting for some kind response besides a weird laugh.

In defeat, I muttered out, "Fine. I'll officially tell him I'm going when I see him."

"Good! See? Was that so hard? We're going to do some major shopping because I don't know about you, but we have to look absolutely amazing for this party!"

Vanessa let out a gleeful giggle, putting her attention back to the magazine. That was my best friend.

As I headed into work at Legends Hotel this fine morning, I had a cup of Brightside Café's famous hazelnut coffee in hand, hoping I'd run into Bryce. I did owe him after drinking more than half of his. Why did it felt like I always owed him? Usually, I've noticed that the Valentino's arrived around this time. Not that I'm excited or anything, I just didn't want the drink to go to waste.

Actually, what was I talking about? I could just drink it myself if anything.

Waiting in the hotel lobby, I spotted Bryce coming from the re-volving doors. People would pass by and greet him, but something was off about him. Bryce didn't look like he was in the mood at all — he usually killed all the ladies with that smile of his.

What happened?

Bryce's facial expression was dark, and there was a cryptic frown upon his lips. He ignored practically everyone. This was bad. Taking a deep breath, I only hoped he wouldn't vent out his wrath on me because all I wanted to do was deliver this cup and tell him that I was going to his birthday party.

That was all.

"Bryce!" I said his name loud enough for him to hear.

His once well-defined blue eyes were dull as he gazed up at me. When we were face to face, his eyes went on the cup I was holding then back at me. Handing him the cup, I tried to put on a smile.

"Here, it's hazelnut coffee. I know I owe you for last time."

All of a sudden, there was a slight transition in Bryce's lifeless expression as he slowly took the cup from my hands. Before drinking it though, Bryce paused.

He asked with all seriousness even though there was a smirk appearing, "Hold on... this isn't poisoned, right?"

Of course, he would.

I replied dryly, "No! And also, I just wanted to tell you that I'm going to your party."

After taking in a sip of the drink, a satisfied smile grew on Bryce's lips. It was pleasing to see the change. He kept his voice low.

"I kind of knew that. I asked your parents, remember?"

Hearing the tone of his voice, I questioned hesitantly, "Is... everything okay?"

Bryce shrugged.

"I didn't mean it in a bad way. It's refreshing to hear good news every now and then, Daisie. Since you asked, my mom is making me fly out to New York the day before my birthday. Last minute business piling up. It's nothing new though, she never really gave a crap anyway."

I didn't know what has become of me, but I felt sympathy towards Bryce. No wonder he wasn't in mood. All of a sudden, the delivery boy chuckled softly.

"I'm surprised that even you noticed something was wrong. Don't think anything though, I'm just not in the right mood right now... but this," he lifted the cup and expressed, "thanks, Daisie."

Saying that it was no problem, I think it was always an accomplished feeling when you could make someone feel better. Even if it was Bryce Valentino, he was a human being too.

Unintentionally, I found myself staring into Bryce's mesmerizing sky blue eyes. I always wondered why Bryce had such sparkling glacial blue eyes compared to the other Valentino men who bore midnight blue eyes.

"You've been staring at me for the longest time. What's wrong?" Bryce's question bought me back to reality.

My eyes dropped to the floor as I mumbled, "I-I just couldn't help but notice how different your eye color is from your family."

An entertained laugh escaped from Bryce. He smirked.

"I thought you were going to tell me I look handsome today. Anyway, I got my eyes from my grandfather. He passed away last year..."

The sudden change in Bryce's voice got me back to look up at him. Hearing him talk about his grandpa tied knots in my stomach. The look in his eyes showcased sadness as if Bryce was recalling back memories of him.

Blinking, I stammered, "I'm sorry. I bet he was an amazing person."

He nodded in agreement.

"He was and always will be. He started Phoenix Empire, you know that? With my grandma.. And don't be sorry, I can't help but miss them," after a moment of silence, Bryce cleared his throat and mentioned, "I have to go. I'll see you on my birthday."

As I waved goodbye to head up to Symphony's, I was stopped when Bryce called me the usual "Daisie". As I looked over my shoulder, his once annoyed facial expression was non-existent.

Bryce had a smile on — though very small — which still made me smile back.

Bryce's voice rubbed against my ear drums as he complimented, "You're really something, you know that?"

Oh no.

I fidgeted back, looking straight ahead, and hoped he wouldn't see my cheeks transform into tomato red. How embarrassing was this? My heart quickened two times faster or so — I couldn't even tell at that point. Every single time, Bryce's words would affect me like this. When I glanced back, Bryce was already gone.

The whole time at work, my ears constantly replayed Bryce say "you're really something, you know that?".

Over and over again.

Even as I walked to the parking lot, my mind would go back to that moment. Seeing his face soften after talking to him made my heart skip a beat. What was the matter with me?

I told myself repeatedly, "This is nothing, this is nothing."

After a moment of non-stop pacing, I finally got his words out of my head.

Exhaling, it was already night fall. The mild summer wind breezed towards my way. Summer was never really my favorite season. The heat always killed me, and I didn't like the fact many girls tended to wear less because of it.

Grabbing my car keys out of my bag, I noticed a figure walking to their car through my peripheral vision. This wasn't something new, but what made me fully look was finding out it was Bryce walking to his car. Squinting my eyes, the lamppost revealed him more, and he probably didn't notice me there.

Debating whether or not I should get his attention, I resisted because I didn't want him to think I was waiting for him or anything creepy like that. Turning away, I found myself looking back at him again anyway. This time, Bryce was much more closer, but why did his face look like he was in pain?

Bryce looked bothered especially with his dark eyebrows knitted sharply, and his lips curved into a frown.

Ignoring what I decided earlier, I ended up putting my car keys back in my purse and headed towards Bryce. As I got closer and closer, I watched as Bryce placed his hand on his neck — as if he wanted to check if he had a high temperature. The delivery boy probably heard the sound of my footsteps and gazed up. My eyes jumped, clearly seeing a sickened expression on his face.

Bryce coughed out, "Daisie..."

Before he could say another word, Bryce abruptly closed his eyes, and his legs stumbled. Dropping my bag onto the ground, I ran as fast as I could to catch him before falling onto the cement.

I shouted through panic, "Bryce! Don't faint on me!"

Luckily, I managed to catch him on time even though I ended up falling onto the floor. His body was as hot as an oven, and the light from the lamppost revealed beads of sweat across that handsome face. Bryce winced as his teeth chattered against together.

Gasping, today was definitely not his day. Bryce Valentino was sick, and I had to be the one to save him.

I cursed under my breath, "Shit, shit. What am I going to do?"

Bryce was still in my arms, trying to level his breathing.

I tried asking, hoping he'd regain conscious, "Bryce? Bryce? Can you hear me? Do you need to go to the hospital? Wait, I'll take you back to the hotel! Is your parents here or at home? Hello? Answer me!"

It was stupid of me to be shouting at someone who was clearly not in the right state of mind.

The only words that managed to escape from Bryce's lips before reaching deep slumber was, "Home..."

Where exactly was home?

Reaching for his car keys that he dropped onto the ground, I pressed the alarm to find the car Bryce was using. It was just a few feet away. Trying to get back up on my feet, I tried pulling up Bryce, and boy, this was difficult. Unless I was just that weak.

Supporting him up with my measly shoulders, my stomach dropped knowing that Bryce owned the most recent Ferrari. I gulped down hard, staring at the red beauty. What hauled my attention over was the GPS system that was attached. Maybe that would have a some kind of home address.

What was I thinking? I couldn't drive his car!

But, this was the only way.

My mind was being thrown in many directions, losing sense of right from wrong.

Opening his car door, I gently placed Bryce onto the passenger seat and let out a tired sigh. Quickly, I grabbed my purse and sat in the driver's seat. My hands were shaking from anxiety as I placed the key into the ignition. I couldn't mess up. This car had to be a half of million dollars — I'd be paying my whole life if anything went wrong.

As the engine of the Ferrari started up, the GPS system turned on as well.

A robotic female voice spoke, "Welcome back, where shall we go?"

How fancy.

Snapping out of it, I stuttered, "U-uh... home?"

To my surprise, Bryce seemed to have registered his home address. The GPS system comprehended, opening up the directions. This car is way too cool.

Calm yourself. Bryce's health was in stake!

The voice commanded, "Start by making a left."

Just hope that I was doing the right thing.

Chapter 13

Not even thinking things through, I was driving Bryce's expensive Ferrari as he was passed out sick.

Following the GPS system's directions, I scolded myself, "Maisie Lockhart, you are definitely being stupid right now."

After making the last right turn, I found myself heading towards a top-notch condominium tower. Shocked, I was expecting a huge mansion of some sort. Supporting Bryce with his arm over my shoulder, I stumbled clumsily while we made our way in. The lobby of the tower was clean and modern, having a monochromatic color palette.

The young and short receptionist noticed me carrying their resident in and quickly ran towards me. Her brown eyes widened as she gasped.

"Is Mr. Valentino alright?"

I explained, "He's sick... Can you call his family?"

Damn, I should have done that in the first place.

The receptionist assisted me to his condo and told me that he lives here by himself. This was home? Bryce didn't live with family.

Opening the door for me, I was in awe of the loft style home. It looked exactly like something from a magazine from the open space to the touch of factory brick. Everything looked so urban. Before the receptionist left, I reminded her to call his family.

I wasn't a doctor, but I knew the basics of lowering a fever.

Placing Bryce onto his black leather L-shaped sectional, I quickly took off his blazer for him to breathe better. This wasn't a tour, so I rapidly tried to find some medicine. I checked the medicine cabinet after searching for the bathroom and grabbed everything that would be helpful.

Pacing to his kitchen, this was like Mom's dream — all black appliances and steel counter tops. I managed to find a cloth I could use to cool Bryce down with and placed some ice into a glass bowl. It was weird enough I was going through Bryce's things, but his fever needed to go down somehow.

Walking back to Bryce, I placed my hand on his forehead, and he was still burning up. The delivery boy was in a deep sleep, but his face still expressed pain. Wrapping the ice in the cloth, I immediately placed it over his forehead. Following what Mom usually did when I was sick, I proceeded with giving him cough syrup and fever reducer. As I got up, I looked around for a blanket to place over him.

Tapping my chin, I wondered, "If I was a spare blanket, where would I be?"

Searching through the oak wood closets by the hallway, I luckily found a comfy white blanket.

Sorry for going through your stuff, Bryce.

I ran back and made sure he was kept warm. Once I finished, I checked his temperature, and it was still high. Trying to calm down, I reasoned with myself that the medicine probably hasn't kicked in.

Throughout the time I waited, I wondered where his parents were. I was sure that I reminded the receptionist many times to call them. Gazing sadly at the sleeping Bryce, he had to have gotten sick because he was overworked. I paced back and forth, hoping I didn't kill the Valentino.

As time passed, I gradually noticed there wasn't any sweat visible anymore, and it appeared like Bryce was breathing more evenly. Grabbing the thermometer, I checked his temperature again, and it was hitting normal. Letting out a relieved smile, his fever was going down.

Losing track of time, I searched for my phone until I realized I left my bag in Bryce's car. That was just outstanding. Finding the nearest clock, it has been four hours, and no sign of his parents either. Walking towards his kitchen, I knew that if someone lived in a luxurious condo, the telephone line would connect to the front desk.

As expected, I found the wireless phone sitting on the counter top and dialed the receptionist. I asked whether or not she called, and she told me that the Valentino's had a business meeting but will soon be on their way. It worried me that if no one was with Bryce, what would have happened? His parents wouldn't leave the meeting, knowing that their son is sick? Well, it wasn't my place to judge.

Rubbing my eyes from exhaustion, I walked back to Bryce. At least his fever has gone down, and his skin color was coming back. Looking over him, I quickly stepped back once I noticed his eyes were beginning to open. Those thick dark eyelashes revealed his captivating sky blue eyes.

Bryce coughed, his voice was raspy.

"What —"

Indicating for him to just relax, I explained, "You're sick, Bryce. You fainted at the parking lot, and I took you back to your place. After some medicine and rest, your fever finally went down."

Bryce looked like he was in disbelief.

Yes, even though he was a Valentino, you was still human.

Bryce felt his neck first before answering, "You... you did all of this?"

Laughing hesitantly, I nodded.

"Yeah, I didn't know what I was thinking. I kind of panicked, and when I panic, I tend to not think clearly. I should have taken you to the hospital."

The atmosphere grew slightly awkward since his now lively eyes were gazing up at me. Bryce slowly got up, and I carefully assisted him. My eyes looked away when our faces got so close.

After handing him a bottle of water, Bryce said once he was done taking a gulp, "Thank you."

Giving him a smile, it was relieving to see him somewhat better. I nodded.

"You don't have to thank me. You got sick out of exhaustion, I bet."

Bryce shook his head.

"I got an allergic reaction earlier today."

Scared, I immediately thought it was because of the drink I gave him. It couldn't be though. My face was probably giving it away, and Bryce twitched into a smile.

He casually explained, "It's not you. My mom gave me some drink that would supposedly help my already sore throat earlier. She probably forgot I was allergic to cinnamon, and I wasn't able to breathe for a while. Guess, it made it all worse."

Speechless, I didn't know what to say. As Bryce glanced around his loft, he chuckled lowly.

"I can't believe you actually did all of this...."

I asked to make sure, "You really are feeling better though, right?"

"Yeah. Thanks to you, Daisie."

Bryce soon gave me a surprisingly warm grin. My heart beat quickened, and I momentarily glanced away.

Tucking my hair behind my ear, I stammered, "I-I'm glad. Making you feel better was definitely a challenge."

Bryce took another sip of water and complimented, "Wouldn't have asked for a better doctor."

My cheeks were probably turning red, making me the sick one.

As I was about to comment on that, the main door rapidly opened, and in came the Valentino's. Bryce's father and mother, and even Logan and David were rushing in. What looked like a real doctor trailed from behind. All of them seemed shocked to see the two of us having a casual conversation.

Bryce's father acknowledged me before talking to Bryce, "Are you okay, son?"

Mr. Valentino motioned the doctor to quickly come examine Bryce.

Standing up, I politely excused myself since I knew it was time for me to go. Giving Bryce one last look, his sky blue eyes were only stuck on me. He looked bothered by the sudden interruption. I was slightly afraid to deal with whatever Bryce's mom was thinking. My eyes couldn't help but look at her reaction. Her brown eyes were cold, but she glanced off to accompany her son. Both Logan and David approached me with concerned faces.

Explaining to them, Logan nodded his head.

"Did you really take care of Bryce all by yourself? Thank you again, Maisie."

Shaking my head, I murmured, "No, it's perfectly fine. It's just good to see he's doing better."

The two thanked me once more before David went off first to see his cousin. Logan looked at me and smiled gently.

"You look tired. Get some rest, okay?"

Nodding my head, I watched Logan who soon followed after to see how Bryce was doing. Looked like they got everything covered. About to leave, I was then stopped when I heard —

"Maisie, can I speak with you?"

My stomach flopped, knowing that voice belonged to none other than Bryce's mother. Gulping, I took a confident deep breath before turning around. I nodded my head solemnly, and the two of us walked outside Bryce's condo. Nervousness soon occupied me.

What did she need to talk about?

Once Monica Valentino closed the door shut, her piercing eyes laid upon me. I wasn't going to lie; Bryce's mother was absolutely stunning. The designer business clothing perfectly suited her tall and slim figure. Her raven, black hair was tied up nicely in a bun, giving her a strong and professional approach.

His mother then remarked, "You should have known to take this matter in professional hands."

I lowered my head slightly, apologizing.

She continued, "I thank you for what you did, but I don't want to see this happening again."

Instead of waiting for a response, she handed me a white envelope from her Louis Vuitton purse.

Not taking it, I questioned respectfully, "May I ask what that is?"

Bryce's mother explained coldly, "It's money. Take this, I'm sure it's enough for you to quit your job at the hotel."

Surprised, I couldn't believe what I was hearing.

Shaking my head, I replied, "I... can't take it. Please, let me keep the job."

After a moment, his mother nodded.

"Fine, but listen to me when I say this, you need to leave my son alone. I don't want to see you with him anymore. You're a bother to my family. Ever since you came, all he's been doing is getting himself into more trouble. I'll let you keep your job, but you must act like you have no relations with Bryce. I also ask of you to not attend his party. Leave him alone, you got that?"

My heart gradually clenched by her words, and I was fighting back the tears that were forming in the rims of my eyes. In the end, she was Bryce's mother. As much as I wanted to resist, I nodded my head. I wasn't going to let her buy me out with money, but it killed me that I had to do this.

I then said, my voice broken, "I'll do that, Mrs. Valentino."

Bryce's mother gave me a nod.

"I heard you left your car at the hotel. A driver of mine is waiting outside to take you back."

Without waiting for a reply, she turned and walked back inside. It took a while to take in everything she just said. No one has ever spoken coldly to me before like that.

Why did she hate me so much? I should have asked her that.

Taking the elevator door down, I found the driver outside. I told him not worry about me and chose to ride the bus with the spare change I had in my pocket.

Nothing was making sense. As much as I held it in during the bus ride, I couldn't help but let the tears fall. It was usually hard to make me cry, but my strength somehow weakened whenever Bryce's mother was around.

To make things even better, I wasn't able to get into my car anyway since I left my bag with everything inside of it inside Bryce's car. I was so screwed right now. Wiping my eyes, I hopelessly stood in front of my car as my mind replayed the conversation with Bryce's mother. I wasn't even able to properly say goodbye to Bryce.

All of a sudden, bright headlights flashed my way. The car engine of a slick, black Lamborghini shut off and out came Logan with my bag in hand — the familiar brown leather caught my attention. Relieved and grateful, I hoped Logan wouldn't notice my watery eyes.

Logan approached me with a smile on his face.

"You forgot this."

Lowering my head so he wouldn't see, I thanked him as I took the bag. Suddenly, I felt Logan's hand gently lift my chin up.

Oh, crap.

Logan's dark blue eyes grew concerned.

"Maisie, why are you crying?"

Shaking my head, I faked a laugh and explained, "Nothing, probably just allergies. Thank you for bringing this to me. I-I should get going now."

Instead, Logan stopped me, giving me that "I'm not taking your bull crap" look. Letting out a sigh, I made up a white lie.

"I was crying because I thought I lost my purse and wouldn't be able to get home. Thanks to you, I feel much better."

Despite it making me sound like a cry baby, I was completely honest about the last part though.

Logan examined me for a while before replying, "You don't have to cry. I'm here for you, okay?"

Giving him a smile, I thanked him again, "I'm grateful for that."

Logan gave me a reassuring smile before the two of us headed off.

As I drove back home, I tried ridding away what Bryce's mother said. But I couldn't. I had to leave Bryce alone because I was a bother. The more I thought about it, she was right. Bryce did get more into trouble because of me. It wouldn't happen again. Making sure I looked completely fine from the car mirror, I locked my car and headed in home.

Checking my phone, I discovered I had so many missed calls from Mom and Pops. When I checked the time, it was already eleven. I was supposed to be home at six. Hearing a light switch flicker open, I prepared myself knowing that it was either going to be Pops or Mom — or both.

Pops revealed himself from the hallway. His soft brown eyes were filled with relief.

"Maisie, where in the world have you been?"

Explaining myself, I said honestly, "Pops, I'm really sorry. I didn't have my phone on me but Bryce got sick, so I stayed with him. I should have called. I'm really sorry."

Pops moved closer towards me and nodded, understanding.

"We were all worried about you. Even Vanessa didn't know where you were. Is everything okay, Maisie?"

I nodded my head, even if it wasn't close to being true.

What was I thinking when I thought Bryce's mother would actually welcome me in open arms for taking care of Bryce?

Then again, I blamed my wishful thinking.

Chapter 14

It has almost been two weeks, and I followed exactly what Bryce's mother said.

The weekend of Bryce's birthday, June 7th, I lied to Vanessa saying that I couldn't make it to the party because I was stuck taking care of the market. The same night, Mason stopped by as I was closing the market, finding me there instead of Mom or Pops. Even my younger brother thought I was going.

I found out that Vanessa called Mason, asking if he could do another favor, but Mason was playing at some local café. Guess everything all worked out.

Throughout the past few days, it was like I literally had no connection with Bryce. In the back of my mind, I worried about him. The last time I saw the delivery boy was the night he got sick, and it bothered me how I didn't get to greet him a happy birthday. My mind was going to explode from over thinking.

Each time after work, I always found myself walking outside to Legends Garden. This place always made me feel better, and I found sanctuary here. The flowers, the atmosphere, everything about it were so welcoming. Sometimes, the sudden memory of Bryce first taking me here would reappear.

Three days ago, I even had an interesting conversation with one of the "flowers" here at the Garden.

Okay, I swore I wasn't crazy. I really did.

Despite me telling Vanessa the real truth the day after Bryce's birthday, it was still bothering me. Vanessa wasn't too happy about my secret, but she was more upset by the fact Bryce's mother told me to back off. When I asked how Bryce's party went, Vanessa looked bothered.

She revealed that even though everyone was having a good time, the birthday boy himself looked upset and left within an hour.

Anyway, this odd conversation with the flower went like this.

I was staring at the daisies for a good five minutes and involuntarily spoke to it, "What am I going to do?"

What made things even more bizarre was when a voice replied back, "Who's this flower talking to me?"

The voice sounded low and masculine — had to be a boy.

Confused, I looked left to right and finally pointed to myself, "Me...?"

I went along with it.

"I'm a daisy, a completely lost daisy."

The voice replied, "Looks like we're the same."

Instead of thinking this was all weird, I continued talking to the flower.

I asked, "Could you help me? Daisy to daisy."

"I guess. What's wrong?" The voice replied in a light tone.

"I've been told to stay away from a certain person. The one who told me to stay away doesn't like me much. I'm not sure if I did anything wrong though."

"Well, you must be pretty dumb to follow what the person says," the voice answered, scolding me.

Raising my eyebrows, I scoffed, "Wait, so it's my fault? I just feel like the person was right. The person they are looking out for, I've been a bother to them. That person shouldn't surround themselves around daisies like me; that person probably fits well around pretty roses instead."

"You're a very confusing daisy. So, what you're saying is you don't think you're good enough for that person? Did you ever think that person feels different about you?"

Shrugging even though the voice couldn't see me, I responded glumly, "I don't know. I never got a chance to talk to that person... I even missed their birthday."

"I'm sure that person was upset too. You should ask the person. You'll have a peace of mind when you do," the voice suggested.

Thinking about it, the daisy was right.

Observing the area, I wondered who this voice actually belonged to. I figured the voice was standing straight ahead. Too bad a vine wall was separating us.

Well, maybe it was for the best. It was like doing confessions.

However, I shook my head and lied, "I think I need to leave that person alone. He's just a delivery boy anyway."

"For just a delivery boy... he seems pretty important to you."

Before I could answer, my cellphone started ringing. The caller ID was blinking Mom.

Turning back to the "daisy", I announced, "I'll think about what you said. You've been a big help. My fellow daisy, I have to go now."

I didn't tell anyone about this conversation though, not even Vanessa. Just reliving that particular moment was starting to question my sanity.

"Maisie! Hold on!" a voice poked my thoughts away.

Stopping myself in the middle of the hotel lobby, I quickly looked over my shoulder and found Logan waving to get my attention. Ever since he saw me crying that one night, he had a hard time letting the subject drop. I told him many times that I was okay, but I knew he was reading past my tainted expression. Guilty, I've been avoiding Logan just as much.

Seeing the sight of him was kind of surprising. Logan wasn't wearing his everyday business attire. Instead, Logan approached me wearing casual clothing — he looked like one of those trendy models I saw in Vanessa's fashion magazines.

Smiling, I waved.

"Hey Logan. I'm just about to go home. What's up?"

When we met at a reasonable distance, his midnight blue eyes glowed from the sunlight. Logan chuckled, running his hand through his jet black hair.

"I don't know how to say this, but I'm getting the feeling you're avoiding me."

Going along with his laughter, I shook my head and replied, "Me? No, of course not! I'm a little surprised seeing you not in work attire."

Logan looked down at his clothes then back at me. He grinned.

"I had a meeting early this morning, but that's all. No work for the rest of the day."

This must be a once in a lifetime opportunity. I had to admit, even though I've been keeping distance from the Valentino's, I noticed how occupied the three were becoming.

Once, I overheard my coworkers saying how the Valentino's deal with their family business from early morning to past midnight. Just staying up during the day got me exhausted already.

Nodding, I gave him a smile.

"That's great news. Any plans for you?"

As I waited for a reply, I noticed Logan cleared his throat and looked away briefly. Thinking something was wrong, I angled my head curiously.

Finally, Logan looked back at me and kindly suggested, "Actually, I don't. Since I saw you, I thought maybe we could spend the day together."

Shocked, I bit my lower lip, but it sounded like a good idea. Logan has been there for me even if I did try to avoid him this past week. I smiled gently, telling him that I'd love to.

Logan grinned and said, "Maybe I could get you to fully smile, huh?"

We decided to go around the fun and games floors of Legends Hotel. When Bryce showed me around, my mouth dropped with amazement seeing the three floors of cosmic bowling and arcade games. The place was huge, and it attracted all ages. For a pair hitting their twenties, it definitely made me feel like a teenager again.

Once we got there, I suggested we go bowling first. The bowling alley occupied one-third each of the three levels. I haven't bowled in forever, but it didn't stop me from challenging Logan. Humiliation swam over me when Logan managed to get four strikes in a row.

Logan joked as I was reaching for my bowling ball, "Should we put the gutters up?"

Glancing up at the screen, I had a lame score of 20. I needed to catch up and make the Lockhart family name proud!

Shaking my head, his taunt did cause me to laugh. Just by bowling with Logan, I was effortlessly happy. Towards the end of our bowling match, I managed to redeem myself by getting three strikes in a row. Overall, Logan hit over 200 while I barely hit the 100's. Despite me losing, Logan encouraged me by giving a high five.

Heading out of the bowling alley, what caught my attention were the pool tables from the next area of the floor. Suggesting those next, Logan nodded with a small grin and off we went. Stumped on the last ball, Logan snagged the win once more, and I congratulated him — even if I didn't like losing. I noticed how Logan would purposely mess up sometimes so I could catch up, but I didn't want any of that.

Throughout our time here, various girls would giggle to their delight, seeing one of the handsome Valentino's walk around. What they frowned upon was the fact I was with him.

Oh well, deal with it.

As we entered the fun filled three-story arcade, I knew there was one thing I could show exceptional skills at — the basketball game! And, I did. Logan looked at me with astonishment when the final scores announced 72-54.

He complimented with a chuckle, "Didn't know you had it in you."

I shrugged, thanking him, "Basketball was my favorite sport in high school."

The hours past, and we spent the rest of the afternoon playing in the arcade from the racing games to scoring tickets. It has been a long time since I got in touch with my kid at heart. I couldn't express enough how much I laughed and smiled because Logan took me here.

When we grew tired — which I never thought was possible — we headed back downstairs to the hotel lobby. Instead of parting ways, I asked if we could take a walk around Legends Garden. I grew such a strong attachment with that place.

Walking side by side through the Garden's cobblestone walk-ways, I smiled.

"Thanks for taking me, Logan. It really made me feel better."

Did I just seriously say that?

Logan caught that and said through a sly grin, "See, I knew something was still bothering you."

"I... didn't mean to say that," sighing, I asked, "Logan, you don't feel weird hanging around with me?"

Hearing his shoes pull to stop, Logan shifted his head to look at me.

"What do you mean, Maisie?"

Grumbling, I only stared at whatever was in front of me.

"Uh, how do I say this? Cause... I'm not like you and your family."

"Maisie, you should know it's not status and money that makes us friends. It's because of who you are. Hold on, is this why you've been avoiding me?"

Logan appeared confused.

Muttering to myself, I scolded, "You should have kept your damn mouth shut, Maisie."

Putting my attention back at Logan, his face was bothered now. I sighed in defeat.

"I'll be honest with you... kind of."

Suddenly, I felt Logan's hand reach for my shoulder. Gazing up at him, he was like a skyscraper compared to me.

Logan said with a kind smile, "Growing up, my grandma once told my cousins and I that we must be people with quality. She said a person may be rich and filled with connections, but if they have a cold heart, they are as low as having nothing. Even people with less can express more character thus making them truly worthy. Our grandma told us that there are very few people surrounding us, having that quality and those are the people who'll make you appreciate life more."

Logan's dark blue eyes gazed down upon mine.

"And she's exactly right."

Taken back, I couldn't help but stare at Logan in admiration while he was talking about his grandma. It bought me back to the time Bryce mentioned about their grandparents. They must have left a huge impact on them.

He added through a laugh, "She even told us when we find a girl, she has to be someone who, not only can help uphold our company, but has that quality as well."

Stammering into a sentence, I said with all seriousness, "You'll find that girl, Logan. Especially with your personality."

His eyes lit up as he replied, "I think I —"

"Did you really think you could get away with driving my car?"

Was that?

Being interrupted, Logan's eyes immediately widened when he spotted who that voice belonged to. Following Logan's gaze, my heart jumped. It was Bryce!

As always, Bryce was handsome from his face to the way he carried himself — even if he did have that signature glare on. Not knowing what to do or say, Bryce continued to stare me down.

His arms were folded and demanded, "You. Me. Talk. Now."

Without waiting for a reply, Bryce marched towards me and grabbed onto my wrist. I resisted, flashing a look between Bryce and Logan. Logan's eyes darkened as he reached out to break Bryce's grip.

"What do you think you're doing?"

Bryce replied coldly at Logan, "I need to talk to her. It's obvious, right?"

Logan talked back, just as harsh, "Let go."

The two were giving each other such fatal stares.

Breaking the sudden tension, I barked out, "Bryce! Let go of my wrist, and I'll talk to you!"

Guess it was time to follow that daisy's advice. The two broke off their stares, and I felt my blood circulating properly on my wrist again. Bryce's glacial blue eyes darted at Logan before looking at mine.

"You ready?"

Perplexed, I couldn't believe Bryce was doing this. He didn't have to make things so dramatic. Now, it seemed like Logan and him weren't on good terms again. I sternly nodded my head in reply.

Before going, I glanced back at Logan and gave him an apologetic look for leaving him so suddenly. As a response, Logan's jaw only clenched tightly before he nodded shortly. Having an inner battle with myself, I wasn't supposed to talk to Bryce.

Yet, there was hidden happiness inside of me as I walked a step behind him.

Chapter 15

"This delivery boy..." I grumbled under my breath as I followed him.

Bryce and I stopped walking once we reached the outside of an abandoned green house towards the lonesome side of Legends Garden. Once Bryce turned around, he didn't have that tensed glare anymore. Instead, was that infamous smirk that seemed to be permanent on his face.

Folding my arms, I commented about what he did, "What was that about?"

"Sorry, did I ruin something important?" Bryce taunted with a smirk.

Thinking back at that moment, Logan did look like he was in the middle of saying something. Bryce over here just had to "rise from the dead" and come out of nowhere. When I didn't reply back, Bryce started to chuckle softly.

As Bryce shook his head side to side, he preached, "I didn't like what I was seeing."

My eyebrows scrunched together as I inquired, "Bryce, what are you talking about?"

Raising his hand up, Bryce gestured to forget about it. His blue eyes now jumped at me, and he gave me a sideways grin.

"Daisie, you act like you're the victim. I seriously thought you died. Explain."

As I continued to stand there dumbfounded, I eventually realized the delivery boy must have been talking about how I made myself disappear this past two weeks. Ignoring that, I wasn't going to let Bryce get away with what happened.

I stated dryly, "What you did was rude."

"Look who's talking," he retorted in a clever tone.

Biting my tongue, I soon replied, "Okay, I'm sorry Bryce Valentino for missing your birthday. I'm sorry for driving your expensive Ferrari without permission. I'm sorry for not saying sorry to you earlier. I'm sorry for making it seem like I died. I'm sorry."

As soon as I finished, Bryce inched his face closer to mine. As I took a few steps back, I felt my back hitting against the glass wall of the greenhouse. Great. I was about to be surrounded by Bryce — once again. Squinting my eyes, I waited for some reply.

Bryce stated, his breath smelling like peppermint, "Actually, I don't care about you driving my car, but to miss my birthday, that's very unforgivable."

Why did he have to smell so good?

Not only his breath, but his masculine yet light cologne was drawing me in.

Mentally shaking my head, I bit my lower lip before settling a peace offering, "I'll buy you hazelnut coffee everyday as an apology and a gift."

Those sky blue eyes blinked mockingly, and Bryce commented, "That's it? All the hazelnut coffee in the world isn't going to fix it."

Glancing away, I murmured, "I had my reasons, Bryce. I really am sorry."

The sudden memory of my conversation with his mother reappeared — those cold brown eyes were inevitable. Suddenly, Bryce's voice lightened.

"I know."

When I finally looked back up at our close distance, his lips stretched into a close grin.

Bryce then revealed, "I am just a delivery boy, right?"

My eyes widened hearing him say those words like that. He was mocking me. My private daisy to daisy conversation was with Bryce this whole time? How humiliating could this get? How could I have not recognized his voice?

As my stomach was turning, I lowered my head.

"Fuck. It was you this whole time."

Bryce chuckled at my response.

"Sure was. Looks like you weren't even going to take my advice. That is also unforgivable."

Leveling my eyes with Bryce, I was about to answer until he stopped me by abruptly placing his two fingers over my lips.

What in the world?

He continued letting himself talk, "Never mind that, Daisie. As a late birthday present..."

A sudden change shifted in his expression. Bryce looked absolutely alluring. My eyes widened seeing his lips stretch into a grin like that. As Bryce moved his face closer to mine, my heart thumped so loud, I was worried I wasn't the only one hearing it. Bryce's eyes twinkled.

"Can you be..."

His voice drifted off, causing me to cringe with anxiety.

The suspense was killing me!

With the way Bryce was going with his sentence, 'can you be', could this be?

Was he going to ask me to be his girlfriend?

Preparing myself, I was growing a smirk on my covered lips.

"...the one to tell me who you saw first?"

Rapidly lifting his fingers off my lips, Bryce waited for a response. My smirk dropped into a surprised frown. Of course, he would!

Confused and disappointed — I hated this feeling — I blinked.

"What?"

Bryce folded his arms, finally taking a step back to let me breathe perfectly again.

"Me or Logan?"

Where was this going? Recalling back anyway, it was Bryce. He was the delivery boy after all.

I answered quietly, "Uh, it was you."

After hearing that, a satisfied grin grew on his lips.

Bryce said through a triumphant grin, "That's what I thought."

"Is that all?"

The question slipped out of my mouth. Nodding, Bryce gave me a vacant expression.

"Why? Did you think I was going to ask something else?"

Quickly shaking my head no, Bryce stared momentarily until he ended up chuckling to his entertainment. I never felt so embarrassed. As I was feeling miserable, Bryce eventually stopped. His voice altered to a more serious tone.

"By the way, you don't have to worry about that person anymore."

Taken back from the sudden mood change, was Bryce talking about his mother? My eyes gazed back up at him, finding Bryce looking completely sincere.

Pursing my lips, I muttered out, "So, you know."

To think we'd have a serious conversation.

Bryce let out a light laugh and pointed out the obvious, "Really Daisie? You pretty much confessed everything to me, remember?"

Damn it, this conversation was making me look bad.

Bryce's voice partied with taunt, "Didn't know you missed me so much."

Rolling my eyes at him, I ended up mocking him back until Bryce rapidly shot me a glare. I guess this meant that everything was allright between us? No matter what, I knew nothing was going to change between his mother and me though. Because I was drifting off, I didn't notice that Bryce was walking away already.

When I called out to Bryce, he stopped and glanced over his shoulder.

"Happy birthday, Bryce. Even if I'm late."

Saying those words released the stress in my heart as I smiled.

A smirk appeared, and Bryce reminded, "Thanks, Daisie. But don't you forget to give your delivery boy his hazelnut coffee."

Shouldn't he be the one doing the deliveries?

But what caught my ears was 'your delivery boy'.

"Who does he think he is?" I blurted out loud, walking towards my family market.

Bryce Valentino was always going to be the unpredictable kind. During my whole car ride, I reminisced about my conversation with my fellow daisy who turned out to be Bryce.

"I'm sure that person was upset too. You should ask the person. You'll have a peace of mind when you do."

How did he even find me? I was positive Bryce was busy. Suddenly remembering what Vanessa said about Bryce's birthday, was Byce upset and left early because of —

No. That couldn't be right.

Slapping my cheeks, I told myself, "Stop assuming things, Maisie."

"Maisie, it's you! It's been a while!" A cheerful, boy voice called out to me.

Lifting my head from staring at the cement ground, I found one of Mason's band mates and close friend, Alec Kingsley. Unlike Mason's other band mates, Alec was definitely the more happy-go-lucky kind of guy. He was exactly Mason's height — nearing six feet — and shared the same physique. Although, Alec had shaggy blondish brown hair and crisp hazel eyes.

Giving him a smile, I washed away my past thoughts.

"Hey Alec. What brings you here?"

What I didn't notice was Alec carrying his guitar bag. He grinned.

"Mason called band practice here."

My eyes widened.

"At the market?"

Alec gave me a nod and beamed with excitement, "Yeah! It was way cool. The customers had a good time."

Amused, I was picturing the reactions of the customers. I must admit, their sound was enjoyable to my taste. They ranged from rock to frequent pop rock.

Adjusting my purse on my shoulder, I asked, "How've you been?"

The boy appeared to be shocked from my simple question.

He stammered, "I've been good! Just looking for some colleges. Hey Maisie, you should come by and watch us sometime. You know, show some support to me — Er, I mean the band — and Mason, of course!"

Completely forgetting that Alec Kingsley had a huge crush on me during my last two years of high school, I ended up nodding my head anyways. The guilt trip reached me because the last time I saw Mason and his friends perform was — wow, I didn't even remember.

Alec's hazel eyes soon illuminated eagerly. The grip of his guitar tightened — so tight it looked like it was about to break. His voice rang a notch.

"You'd really come watch us?"

I managed to grin.

"Sure. You're right, I need to show some support."

Alec's cheeks flushed red, and I started to feel guilty because it appeared like I was getting the kid's hopes up.

"Alec, you're not going home yet? Oh, Maisie!" Now, that voice belonged to my brother.

Mason was closing up the market, and that was when I looked at the time on my cellphone. It was already ten o'clock. My brother approached the two of us, carrying a bag containing his electric guitar on one shoulder and carrying his acoustic guitar with his hand.

Curious with our talking, Mason glanced over at Alec. That look which I knew what kind of telepathic thoughts they were sending each other. Alec soon waved at me.

"Well, nice seeing you, Maisie."

"Whenever your guys' next performance is, let me know," I said with a smile.

Grinning widely, Alec nodded and turned his attention back to Mason. The two did their signature handshake, and as soon as Alec disappeared in the night, Mason started laughing.

"Seriously Maisie? You're going to watch us?"

Folding my arms, I frowned a little.

"You act like I don't care. And, I didn't want to reject him after the millionth time."

He snickered out, "I know. Anyway, why are you here?"

"Taking you home, of course."

As the two of us walked back to my car, I decided to start some small talk with Mason.

I shortly broke the silence, "So, have you decided what you want to do yet?"

Mason fixed the strap on his shoulder and nodded. I briefly assumed he was thinking of taking a music major.

He replied, "I want to be a doctor, Maisie."

This made my heels pull to a stop. Giving him a bewildered look, his answer left me in disbelief. However, Mason stared back at me with a serious face — the exact face during the time he admitted to me that he liked Vanessa.

Raising my eyebrows, I wanted to clarify again, "You want to do what?"

"I love music — don't get me wrong — but, I want to be the one to help people for a chance. Like you, Maisie. You gave up going to college to help me and Mom and Pops —"

"Mason, you shouldn't have to bring that up," I interrupted.

Mason shook his head and pressed on, "Come on! You don't have to pretend around me, Maisie. You sacrificed so much for us."

I replied, "It shouldn't affect your dreams, Mason."

Mason turned me with his hands to completely face him.

"Fine, music is one of my dreams. Don't you believe me when I say becoming a doctor is my dream too?"

Biting my tongue, I eventually gave in noticing how genuine Mason was about this. Mason wanted to be a doctor — he would make a great one, I already knew it. Sighing, I gave out a tiny smile.

"Okay... I'm sorry for what I said. I just thought you wanted to stop playing music just to pay me back or something."

Mason's face brightened as he snorted a laugh.

"Maisie, who says I'll stop doing music?"

Giving him a look, I joined in his laughter. Mason would be the best guitar playing doctor then. Happy to know about his choice, we both continued walking.

Then, Mason asked me a question, "How's you and Bryce, by the way?"

"What about?"

"Do you think I'm that dense? You've been avoiding Bryce, even Logan for a while now," he muttered his observation.

Shrugging, I responded honestly, "We're okay. There are times where I just want to strangle him, and there are times where I actually miss that delivery boy."

Hold on a second, was I seriously just admitting that to my younger brother?

"It looks like he's tugging your heartstrings," Mason stated a matter of fact.

Hearing something about strings made me think he was talking about music. I shook my head.

"I don't understand guitar talk."

"Heartstrings. Heartstrings, Maisie," Mason emphasized more slowly and loudly as his eyes widened.

"What?" I asked, still confused.

Mason flashed me a glare, thinking I was joking with him. But honestly, I had not one clue about what he was talking about.

Letting out an exasperated sigh, Mason explained, "Heartstrings are your strongest affections."

Tapping my chin, I claimed, "Heartstrings, that's something I never heard before."

Even though I seriously wasn't playing around, Mason threw his hands out in frustration, causing his guitar to lightly hit my left side.

"Maisie, you're missing the point! You like Bryce Valentino! And, I have a feeling you're tugging his heartstrings too."

Scoffing in disbelief, Mason had to be kidding me.

Fishing out my car keys, I corrected Mason even though he didn't appear to be listening, "No heartstrings are being tugged right now."

But that, my friends, may be the biggest lie I told at the time.

Chapter 16

Today, Mom and I were taking care of the market. The two of us were occupying the front counter for the most part since it was another one of those slow, unproductive days.

As I was busy cleaning the windows, Mom called to my attention, "Maisie, so Mason told me you're talking with the Valentino's again?"

Laughing, I sprayed some window cleaner onto the glass and rubbed the cloth in a circular motion.

I replied, "What else does Mason reveal about me?"

Hearing Mom chuckle, I finished cleaning before walking back to her. Placing the cleaner and cloth into the drawer we kept by the front counter, I turned back to face her.

Nodding my head, I continued, "Yeah Mom, I saw Logan and Bryce a few days ago. Logan's okay, and Bryce is still his usual self."

Mom gave me a tiny smile and tilted her head, asking, "Maisie... do you like Bryce?"

I abruptly shook my head.

"Don't listen to what Mason says."

"Oh honey, I'm not following Mason's words. I'm asking you."

Pausing for a moment, I blinked away momentarily and reassured her, "I don't know, Mom. He's sarcastic and conceited... but surprisingly kind... and always unpredictable."

As I was rambling on and on, I noticed a fully sized grin form against Mom's lips and I sighed to stop myself.

Mom replied, "Sweetie, as long as Bryce treats you right and makes you happy... that's all I care about. But, you have to tell me if something is wrong, okay? I know you resisted dating."

She was probably referring to all her failed attempts of hooking me up with the customers here. Still, I felt guilty because I never told anyone besides Vanessa about what Bryce's mother had said to me. I just knew it was unnecessary drama. No one needed that.

As I nodded my head, I quickly changed the subject, "So, Mom, how did you fall in love with Pops?"

All I really remembered was that Pops and Mom were best friends ever since they were little, but that was really it. Her almond shaped hazel eyes lit up as she smiled warmly, probably recollecting that memory.

Mom answered, her face was expressing joy, "You know that your father and I were very close friends when we were young. I developed stronger feelings for him during high school, but I always thought we would just stay as friends. What we didn't know was that we were both in love with each other, but chased after the wrong people during that time. In the end, your father was always the love of my life. He was there for me through thick and thin, in light and in dark."

Mom's eyes started to water until she started to giggle like she was reliving her high school self. I gave her a huge smile and hugged her. Best friends who became soul mates. It was truly something we read in those romance books.

"Maisie! Maisie! Oh my god!" A voice came barging into the market.

Our embrace broke off when the two of us found Vanessa rushing in, completely out of breath. Surprised out of my life, this was the first time I had seen Vanessa in this state. Her usual neat honey brown hair was now a mess, probably from running, and her face looked a little creepy — cause she was smiling widely.

Vanessa exposed her bright, white teeth. That meant something good happened.

Like, very good.

When Vanessa caught sight of Mom, she chirped, "Mama Lockhart, how are you?"

Mom beamed, "Good as always… Is everything all right?"

As Vanessa was fixing her hair, I reached out to help the missed strands. Giving her a confused look, she soon started jumping up and down before she pulled me into a bear hug. What on earth? Vanessa started twirling me in a circle to a point where I was getting nauseated. The entire time, Mom was laughing at the sight. My expression, however, was stale. While she was spinning me, Vanessa was just laughing non-stop.

Did she just want to throw me around and laugh at my rag doll reflexes?

Completely shifting my feet sturdy onto the floor, I shouted, "Vanessa, what is wrong with you?"

Vanessa's face simply glowed with happiness. This kind of joy was unexplainable to Mom and me. The thing that was scaring me was the fact Vanessa wasn't saying anything. Nothing came out except loud, happy giggling. Glancing back at Mom, she looked just as confused.

Clapping her hands, Vanessa managed to squeal out, "He asked me, Maisie! He asked me!"

Her green eyes started to tremble until real tears started to pour out.

"Who asked you? Wait, David?" I asked, becoming excited.

Mom handed Vanessa a tissue, and Vanessa thanked her before responding.

"I'm so happy right now!"

She went on about how her date yesterday night with David was the best moment of her life. Oh, that was right. She said she would call me but I fell asleep at 9 — grandma status, but I had a long day in my defense.

Throwing her hands out, she beamed, "David asked me to be his girlfriend! We're officially together now!"

My mouth dropped from surprise, growing happy for her. I just knew that moment was going to happen! Seeing Vanessa like this was something new. Throughout her sixteen boyfriends, not one has made her this happy before.

Now, I pulled her to a hug and rejoiced along, "I knew he would! I'm so happy for you, Van!"

Vanessa returned the hug, except much more tighter and kissed my cheek lightly before running to Mom and planting a kiss on her cheek too. If she continued going around kissing people, that may become a problem.

Mom stroked Vanessa's hair happily, her eyes expressed the same happiness.

"Oh sweetie, look at you!"

Vanessa blushed, recalling about how he asked her.

David Valentino, being the romantic guy I knew he was, took Vanessa to that exquisite restaurant on top of the hill, Spotlight Grove. Turned out, he rented the entire place just for them. David and Vanessa had dinner at the best spot of the place. The balcony where you could see all the city lights and eat food made by high class chefs. Vanessa started tearing up again when she reached the part where David had went through all the trouble just to ask her.

She shook her head happily, cheeks red.

"It was like he was proposing! I told him a simple question will do, but he went all out!"

Usually, I found this cheesy when I overhear other girls talk about stuff like this, but I couldn't help but join the excitement with Vanessa and Mom.

Vanessa said through her smiling, "Maisie, David is the one. The one."

As I was about to reply back, my phone started ringing. Way to ruin the moment. Letting out an annoyed sigh, I checked my caller ID.

It was my coworker, Rachel. Picking it up, I casually greeted her with a "hey".

"Lockhart, can you please do me a big favor?"

The frantic tone contrasted her typical upbeat voice.

Confused, I replied, "What's wrong, Rach?"

"My tooth! My fucking tooth chipped off, and I have to go to the dentist, like right now!"

There was a part of me that wanted to bust out laughing, and another part that reminded me to act like a civil lady and understand the poor girl's situation.

Keeping a collected attitude, I casually asked, "What did you do?"

Rachel whined on the other line, "Don't laugh, okay? But I was laughing, and at the same time, I was about to drink a glass of water, and then I accidentally hit my tooth against the glass cup, and it chipped my tooth! I can't believe this is happening to me. Please Lockhart, can you cover my shift? I just can't go to work with a half tooth!"

Quickly cupping the receiver, I released all the laughter, although I did feel bad for Rachel at the same time. Vanessa and Mom both looked at me with curious faces until I composed myself and placed my cellphone back to my ear.

I answered, "Yeah, don't worry about it. I hope you'll be able to fix it, Rachel."

Letting out a depressed sigh, she mumbled, "Thanks Lockhart, I owe you. Well, I have to go now, my tooth needs help asap."

Telling her that it was no problem, we bid our goodbyes and hung up. Back to Legends Hotel again. When I told them I was covering a shift, Vanessa clapped her hands again, saying how she had to go over there anyway.

Before leaving, I kissed Mom goodbye, and she whispered teasingly, "Don't spend too much time at the hotel, okay?"

Vanessa and I laughed in unison before heading out.

My best friend offered with a smile, "I'll drive you there and wait for you to get off."

Stunned, I joked, "This is something I could get use to."

Vanessa stuck her tongue out playfully in return.

As Vanessa and I walked through the revolving front doors, I was beginning to get tired of seeing this hotel almost everyday. Unbelievable, right? Something as glamorous as this, who would get tired of this place? Maybe because instead of being the guests who came here to have fun, I was stuck working day and night.

Vanessa was looking around the hotel lobby, probably in search of David. Looking at the time on my phone, it was almost Rachel's shift.

Tugging onto the sleeve of Vanessa's dress, I motioned, "Van, I'm heading up for work, okay? I'll call you. Maybe you should call David too, so you don't look so lost."

I giggled at my last sentence, and Vanessa jokingly gave me a sour face. We both hugged each other good bye before I adjusted my feet, ready to head to the elevators.

"You show up here without my hazelnut coffee? Seriously, Daisie?"

Only one person would say that or call me that.

Glancing over my right, I found Bryce standing there with a mocking grin smacked on his face. Quickly turning away, I knew I should have stopped by Brightside Café before coming here.

Wait a second, why was I getting so scared of Bryce?

Looking back, Bryce had his dark eyebrows raised, waiting for a response. This time around, David was standing next to him with a friendly smile.

Where was Vanessa?

Clearing my throat, I replied sternly, "I—I..."

"David!"

Vanessa, I love you so much right now.

In came Vanessa to the picture.

David grinned brightly at the sudden sight of her. My eyes caught them embrace each other romantically. It was like the world only consisted of the two of them — very cute.

When I noticed Bryce's reaction, he appeared to be rolling his eyes before locking them onto me. Those icy blue eyes made me jump. Bryce took a couple more steps towards me, leaving Vanessa and David alone. He folded his arms once he approached me. My eyes slowly gazed up to look at him.

Bryce smirked, throwing his hand out in between us.

"One hazelnut coffee, please."

Pursing my lips, I replied completely confident, "I didn't have a chance to get one. Sorry."

Suddenly, Bryce fixed his standing position just so our eyes were leveled with one another. Blinking away, I really hated when he did this. Especially since it made me feel inferior.

He scoffed teasingly, "What kind of birthday gift is this?"

"Hey, what's going on with you two?"

Did I mention how much I loved Vanessa right now?

Bryce and I broke our glances and turned our attention to Vanessa and David. The two really showcased their relationship as they held hands. Vanessa leaned in, shooting me a curious look.

About ready to jet off because I didn't like being the center of attention, and plus, I was already late for Rachel's shift, my mission was suddenly aborted when —

"Bryceyyyyy!" A sweeter than sugar sounding voice entered.

Seemed like our conversation just kept adding and adding. However, I wasn't expecting this addition once I noticed who said that.

Standing before us was a tall, very thin girl. No one that seemed familiar. Her soft platinum blonde hair that was curled reached past her shoulders, and she had playful blue-green eyes. The girl had the facial structure of a model — big eyes, full lips, high cheekbones — she was gorgeous. Not only that, but her clothes were something that Vanessa would kill to wear.

More importantly, who was she?

The four of us were gazing at the girl until I realized she called Bryce. She even called him "Brycey".

When I looked for some kind of reaction, I found David's jaw clenching as his dark blue eyes widened while Vanessa looked just as surprised as her mouth dropped. Only then did I notice that my mouth was wide open too. Quickly clamping it shut, my eyes made their way towards Bryce.

I swear I wasn't kidding, but I never saw Bryce looked so disgusted before.

It was like he staring at a pile of shit.

The girl whipped her shiny, blonde hair and batted her eyes innocently.

"Why aren't you happy to see me? It's been ten years! I'm sorry I missed your birthday, Brycey! Aunt Monica told me I'd be the perfect surprise!"

Now, all of us were looking at Bryce and his disturbed facial expression. His usual spirited blue eyes appeared to have lost the life out of them.

Bryce's only words were, "You have got to be kidding me. What kind of birthday gift is this?"

Chapter 17

"**Y**ou have got to be kidding me. What kind of birthday gift is this?"

You could just imagine the look on all our faces hearing that. Never did I see Bryce look so downright disgusted.

The girl blinked her blue-green eyes numerous times and pouted. Maybe she couldn't comprehend what she just heard.

She let out a whine, "You hurt me, Brycey!"

Bryce appeared to be sick in the stomach. He shook his head vigorously, indicating that he was leaving.

"I got to go —"

Before Bryce could even make a move, the girl grabbed him by the arm and smiled.

"Help me carry my bags up to my room, Brycey! Let's catch up."

"You're not the queen over here," Bryce spat out, not bothering to look at her in the eye.

The annoying girl wouldn't budge as she was clinging onto him like monkey bars. Glancing back at David and Vanessa, the two were just standing like statues. David seemed like he knew who the girl was. Once Vanessa noticed my staring, her green eyes widened.

She mouthed out, "Model!"

The girl was a model?

When I fixed my attention back to Bryce and the girl, he managed to pull away from her grasp while taking a few steps back in retreat. The girl put off her undivided attention on Bryce momentarily and settled her large blue-green eyes on the three of us. She flashed a smile, catching David as she stated how much she missed him too. Before David could react, Vanessa and I watched the girl hug him tightly.

David said slowly through their embrace, "You... dyed your hair."

She let go of David and twirled around.

"I know. It's pretty, right? My manager told me blonde would enhance my look compared to my brown hair!"

At the same time, Vanessa was throwing a 'back up, bitch' face at her.

Finally, the girl acknowledged Vanessa's — along with my — presence. She was quite tall, probably 5 foot 9 or 10, somewhere along those lines.

The girl asked with a sly grin, "Do you know who I am?"

The pitiful greeting was very far from a hello, or nice to meet you. Shaking my head no, my head angled to Vanessa. Surprisingly, she nodded.

Vanessa gave a blunt reply, "You model in Europe. Candace Reynolds."

"Candy," she corrected, her eyes turning into thin slits.

My friend countered back, "Sorry. Heard you were just starting out."

Her rebuttal caused me to stifle a laugh. Vanessa was usually bitter towards any girl who decided to be a smart ass with her. Candace "Candy" Reynolds didn't find this very funny though.

Candace gritted her teeth together.

"I am one of the best models in Europe. I. Am. Famous," she stressed her last sentence sharply.

David stepped into the conversation, calming the fire.

"Candace, this is my girlfriend Vanessa Montgomery. Be good to her."

Even though the two exchanged sweetened smiles, I could read way past Vanessa's eyes. She didn't like her at all. And I didn't either. Ms. Candace Reynolds already gave me the vibe that she was "royalty trash". I could hardly stand someone who looked down upon another. Candace turned away, focusing her attention on me. She probed me as she glanced from head to toe.

So, what? I wasn't wearing my best outfit.

Candace concluded, "You're that worker. Go carry my bags."

Not only did I give her a look of disbelief, but so did David and Vanessa — even Bryce.

Did she want to pick fights with ever girl she met?

Scrunching my eyebrows together, I reasoned, "That's not my job. A simple hello would do. Are you not capable of that?"

Even if I was being a little rude, this girl's attitude wasn't working for me at all. Past Candace, I noticed Vanessa giving me a thumbs up.

Candace muttered out, "Aunt Monica was right. You're nothing but a bother."

Excuse me. What did she just say?

Her once innocent eyes stabbed right through me as her lips rose into a sly grin. Giving her the cold shoulder, I completely ignored her words and looked away. Suddenly, the sound of Candace's footsteps marched towards me, and she grabbed my upper right arm.

The pain electrified since she was pressing onto my still-in-healing cut. Remember the damage jackass Jason caused? As I winced, she found amusement to this, thinking I was weak.

I coughed out, "Let go of my arm!"

But nothing. The two-face even decided to press harder.

From behind, Vanessa looked like she was ready to pull onto Candace's golden hair until someone else harshly broke off Candace's hold. A gasp escaped from me when it turned out to be Bryce. Once Candace finally let go, I instantly placed my hand over my arm. Vanessa was soon by my side and gave Candace, who was now standing so innocently, the nastiest look. David didn't look pleased at all either.

Candace's voice came out insincere.

"I just wanted to get her attention, that's all."

Bryce's expression darkened as he warned, "Candace, don't ever think about laying a finger on Maisie again. You need to apologize because she's still recovering from a injury. Don't play all nice and shit because I know that's not who you really are. God, you're so annoying!"

I couldn't believe Bryce was defending me again.

Several people walking through the lobby had been watching everything.

How wonderful.

After his shouting though, Bryce picked up Candace's luggage anyway, storming off without looking back. Once Candace noticed, she happily followed behind him, finding success.

I officially hate Candace Reynolds.

Exhaling sharply, I couldn't believe this was happening. Especially in public.

Vanessa was gently rubbing the side of my arm, her voice concerned as it bought me back to reality.

"You sure you can go to work, Maisie?"

David was also by my side and suggested, "You should go home. I can deal with the manager."

As I took in their encouraging faces, I shook my head in return. So-called model, Candace, wasn't going to stop me so easily. Giving them a smile, I shook off the pain.

"No, it's okay. I have to cover a shift for my coworker anyway."

Not only did I get into trouble for being fifteen minutes late to work, I was now fuming at how badly this day has become. All because Candace Reynolds came in the picture. To think that a pretty girl that looked like a model was actually a model.

A stuck up, Bryce-fanatic one at that too.

What bothered me most was how Bryce still carried her bags. Just by the moment he caught sight of her, I knew he didn't like her.

So, why? Was he just being a gentlemen?

Candace didn't deserve it.

No, I was not jealous.

Slamming my locker door in the changing room, I let out an irritated sigh. My mind wouldn't let go about what happened. It seemed like Candace was closely tied to the Valentino family. She even called Bryce's mother "Aunt Monica". Not that I cared.

When I snapped out of my thoughts, I noticed my coworker was glimpsing curiously at my direction.

I explained tiredly, "Not a good day, Kristen."

Kristen gave me a look of sympathy since she also overheard me being scolded by our more uptight manager, Mr. Randall King, earlier today. I missed Manager Gray, who was currently on a five week vacation in Hawaii. Lucky.

Fixing her dirty blonde hair that was tied up into a ponytail, Kristen joined my sighing. Her forest green eyes soon enlarged.

"It's okay, Lockhart. We all have those days," she then whispered, "Word's going around saying that you got into a fight with that model."

Surprised, news did travel fast around here.

Kristen went on, "Did you really punch her in the face? Apparently she was bawling her eyes out in her hotel room."

Huffing, I couldn't believe what I was hearing. What a lie!

Placing my hands on my hips, I said in my defense, "Of course not! She started the whole argument. That's all that happened."

Kristen nodded her head, "I figured. She came in earlier today and was a complete brat."

Picking up my bag, I muttered in a bitter tone, "Now that doesn't surprise me.. See you later, Kristen."

"Be careful, Lockhart. She's very close to the Valentino's, she could destroy you," Kristen's voice rang with worry.

Candace Reynolds could fucking try.

Making my way down the elevator, I hoped that I wouldn't run into anyone. People were already giving me looks from Candace's "sob story". Sending Vanessa a text, she instantly replied saying that she was outside by the parking lot. I was just ready for this day to be over.

Once the elevator doors slid open, I walked out but was unexpectedly stopped by a little girl. She was staring up at me, and I couldn't help but notice how much she resembled Candace.

Was everyone just starting to look like Candace Reynolds to get in my head?

The little girl looked very adorable though, wearing a white bow on her head. She had straight, light brown hair that ran along her rib cage. However, her facial features from her blue-green eyes, nose, lips to face structure bore resemblance to that two-faced model.

Why was I comparing this poor girl to Candace?

Not taking another step, I glanced down at the nine or ten year old.

"Hi. May I help you?"

The little girl held her hand out.

"Carlianne Reynolds. Call me Carly. Actually, I'm here to help you."

Reynolds.

Call me crazy, but she had to be related.

Taking her tiny hand slowly, I questioned, "Nice to meet you Carly. If you don't mind me asking, are you related —"

"Yes, please don't say the name. I'm not on my devil of a sister's side," she interrupted, folding her arms.

This little girl kept taking me by surprise.

Carly's large eyes looked up at me, and she sighed.

"I just want to tell you that Candace is a dummy. I heard what happened when she was crying earlier. I swear she acts like she's five. Anyway, I know the truth, and I'm here to support you, Maisie Lockhart."

Why did it feel like this little girl was my defense attorney? She was speaking so maturely. One could mistake Carly as the older sister if you put them both behind screen doors. Nodding my head hesitantly, I was somewhat confused by her actions.

"That's really sweet of you, Carly. But you don't have to go through all -"

Once again, I was being cut off.

Ever since I step foot at the hotel today, I wasn't able to respond fully like a grown adult.

Carly shook her head.

"I don't want to hear it. Listen up, Lockhart."

Having no choice, I listened to her random lecture.

Carly revealed, "Us Reynolds' are close to the Valentino's. Auntie Monica is my mom's best friend. They both want Candace and Bryce to marry each other and live happily ever after. Gag me with a spoon. It's been their dream ever since they were in college and both finally pregnant. Anyway, you can see how desperate my sister is with Bryce while Bryce hates every bit of her."

"Before I was born, I heard stories when they were my age. Candace forced Bryce to play a fake wedding, making his poor cousins do the ceremony. I could see why Bryce is so traumatized. It's been ten years since they last saw each other because my family moved to Europe so Candace could become a model. You'd think they would give up, but even up until now, my mom and Aunt Monica are forcing the two to get along."

She swayed her index finger at me, smirking.

"Now, this brings you in the picture. Candace sees you as an opponent. She will do anything just to get rid of you. But you,

Lockhart, need to stay strong. I'm here to help you! Even if I'm going back home in a month, we're going to beat Candace!"

Soaking this all in, this confirmed even more that Candace Reynolds was a straight up lunatic.

Raising my eyebrow, I inquired, "Beat Candace at what exactly?"

"Everything. You're better than her. Plus, you're going to win Bryce's heart in the end."

Carly gave me a smile of satisfaction.

Bryce again.

I shook my head reassuringly.

"I don't like Bryce like that. I don't want to get involved."

A shudder ran up my spine, remembering how I had such a bad note with Bryce's mom.

Carly waved her hand around and stated a matter of fact, "Nonsense. I don't have to be there or see to know that you like him."

I stated firmly, "I don't. Anyway, some rumor is going around about Candace and me. What really happened?"

Carly rolled her eyes at my comment about Bryce, and then answered, "Don't worry, I'll do damage control. The crybaby was crying because once Bryce dropped off her bags, he didn't bother to say another word to her and went off. She deserves it, right? I heard that she was pressing against your injury. I'm sorry about my sister's lack of brains. She thinks her non-existent muscles were hurting you, what a joke!"

Telling her it was fine even though I did hate the fact Candace violated me like that, I questioned, "Carly, why are you so against your sister anyways?"

The little girl pursed her pink colored lips.

"I never liked her ever since I was born on this planet. Well, I think so. Candace and I never got along. She's too busy thinking about herself and how her so called wedding is going to go with Bryce. Annoying."

After a moment, Carly announced, "Looks like I have to go. My bubble bath should be ready by now."

A giggle escaped from her, "Lockhart all the way! Nice meeting you, Maisie, bye!"

As Carly gleefully skipped off to the elevator, I watched her dumbfounded, still unsure if this whole conversation happened. This little girl was like a complete adult. I was surprised being approached by Candace's younger sister like that. Carly liked me more than her own flesh and blood?

Well, I had nothing to complain about.

Bring it on, Candace Reynolds.

Chapter 18

Something was definitely weird.

When I came into work today, Manager King apologized for yelling at me. He never took back what he said to his employees. Not only that, but in the locker room were flowers from Candace.

A bouquet of beautiful, red roses with a tiny card that said in her curly-shaped writing:

I'm sorry for what I did to you. Please forgive me. Let's be friends.

Love, Candace.

This had to be a sick dream.

However, it wasn't. I pinched myself many times to wake up, even asked Kristen to slap my face a few times — she wouldn't though — and it was all true. Manger King and Candace asking for my forgiveness? It wasn't April Fool's day; it was almost July. So that couldn't be it.

Assuming that Carly forced Candace to drink some potion that made her suddenly nice — though highly unlikely — or smacked some sense into her older sister — I would love to see that happen — I had a hard time believing this sudden burst of friendliness.

It has only been a day since she made me look like a bad guy.

Ending my shift, I was checking my cellphone and noticed I had a missed call. It was just an unknown number.

Checking my voice mail, a familiar voice spoke, "H-hey... Maisie! It's A-A-Alec. Um, you didn't pick up... your... your phone. Ha..ha..ha, obviously. Man, what is wrong with me? Uh... so... so.... I just wanted to t-tell you that we're performing at L-L-Lucky House Café tonight at 6. If you're... free... did you want to come and watch us? O-okay... that's all. Oh yeah... if you're wondering... Mason gave me your n-n-number. I hope — err we hope to see you there!"

Wow, I never heard Alec stutter that badly before.

If I remembered right, he was the one with the most confidence when performing. Nonetheless, it made me release a laugh hearing him.

Mason, you're dead though.

Looking at the time, it was 5:15 PM. Lucky House Café wasn't too far so, I'd make it in time. After saying bye to my coworkers, I headed down the elevator. As the elevator doors slid open, my lucky self spotted Bryce and Candace. What surprised me was seeing Logan there too.

The three appeared to be simply standing there with their attention towards the lobby.

Please not for me.

How I wished I was invisible.

Before I knew it, the doors were about to close on me until I let out a loud yelp, shoving my hand out. My shout caught their eyes, and now my existence was known.

Bryce's annoyed face grew tender when he watched me exiting out the elevators. Candace's cunning eyes were on her bouquet I was holding, and she held a mischievous grin. Maybe I should have just thrown it away to anger her more. However, it was good seeing Logan ever since the time Bryce took me away without a choice. It has been that long come to think of it.

Logan gave me a friendly wave once I reached the three at a reasonable distance.

Candace was the first one to speak up, her voice was sugar-loaded, "I see you got the flowers, Maisie."

Feeling a tad uncomfortable, I nodded.

"Thanks. You didn't have to though."

"Of course I do. I have to show my love to the needy, right?"

Candace's blue-green eyes batted innocently.

How I wanted to punch that nose so badly.

Giving her a sweet smile back, I countered, "How thoughtful. You know, funny this is that I do too. Looks like you need this more then."

Handing back her bouquet, Candace flashed me an appalled expression while Logan and Bryce stifled a laugh from behind. Keeping her chin up, Candace harshly snatched the roses from my hands.

She spat, "Fine then."

Her voice shifted in a sweet matter unexpectedly.

"Maisie, what are you doing tonight?"

Shrugging, I gave her a blunt reply, "I'm going to watch my little brother perform. Why?"

Candace's lips stretched into a bragging smile.

"Oh nothing. We're just going to watch a movie premiere. It's a red carpet event, but looks like you're busy."

"Wait, Mason's show is tonight?" Bryce entered the conversation, disregarding what Candace said.

Logan was eying Bryce curiously, and Candace exhaled sharply for being disrupted. When I nodded my head, Bryce clicked his tongue.

"I forgot it was tonight. Let's go, Maisie."

Before I could even say anything, Bryce was motioning me towards the lobby entrance, leaving Logan and Candace behind. As I looked over my shoulder, I caught a very angry Candace, and once again, I was leaving Logan without properly talking to him. I was such a bad friend.

Once we made it outside, I fidgeted to stop Bryce from controlling me like a robot.

"What the — Bryce! Let me go!"

Huffing, I flipped towards to face him, my hair whipping along.

Bryce folded his arms and declared, "You, Daisie, just saved my life."

There he goes again calling me "Daisie". He seemed to know my real name. Why did he still call me that?

The voice in my head remarked, "It's his special name for you, duh."

Be quiet, voice.

Confused, I raised my eyebrows.

"Save your life? How?"

"I forgot you're a little slow. Candace, who else?"

"So this whole thing was just an excuse to avoid her?"

Bryce replied honestly, "Not really, I don't mind seeing Mason perform."

"What about Logan?" I asked, growing concern that he was left with that psycho model.

Bryce shrugged in reply, saying how Logan can take care of himself. Without letting me have a say in anything, Bryce and I were both sitting in my car driving to Lucky House Café.

Feeling a bit weird about everything, I asked through the silence, "So, Candace —"

"Let's not talk about her right now. She's making my head explode," Bryce muttered, looking outside my car window.

"Have you met her little sister, Carly?" I questioned anyway.

Bryce nodded.

"Yeah, she looks a lot like Candace when we were that age. But Carly is ten times — even more — better than the person Candace will ever be. So, can we please stop talking about her?"

Zipping my mouth shut, Bryce was right. To think that Candace's flowers would be a sincere apology. I knew it was just a publicity stunt. Hitting close to Lucky House Café, I parked my car after fighting for it. The place was packed. Bryce was following behind me once I locked the car.

Before we went in, Bryce reminded, "Don't think I forgot. You were going about another day without giving your delivery boy his hazelnut coffee."

Forgetting about Candace and everything else, Bryce's words made me twitch into a smile as he returned with a grin back. As he opened the doors for me — yes, he could be a gentlemen — I nodded.

"This cafe has pretty good hazelnut coffee."

Lucky House Café was your not so average cafe. It had a laid back feel to it — huge and spacious, with comfy sofas scattered around. It made you feel like you were home, relaxing in front of the fireplace. There was also a leveled deck inside with proper wooden tables and chairs where people could dine or study. It was best known hosting performances for local, aspiring bands. They had a designated stage just to emphasize the attention on them.

As Bryce and I were standing side by side, I instantly spotted Mason, Alec and the rest getting their instruments and equipment ready for the performance. About to wave down a waiter's attention, Bryce suddenly stopped me.

He grinned.

"I want you to get our drinks. I'll find us a spot."

Nodding along, I made my way towards the register. Before going, I made sure that Mason knew I was there.

Immediately, I noticed a hoard of high school girls giggling as they stalked — I mean excessively admired — my little brother and his friends. The group of ten were all talking loudly to get their attention but looked like it wasn't working. Mason had his mind on the equipment while Alec and the other two, Travis and Nick, were busy tuning the instruments.

Moving closer to the stage, I casually called out to Mason. Looking up, Mason grinned widely.

"Hey, Maisie!"

Following Mason were the other three. There was a tint of red growing on Alec's cheeks. Oh gosh.

Giving the four some support because the café was filled, I smiled.

"Kill it tonight, okay?"

Alec jumped in, almost dropping his guitar, "Just for you, Maisie!"

Nodding as I laughed, I turned around only to find a bunch of evil stares directed at me. Lifting my hands up, I rolled my eyes at the high school girls.

"Chill. Mason is my brother, so stop crapping your pants."

As I was walking off, I heard the girls gasping and whispering how they had to be nice so I could give them his number.

Was this how crazy girls were nowadays?

Actually, I needed to get back at Mason for giving Alec my number.

After ordering two hazelnut coffees, I found Bryce sitting in one of the black leather sofas. The delivery boy chose one of the farthest spots here. Maybe he wanted to keep a low profile. Heading towards him, I noticed a huge smirk that was etched onto his face.

Handing him his drink, I asked before taking a seat, "What's so funny?"

Bryce took a sip before speaking, "I wonder what will happen to you when those girls find out you're here with me."

He probably witnessed the whole thing.

Snorting a laugh, I was close to spitting my drink out.

"Don't get too cocky now."

Bryce noticed everything, and he chuckled.

"Very graceful, Daisie."

Our conversation was put to a stop when the lights of the café dimmed, and the spotlight was on Mason.

He was standing by the mic and spoke confidently, "Hey every-body, I can tell it's going to be a good night. Take a seat, relax and enjoy."

Has my younger brother grown or what?

All of a sudden, you could hear the room fill with happy sighs coming from the lovestruck girls which made me wince. Mason walked back, and the spotlight emphasized the whole group now.

When Mason got his guitar and motioned the guys, the sound of their music scattered. They have gotten a lot better since they started out.

The guitars, drums, and singing synchronized perfectly as one. From the corner of my eyes, I even caught Bryce tapping his fingers against his leg. Everyone had their undivided attention on them. I smiled at the sight — I couldn't help but be proud.

After performing two songs perfectly, the crowd, including Bryce and me, stood up to give them a round of applause. This time, Alec took the mic. He was filled with charisma which opposed the anxiety he has around me.

Alec's calm voice echoed.

"You all having a good time?"

Shouts and screams blended together. He chuckled, his hazel eyes soon searched the area.

"This song… is dedicated to someone who's one in a million to us. This is for you, Maisie."

Back it up.

Did Alec just say my name?

Mason and his friends all held the same grins and started playing. This was probably the sweetest thing someone has done for me. I was probably going to get murdered by raging high school girls after. Brightly grinning, I glimpsed back at Bryce who had a very dry expression on his face.

What a kill joy.

Once they were done playing, everyone stood up again in applause, and I was clapping happily. Mason and his friends played two more songs, and their successful performance came to a close.

As they were packing up, a rush of girls were running towards them.

Turning my attention to Bryce, I asked casually, "They did great, didn't they?"

"You're still blushing. Do younger guys attract you?" Bryce bluntly pointed out.

"Ew, no! That's just a sweet thing they did." I retorted, twitching a smile.

When the crowd cleared away, Bryce and I got up from our seats to personally congratulate the four.

Giving Mason a high five, I beamed, "You really make the Lockhart family proud."

Mason stuck his tongue out.

"I try — Bryce! I didn't know you were here!"

The two did the usual "dude" handshake. Bryce gave Mason and the rest a friendly grin.

"Nice job, what's your band name?"

Alec answered this time, "We... actually don't have one yet; we're just doing this for fun. Hey, you're one of the Valentino's! Are you Maisie's boyfriend?"

Instantly, I shouted out, "He's just a friend!"

Bryce smirked.

"You should be honored."

The guys laughed in unison, leaving me with a stale expression. Alec appeared to be sighing in relief though. After moments of talking and thanking them for dedicating a song to me, I figured it was time to go. When I asked Mason if he needed a ride, he answered that he was hitching one with Travis. Nodding my head, I told him to be safe while Bryce and I were heading out.

Alec waved.

"S-see you n-next time! T-thanks for coming, Maisie!"

Waving back, my smile dropped when I heard Bryce say, "You're about to hit the door."

What door?

Oh, fuck.

When I turned straight ahead, I was welcomed by the glass smacking against my forehead. Even though Bryce assisted me, he was holding in a laugh until he fully released it.

Keep laughing, delivery boy.

As I was rubbing my forehead, he held the door open for me, still laughing. Shooting a glare at Bryce, I gritted my teeth.

"It's not funny."

Bryce chuckled anyway.

"It kinda is.. you okay though?"

Rolling my eyes, I walked out, letting the cold air seep through my skin.

"I'm fine. Thanks for asking so late."

He replied, "At least I asked."

Before I could respond, Bryce was calling Mason and his friends who were walking towards their car.

The four looked somewhat confused until Bryce continued, "I forgot to mention since you guys did a good job today, I think you all deserve a day of unlimited arcade gaming and bowling."

Like winning the lottery, the four eighteen year olds' eyes lit up.

Mason answered, unsure, "Wait, you serious?"

Bryce nodded his head.

"I told you I would, right Mason?"

Travis and Nick both looked like little kids getting free candy in the candy store. Alec grinned ear to ear.

"That would be awesome, man!"

The four all did a high five, leaving Bryce with a satisfied look. I couldn't help but wonder why he was doing this. Random act of kindness?

Mason slapped Bryce's back and praised, "Thanks, Bryce... I think I'm starting to love you more than I love Maisie."

Oh, I understood now.

His friends — including Alec — nodded, agreeing word for word. Suddenly, Mason's brown eyes flashed at me, and he stuck his tongue out.

"Just kidding, Maisie."

Before I could chase after Mason for betraying me, all four of them ran off to their cars. Bunch of runts. When Bryce turned around to see my expression, a triumphant grin grew on his face.

His voice danced with victory.

"I just wanted to show you how easily I can take your 'one in a million' spot."

Darting my eyes at him, I scoffed, "You suck."

Turning away, I mumbled under my breath, "Cocky delivery boy always has to be number one."

"What's that?" Bryce playfully cupped his ear in a joking matter.

"Nothing," I answered, trying to be bitter as I fished for my keys out of my bag.

"Don't see why that Alec kid likes you so much," Bryce ranted out as we walked to my car.

"Excuse me? What's there not to like?" I answered with confidence, hoping I'd get Bryce to be quiet.

Instead, Bryce moved closer — the kind of closeness that would tug my heartstrings. As I waited for a reply, Bryce eyed me slowly from head to toe and soon released an amused face.

Blushing, I barked out, "Sorry for not looking like your lovely Candace."

Bryce took a step back and then threw on a charming grin, surprising me.

"No. Thank you for just being Daisie."

Chapter 19

"**M**aisie, you look absolutely beautiful. Why the long face?" Logan's voice swayed gently into my eardrums.

See, this was not a dream.

It so happened that today — this ruined Saturday — was Candace's welcoming party, and I happened to be cordially invited. At first, I thought it was another one of her sick jokes when she dropped a frilly invitation in my work locker.

Kind of creepy how she knew these things.

However, I eventually found an explanation for going. Candace forcefully partnered herself with Bryce for the night, Vanessa with David — not like they were complaining — and I was with Logan — I didn't mind that either. Not even trying to understand what Candace's intentions may be, I was simply here to accompany Logan.

And, why was Logan calling me beautiful?

I honestly didn't think it was me.

It was my dress.

When I came home Friday night, I found a package waiting for me. I discovered that it was from Carly.

Carly left a note in her kiddie handwriting saying:

Wear this to Candace's lame party. YOU will look FAB-U-LOUS!

Just everything about Carly was shocking, but I couldn't help but love her even though I barely know the girl. She was like a little sister sent from the universe. Literally.

Once I opened the box, there was a dress inside that was extremely jaw dropping. The little girl has good taste.

The dress was a shimmery teal that was above the knees and had enough layers throughout the bottom to emphasize volume. It was strapless and sweetheart shaped with a crystal beaded trim, hugging my body nicely. My chocolate brown hair that was now curled at the ends and black small sequined pumps I wore tied the outfit as a whole.

When I walked out of my room, my parents were in awe before claiming that I looked a celebrity. All parents had to say that to their kids, you know.

Blushing lightly, I shrugged.

"It's nothing. You're not so bad yourself, Logan."

Logan looked very handsome in a nicely fit tuxedo with his hair stylishly fixed up. He generously picked me up from my house, and here we are in Legends Hotel. It didn't surprise me, knowing that Candace's welcome party would be thrown here and hosted by Bryce's mother.

As soon as we came walking in the ballroom, I definitely got that Hollywood feeling. The ballroom was glamorous with a red carpet, an elegant staircase when you walk in from across, tons of paparazzi and guests swarming the place — your typical A-class party.

My eyes widened at how packed the place was. However, I cringed unpleasantly when I saw a banner saying Candy's Wonderland. Was Candace twelve or something? The ballroom was splashed with pink from the balloons to the tables.

Kill my eyes now, please.

"Maisie!" A voice broke my thoughts.

Snapping back into reality, I was formally linking arms with Logan who must have noticed my absent-mind. It wasn't Logan who said that though.

Vanessa was strolling towards me as David followed behind her. The two were holding hands that I smiled at their cuteness. When they reached a reasonable distance, Vanessa's green eyes widened with excitement. She pulled me into a hug until I couldn't breathe.

"You didn't tell me you're going all out tonight! You look so damn gorgeous and tall. I'm so jealous!"

Letting out a weakened laugh, Vanessa shouldn't be talking. Her beautiful little black dress emphasized her figure along with her very straight and long honey brown hair. Her red shoes just made the outfit pop. Something so simple yet elegant could only be rocked by Vanessa.

For the mean time, the four of us were chatting away while picking up the hors d'oeuvres the waiters were carrying in trays as they traveled from place to place. In the back of my mind, I couldn't help but wonder where Bryce was. Searching around the ballroom, many eyes from unfamiliar faces were glancing towards at me which caused me to grow conscious.

Was there anything on my face or stuck in my teeth?

They all appeared to be smiling at me.

Great, I think there was something on my face.

My mood dropped when Bryce's mother and I exchanged glances when I saw her speaking to a group of what looked like executives.

Out of the whole Valentino family, she was the only one who gives me dirty looks. I wasn't too surprised anymore.

"May I have your attention, please?"

The MC of the party had the entire ballroom dimmed, and a spotlight stuck on the top of the staircase.

This had to be Candace's grand entrance. The thought of going to the restroom to miss it crossed my mind, but I was only half-joking. Logan and I locked eyes momentarily, and we both returned friendly grins to each other before fixing our attention to the staircase. It was nice reconnecting with Logan after so long.

The MC spoke into the mic, "Thank you all for coming tonight. Ms. Candace Reynolds would like to thank all for the warm welcome. Now without further ado, here's Europe's rising model, Candy!"

Instantly, the band started playing an upbeat track, and the doors swung opened.

In came Candace with Bryce, her arm grasping tightly to his. Everybody was cheering while the four of us were the only ones with lifeless clapping. Candace did look a superstar from her wavy golden hair to her ravishing makeup that winked in the light. Throwing on that annoying million watt smile, she wore a bright pink strapless dress that was above the knees with a flowing train in the back.

Enough about Candace, my eyes widened seeing Bryce.

Bryce looked incredible in that tuxedo of his and the way his ebony medium length hair was gently style. Just with the way Bryce presented himself made him the real star under the spotlight despite the scowl on his face.

As the two made their way down the stairs together, the cameras were flashing endlessly, and people were flocking over to them.

They looked like a picture perfect couple. Seeing how friendly Bryce's mother was towards Candace made things unbelievable. Why was I getting all frustrated all of a sudden?

Following behind Candace's entrance, the MC introduced Carly, and everyone cooed with delight. Carly was wearing a white, princess-like dress and her light brown hair was curled as she wore the same white bow from our first encounter.

I heard Vanessa squeal out, "She's too adorable! I just want to pinch her cheeks!"

Indeed.

Carly immediately ran towards us with an adorable smile on her face. She rejoiced as she hugged me.

"You're so pretty, Lockhart! What did I tell you?"

Thanking her, I smiled.

"Look at you! You're the pretty one over here. Listen Carly, I can pay you back for the dress."

Carly waved her hands and grinned.

"No need. I told you I'll help, right? Besides, that dress is expensive but don't worry, I get two grand every week from my parents."

She was kidding, right?

The young girl spoke as if it was no big deal, leaving me stunned. Carly soon rushed over to give the rest hugs. Vanessa looked like she was going to faint from Carly's natural cuteness. Carly then looked at Logan and David and smirked.

"You two are very lucky to be accompanied by very pretty ladies tonight."

How adorable.

"Hey, my friends. Glad you can make it!"

Only one person could talk sweeter than sugar.

As we turned, we found Candace and Bryce standing side by side. I glanced quickly at Candace before catching Bryce's eyes at me. His blue eyes widened slightly until he glanced away. Soon, Bryce had a bored expression on his face. I felt bad for him because he was suffering big time.

"Isn't that right. Maisie?" Candace asked, grabbing my attention.

She was talking to me? I was tuning Candace out this whole time.

Playing it cool, I replied, "Sorry, what did you say?"

"I was saying how pretty you look tonight. So pretty that it looks like you're trying to upstage me."

She sneered through a tight grin. Giving her a sarcastic look back, I shrugged.

"Why would I do such a thing? Nothing can be better than a fluffy cloud of cotton candy, right?"

Instantly, Vanessa and Carly cracked a laugh while David and Logan were trying their best to hold a straight face. Bryce looked off to the side momentarily, and I found his lips lifting into a smile. Once again, Candace was left with a sour expression.

She shrugged, batting her eyes which I started to think was a twitch problem.

"I am the star anyways. Let's go, Brycey."

Without a say, Candace dragged Bryce along with her.

Carly grumbled through a sigh, "I won't be surprised if Bryce drowns himself in the pool tonight."

It made us all laugh even though I hoped Bryce wouldn't resort to such a thing.

"Lockhart, I need your help!"

Feeling a sudden tug on my dress, I was laughing at a lame joke Logan had said.

Even if it was Candace's welcoming party, it was fun so far. The food was surprisingly delicious, we all had a few good laughs, and the best reason of all, Candace wasn't actually here with us.

As we both gazed down, it was Carly. Her face fell with worry, and her blue-green eyes expressed a lost puppy. Logan raised his eyebrows with curiosity.

I asked, "What's wrong, Carly?"

"Come with me outside! I lost my bow somewhere!" She wailed a light cry.

Looking at the hair, the bow was nowhere present. Even though Logan offered to help, Carly specifically asked only me. Glancing back at Logan, he shrugged with a smile before saying that he'd be here waiting. Following Carly, I noticed she was heading to Legends Garden.

She lost her bow there?

Carly was holding my hand as she questioned, "It's somewhere there, you'll help me right?"

Nodding my head, it was the least I could do. Walking outside, I had that same sanctuary feeling at the Garden. The cool summer breeze was pleasant, and the entire place sparkled dramatically under the moonlight. As Carly was tapping her chin, we searched around the large perimeter but found no luck.

I asked, looking past a rose bush, "Are you sure you dropped it here?"

Turning back around, Carly disappeared!

Making a complete 360 turn, she completely vanished. Letting out a sigh, I hoped nothing happened to her, and I hope she didn't take me here for no reason.

However, I soon spotted a reason.

Sitting in one of the lonely benches was Bryce.

With a bunch of questions circulating my mind, my feet were walking towards him unconsciously. His attention was on the ground as he supported his head with the palms of his hand. When I called out to him, Bryce lifted his head up, revealing those sky blue eyes. They looked so captivating at night.

Bryce returned with a smirk, "Following me?"

Stifling a laugh, I countered, "You're not the only person here, you know."

Bryce shrugged yet motioned me to take a seat next to him. As I sat down, I sighed, and he seemed to have done the same.

Through our silence, Bryce suddenly asked, "Tell me something, Daisie. Why don't you go to college? You don't seem like a girl who wouldn't go and end up being a brainless model we happen to know."

Even though this was such a random question, I knew Bryce was referring to Candace.

But that subject was something I rarely talked about.

Gulping down, I let out a hesitant laugh.

"It's nothing."

Bryce swiftly turned to look at me, and he wasn't buying my simple answer. Why did Bryce have to be so curious about me all of a sudden? Why couldn't he ask what my favorite color is? Yet, there was something in my heart telling me to say it.

I mean, it was just the two of us at the moment.

Playing with the ends of my curls, I murmured, "There's actually something..."

Instead of responding, Bryce continued to look at me with honest eyes. He was waiting to listen.

Recalling back to that time, I felt a chill run up my spine, "The summer I graduated high school, Mason got into a huge car accident. He was only sixteen years old with a new license. A drunk driver hit him badly. Doctors said it was a miracle that he survived. Mason was in a coma for four months."

"At the same time, we were planning to open our market, but because of what happened, my parents couldn't focus. So, I told them I'd take care of starting the business. During that whole summer, I did everything I could to make Lockhart's Pantry the way it is now. I missed my college deadlines, and all of that, but it really didn't matter to me."

I simply stared at my lap.

"Starting a business is rough, but we made it through. What made things better was just knowing that Mason was alive and would be better. You know I don't tell this to people because I know they're going to ask if I regret my decision. I should have been in college, they would probably say in pity. But, you know what? Just knowing that Mason made it through and that my parents' wish came true is all I need to be happy."

Suddenly, a traitor tear rolled down my cheek and I tried to laugh it off.

"Mason... he can't even put his hands behind a wheel anymore. I've tried many times to help, but he's so scared."

Now as if someone broke down the dam, my eyes were being flooded by tears. These emotions were getting the best of me. Quickly wiping my eyes, I chuckled softly.

"These — these aren't tears. I swear, the pollen in the flowers must be getting to me."

Despite me looking away, I soon felt a warm hand grazing against my cheek. It was Bryce. He was wiping away a tear I managed to miss. As his hand glided gently, my heartstrings were being tugged at the touch.

"A beautiful girl like you shouldn't be crying."

His voice ever so gentle.

Surprisingly, I turned to look at him with widened eyes, and he returned with a warm smile that comforted me oddly.

It was a smile that rarely appeared on Bryce's lips.

For a while, it was mostly silent. It didn't bother me though. Just the two of us sitting side by side was relieving. When I managed to stop crying, I thanked waterproof mascara for saving me from looking like a complete disaster.

"I'm sorry for asking. You didn't have to tell me," Bryce broke the ice.

Honestly, I found no regrets telling Bryce that.

Shaking my head, I muttered, "Don't be. We should go inside, they're probably looking for us, huh?"

The delivery boy looked deeply into my eyes before nodding his head in agreement. As he got up first, Bryce held out his hand in front of me to take. Letting out a small laugh, I took it as we exited out the garden. This kind of company was very different from our usual selves. There were no words that could explain how fast my heart was beating.

When Bryce opened the doors, the party was still lively as ever which contrasted the somber atmosphere we shared moments ago. The bright lights made me squint as I followed beside Bryce.

However, I found myself being welcomed back...

In a not so friendly matter.

Something was splashed up against me, happening in a flash. The color of deep red was now dripping from my neck down, tainting the dress I loved so much. My cheeks flushed, and my heart jumped in a negative matter seeing who did that.

It was Candace with the most surprised look on her face even though behind those blue-green eyes was revenge.

Chapter 20

This was probably an immediate reaction.

I found my hands grabbing onto Candace's hair like no tomorrow.

Instantly, the both of us were being pushed back out to the entrance. The door slammed shut so no one could get out and see or take evidence of what was happening. Everything was blinding for a moment. Frustration, anger, embarrassment were taking over.

"Maisie, you need to let go!" A voice yelled, not belonging to Candace.

"Vanessa, don't get into this!" Another voice shouted.

Vanessa?

Snapping out of my fury, I realized that Candace was helpless as I was tugging onto the strands of her hair while Vanessa was holding her back. The three Valentino's were also there with the most surprised expressions on their handsome faces, trying to stop the three of us in our brawl.

Huffing, I rapidly unleashed Candace's hair and took a step back. Her eyes were wide open as she was gasping for breath. Vanessa eventually let go, and her green eyes were dark. My friend's usual upbeat smile was long gone.

I yelled directly at Candace, tuning out everyone around us, "What the hell was that for?"

Even though the weather was chilly, I was literally burning up. The drink she spilled on me was cascading down my dress, my neck, and it was sickening. I've seen this so many times in movies but to experience it was worse than I thought.

Candace was fixing her posture, and she barked back, "What were you doing with Bryce?"

Her childish motives explained everything.

Whipping my hair behind me, I felt my voice shake from bewilderment.

"Is that it? We were just outside, for crying out loud! You're acting like Bryce is your pet dog, and you're always keeping him tied!"

I didn't know where all of this was coming from. I just had enough.

No one ever messed with Maisie Lockhart.

Candace took a step closer to me, her eyes turning into thin slits.

"Bryce is mine. You need to back off!"

"Candace, you self-centered moron!" A voice broke into our argument.

Everyone's eyes turned to that young yet loudly projected voice. It was Carly. She was coming from the opposite direction as she stomped down our way. The nine year old was breathing heavily, and her once sweet blue-green eyes transitioned angrily.

Candace scrunched her nose in disbelief and let out a fake laugh.

"Carly, this is none of your business! You know what, you're nothing but an annoying little girl who tries so hard to be smart!"

She had got to kidding me.

At that instance, I thought Candace had broken her little sister's heart saying that, but Carly gritted her teeth and argued back, "At least I'm not stupid like you! You're more annoying! All your care about is attention! Maisie did nothing wrong, but you always ruin everything!"

The sisters were at it, arguing with one another. It irked me because Candace was the older sibling, yet she was bringing her little sister down like that. Carly was only nine! Candace was indeed ruining everything — for all of us. My fists tightly clutched together, seeing the two bicker.

I snapped on the top of my lungs "Could you shut up and listen to yourself, Candace? Carly is your little sister, and you're supposed to care about her! Leave her out of this!"

Candace appeared delirious, her eyes now glaring at me.

"You can't tell me what to do. Why don't you look in the mirror and look at yourself, you're a disaster!"

Before I knew it, Vanessa didn't think twice about barging in, telling Candace off. I didn't want to mention all the cursing she was adding. David was already holding Vanessa back from punching the life out of Candace while Logan was holding Candace back. Bryce tried pulling the two girls apart. It was pure madness. The Valentino's had no control of the situation, and I caught their distressed faces. Carly was frightened before her very eyes.

Everything about today was a roller coaster.

I heard the Valentino boys shout out at different times, "Candace, apologize now!"

Like, she would.

Trying to calm the atmosphere, I hated to see this get out of hand any longer. So, I did everything I could to be start being civil and tell everyone it was okay.

This was my fight.

When everyone composed themselves, I retorted coldly at Candace, "You know what, Candace? I don't care how I look like. It can't match up to how much of a disaster you are inside. Now, since you love being all innocent, why don't you go back to your party and act like nothing happened. I'll leave, and you could go on living your happily ever after."

Without waiting for a reply, I took Carly and stormed out of the circle. It was all happening so quickly. I may have been a bitch, but I didn't care. The dress was ruined, my hair was all nappy, and I never felt like complete shit before.

This was worse than Bryce's mother. My mind was spurring in so many directions.

"Daisie... where do you think you're going?"

I felt a warm hand grab mine.

Turning around, we found Bryce with a pained expression on his face. His sky blue eyes were expressing worry, but I had to show him I was okay. I didn't want to burst into tears in front of him again.

Besides Candace's doings weren't worth any of my tears.

Pulling away from his grip, I answered, "I'm leaving, Bryce. I'm sure you could obviously see that."

"I can take you home."

"Don't bother. Go to Candace."

"Why are you being like this?" Bryce asked in frustration.

I countered, forgetting there was a little girl between us, "I don't know if you noticed, Bryce, but that psycho just spilled her drink all over me. She wants me to get away from you. Because tonight's her night, I'm leaving."

"I don't want you to push me away though." He replied with even seriousness.

Hearing that, I felt my eyes widened.

Clearing my throat, I asked, "What are you trying to say?"

After a moment, it was nothing but staring. I could see the lump in Bryce's throat, and it seemed like he couldn't find enough strength to reply back.

"Bryce, you need to control Candace. Logan will help. We'll take Maisie home."

It was Vanessa.

The two of us snapped out of our gazing and turned our attention to Vanessa and David, who were standing to the right of us.

David said in a stressed tone, "People are wondering what happened. Can you deal with it, Bryce?"

Bryce murmured as he took off his jacket, "Do I even have a choice, Dave?"

Wondering why Bryce had taken off his jacket, it sent chills up my spine when he placed his jacket over me. Before leaving, his icy blue eyes were only stuck on mine.

"Take it. I'm sorry about today."

Carly added bitterly, letting go of my hand, "I'm not done with her yet either. I'm coming too."

And just like that, the two walked back into the Legends' ballroom for damage control.

Vanessa went quickly by my side. I felt her hand stroking my sticky, stringy hair. Her eyes were concerned and saddened when she took in the sight of me.

"Maisie, let's get you home. I'll destroy that bitch later."

Taking a deep breath, I tried to shake everything off but just looking down at my dress made my stomach twist all over again. Pulling my attention, I saw how both David and her were worried. I sighed.

"I can't go home like this."

"Don't worry, we'll take your dress to the dry cleaners. How about we get you cleaned up first?"

Vanessa and I expressed grateful expressions.

David Valentino, thank you for the smart suggestion.

Never in my life did I explode on someone like that.

Candace Reynolds pushed it. Just looking back at the moment, I was like a monster at the moment. Word got out about what Candace did and not even Carly could stop the truth from spreading. It was all a bunch of hearsay though. No photos, no evidence could prove her spilling the drink on me purposely and the aftershock.

However, it was only then my family found out. They were furious, of course. That night I came home looking perfectly fine. We went to Vanessa's house, and I "re-glamorized" myself while David took my dress to the dry cleaners.

I reassured my parents that it wasn't intentional.

Yeah, right.

As much as I hated everything about Candace, I didn't want to bring my family into this.

Fortunately, my lie worked because the model told everyone it was simply an accident because she so happened to have lost grip of her drink. Candace had Bryce's mother support on this so it became believable.

Even if our circle knew the truth — it was all unwanted drama.

Besides, I could deal with it myself. My family had other things to worry about. However, Mom wasn't satisfied even if Candace personally apologized to me two days after the incident. I could put up a front, but a strong feeling ran through me that Mom could read past that.

I should have prepared myself better for someone like Candace Reynolds.

Because of everything, I took four days off.

The time off was what I needed to clear my mind from everything. I acted like everything was fine — it was eventually. I avoided the Valentino's ever since. Vanessa assured them, if they asked, that I was still alive and breathing, and there was nothing to worry about. The only calls I did answer was from Carly because I felt bad that the dress she got me was ruined by Candace and how horrible her older sister treated her.

The nine year old wasn't so happy either. Carly told me that she officially disowned Candace as her sister. It made me laugh, but at the same time, they are still sisters.

Today was the end of my sudden "vacation".

My coworkers all generously covered for me, but Manager King needed my presence there — now or never.

As I was leaving for work, Mason tried leaving me some words of wisdom:

"Maisie, don't go there. I hate that Candace."

"I'm not a quitter, Mason. And she can't scare me."

"You don't have to be superman all the time, you know."

"I like to think I'm super women. Don't worry about me."

However, I only thought Mason was worrying about me because he caught me furiously talking to myself at the market.

I swore that my mentality was stable — that was just during the time I was still pissed about what Candace did.

Surprisingly, I found out Mason let go of his huge crush on Vanessa after he discovered she was dating David. At the same time, I couldn't help but feel guilty for not telling him sooner. He has grown up.

Now, it seemed like I was asking for my death wish as I stepped foot in this hotel. To my surprise though, people were actually nice towards me. As if they sympathize me. This feeling was just as worse.

It was only then I heard someone clear their throat and say, "Ms. Lockhart, may I have a word with you?"

Looking around the lobby, I was shocked to see Bryce's father speaking to me.

A little shaken up, I quickly nodded my head but was not antic-ipating what he was going to say. Bryce's father, Curtis Valentino, was handsome at his age and always well spoken of. I could see the resemblance between Bryce and him — they shared similar facial structures, the same tall height and presentation.

Bryce's father had a tender smile on which took a while to take in because I was so used to seeing Bryce's mother scowling at me.

"I apologize for what happened at Candace's party. That was very unfortunate and something that won't happen again," he stated sincerely.

Shaking my head, I put on a friendly grin to indicate that every-thing was all right. His father's dark blue eyes laid upon me.

"If you don't mind me asking, was it really an accident, Ms. Lockhart?"

Gulping down, I assured with an honest expression, "You can call me Maisie, Mr. Valentino. And it really was an accident."

"Well Maisie, for some reason, my son is telling me otherwise. I just want to apologize again and to your family," his father added.

Bryce told him the real truth?

Still, I didn't want to start anything.

Shaking my head again, I reminded his father once more that he had nothing to worry about. I couldn't believe Bryce's father appeared to be worried on my behalf. Bryce's father soon nodded his head.

After a short pause, he asked, "One more thing Maisie, is your parents doing alright? Your mother?"

Slightly confused, I tilted my head but answered anyway, "Yeah, they're doing great. Thanks for asking. Can I ask why?"

Those dark blue eyes lit up, and he let out a soft chuckle.

"Oh no, it's just we knew each other at one point of our lives. That's good to hear. I'm very glad."

After nodding my head with a smile, Bryce's father soon went off to his meeting, and it left me wondering about what connection Mom had with Curtis Valentino. This was surely out of the blue, and I'd definitely find out why soon enough.

Realizing that my shift for work would be starting soon, I adjusted my feet to head over to the elevators. I was put to a stop once I spotted Bryce and Candace from the opposite direction. It took all the strength I had to prevent myself from attacking Candace. I reminded myself I was over it.

The two didn't notice me, and I wanted to keep it that way. From what I could see, Candace was carrying a bouquet of flowers while Bryce seemed to walking a few steps ahead from her with that dry expression he had on when he was stuck with her.

Seeing Bryce bought me back to that night. From the moment of our conversation to when he placed his jacket over me. What kept bothering me was when he said he didn't want me to push him away. As much as I didn't want to, it seemed easier for the both of us if it went that way.

Why was I not happy though?

Throughout this whole time, I was having an inner argument with myself.

That was until I realized the flowers Candace was holding were a bouquet of daisies.

My stomach dropped at the sight of it.

Quickly, I rushed over to the elevators so they wouldn't be able to catch me here. It was still good enough to hear what they were saying as I observed passed my shoulder.

Candace was giggling happily.

"Oh Brycey, you didn't have to. Next time, get me roses. I love those!"

Bryce seemed to be shaking his head, his reply came out dry, "They're not even for you."

Candace stopped on her heels and she whined, throwing her arms out with the bouquet in hand, "What? For who then?"

This caused a few heads to examine the brat.

Bryce didn't stop walking, keeping his hands in his pockets, and answered nonchalantly, "Daisie. I'll get a new one anyway."

She let out a pout and batted her green-blue eyes sadly as she tried catching up to his pace.

"Brycey, I know these are daisies! Who is it for? You never answered me!"

And that explained it all.

Chapter 21

"Yes, it's true…we were friends when we were younger," Mom stammered into a sentence.

Her hazel eyes seemed blank as she spoke. Why was she so hesitant in answering this? Leaning against the kitchen counter, I nodded. I just had to find out as soon as I got home.

Tilting my head, I inquired, "Mom, why didn't you tell me this? You didn't have to go on pretending you didn't know a Valentino personally."

Scrubbing the dishes clean, she sighed.

"I wasn't pretending, honey. He isn't the same person he was long ago."

Taking the dishes from her hand to the drying rack, I pondered with what she said. Curtis Valentino was really nice from what I could see — compared to his wife. Were we talking about the same person?

Shaking my head from those thoughts, I commented, "It seems like Mr. Valentino still cares about you, Mom."

Once she turned the faucet off, it left the kitchen to silence. Suddenly, a smile grew on her face.

Mom replied, "Sweetie, that was back then. I worry about him sometimes too, but I know he's doing great."

And that was that.

Mom motioned me to go freshen up and get some rest after a day of work. Sighing, I knew she didn't want to be bothered anymore by my questions. This left my mind back to Bryce. Those bouquet of daisies were actually for me.

Did he know I was going to be at work?

However, during my whole shift, I didn't bump into any of the Valentino's or Candace. A part of me was sighing in relief. Biting my lower lip, I plopped onto my bed and thought about what Bryce had said.

"I don't want you to push me away though."

The sincerity in his voice and his eyes were making my heart flutter at the memory. These stupid heartstrings Mason had been talking about were tugged badly ever since that moment.

Closing my eyes briefly, the sound of my cellphone ringing got my attention. I reached over and noticed that Carly had left me a text.

Lockhart, I need your company tomorrow. I want waffles.

"Yummy!"

Carly licked her lips in delight once the teenage waiter placed a plate of freshly made waffles with delectable strawberries on top. Her small nose leaned towards the steamy waffles, and she happily stabbed her fork into it, shoving a piece into her mouth.

Watching her in amusement, it was nice seeing the little kid in her appear — she acted so mature, I would forget she was nine. We sat across from each other by the window of Marty's Waffles.

Famous for their — you guessed it — waffles.

Sipping on a cup of hazelnut coffee, I questioned, "So, is everything okay, Carly?"

She nodded happily, the syrup of the strawberries running down the side of her lips.

"I actually thought you and Bryce would have kissed already, but Candace ruined everything! On a light note, everything is going as planned!"

Raising an eyebrow, I placed the mug down.

"Wait... what do you mean?"

In a way, I was still bothered how Candace never apologized to Carly. Instead, Carly just moved on from their argument. Carly's attention was on the waffles for a while, and I realized that she was too preoccupied with her food.

Looking around, no one was here, but I reminded myself that we did come straight here right once Marty opened. Apparently, Carly was throwing a tantrum because no one would fulfill her waffle craving at the hotel. Poor girl. After finishing two waffles, she placed her fork down and chugged a glass of milk.

As soon as she wiped her lips, she answered, "You're still winning, Lockhart! It's only been a week, and you're showing Candace who's boss."

The thing was, I wasn't even trying. Candace just placed herself in bad positions.

Before I could say anything to that, my phone started ringing. Going through my purse, I realized that it was a blocked number. Picking it up anyways, I answered with a dull hello.

"Daisie, where are you?"

My heart thumped.

Scrunching my nose, I asked "Bryce, is that you?"

"I'm the one asking questions here. Where are you?"

I ignored his question, "How did you get my number?"

"I need you here right now," he slightly demanded.

"...What?"

My eyes blinked from surprise.

"Come to Legends."

"No," I simply answered.

A please would be nice.

"Now."

"No." I repeated into the receiver.

Carly was eying me curiously, and I gave her a loose grin.

"Wait, are you mad at me?"

"No."

"Stop saying no."

"Bryce! What do you want?"

"I already told you. I need you, so come to the hotel. Can you not understand English?"

He was holding in a laugh.

"I can't. I'm doing something right now. Bye!"

I ended the call just like that. Tossing my phone back into my bag, I put my attention back on Carly like nothing happened. On the other hand, Carly grew depressed all of a sudden.

"Why are you rejecting Bryce?"

Because of her mood change, she pushed away her plate of waffles like it was nothing to her. Guilt was rushing towards me.

Shaking my head, I explained, "No, it's not like that. He's just being weird. Go on, and finish your waffles."

Carly's once happy face disappeared to a frown.

"Lockhart, you're doing a horrible job right now. Call him back."

As soon as she said that, my phone started ringing again. Sighing, I didn't even bother looking at the caller ID because I already knew who it was.

Pressing the answer button, I answered, "Bryce, I —"

"Bryce called me. Go to the hotel, Maisie," Mason interrupted nonchalantly, smacking his lips like he was eating at the same time.

I complained, "Stop chewing so loud. And I can't. I'm with someone right now."

Mason gasped on the other line and assumed, "Have you already moved on?"

Rolling my eyes, I defended, "No! Since when did you side with Bryce?"

"You know if Bryce was in your position, he'd be there in a heartbeat."

Even Mason was starting to make me feel guilty.

Clearing his throat, Mason said solemnly, "Just go, okay? He really needs you right now."

What was going on with Bryce? Before I could reply back, Mason hung up, and I dropped my phone back onto my bag. Carly had her eyebrows raised through her watching.

"Who was that?"

"My younger brother."

I frowned, sipping on my drink to relax myself.

Carly suddenly beamed, "Is he cute?"

Her frown lifted into a cute little smile that gave me the most wonderful idea. Grinning, I waved down the waiter for the bill.

"Would you like to meet him?"

"Maisie, why do I have to take care of a little girl?" Mason complained on the other line with a hushed tone.

Letting out a pleased laugh, I was in my car heading to Legends Hotel.

"She's not a little girl. Be nice to Carly. Thanks, little bro!"

As he began shouting on the other line, I clicked the end button and grinned. I didn't want to leave Carly alone. She needed company, and Mason would be perfect for that. Seeing the hotel nearby, a sigh escaped my lips as I wondered why Bryce called me here. It has been days since we last saw each other — not counting yesterday.

Picking up the cup of hazelnut coffee from my car cup holder, I locked my car and made my way into the hotel. As always, the hotel glowed from popularity to its looks. Ever since I came back, people looked at me differently. Maybe because of the Candace incident but, I grew to not care. It was like it never happened in the public's eyes.

Suddenly, my phone vibrated in my bag. Opening the text message, it read:

I'm in my office.

Replying back with an 'I'll be there', I then asked how he got my number. It was a matter of two-seconds before I opened a new text saying:

I have my sources.

Typical answer.

Anyway, this would be the first time I'd see Bryce's office. Curiosity drifted towards me as I took the elevator where the offices were designated at. Once the doors slid open, my eyes widened from surprise seeing Logan.

Logan appeared to be in disbelief.

"Maisie? Is that you?"

Chuckling lightly, I nodded my head and suddenly found myself in Logan's arms. Sadly, I had to give him a half hug because of the cup containing hot liquid in my right hand. Logan's brightened expression bought me into a wide smile. When we pulled away from each other, he grinned.

"How are you? Vanessa told me you've been doing okay, but you never picked up your phone."

I apologized, "Logan, I'm sorry I haven't been a good friend to you lately. I shouldn't have made you worried."

Logan shook his head.

"No, I'm glad you're doing fine. Everything's just been hectic. I was actually going to see you."

His eyes then slowly made its way to the cup I was holding.

"I'm happy we ran into each other even if it's like this," pointing at the cup, I then explained, "oh, this is... for Bryce. I kind of owe him."

Catching Logan's jaw clench as soon as I said that, he then quickly gave me a nod, understanding. Clearing his throat, his eyes wandered slightly.

"Well, I guess I'll be going now. We need to catch up, okay?" his voice shifted into a low murmur, "Bryce's office is just a few doors down."

Smiling lightly, I couldn't help but feel like I offended Logan somehow. As we waved each other goodbye, we exchanged places, and Logan took the elevator down.

Adjusting my position, I headed down the lonely hallway. There were rows of endless doors, and to my right was the open scenery of the city. The walls on my left were made of glass that were tinted like frost while the floors were dark hardwood expressing a modern look to the building.

Passing by each door, my heart thumped once I found the words Bryce Valentino on a placard.

I reminded myself, "Stop acting so nervous, Maisie."

Putting on a confident face, I knocked two times until the soothing voice of Bryce replied with a 'come in'.

Pushing down the door handle, I casually opened the door, and I did everything I could to keep my mouth from dropping with amazement. Bryce's office was one word — bright.

The whole wall from across was of glass, so there was an open view of the cityscape. One thing about Legends was all the glass that was used. This hotel seemed so fragile to me. The furniture was all white with accents of black which emphasized the simple yet masculine style of Bryce. Everything looked so neat and organized. The wall of bookshelves to my left, the large desk that was placed beside the humongous window, the nice leather seating area on the right, the stylish decorations, the flat screen T.V.

My goodness, it could be mistaken as a room.

"Amazed? Your mouth is wide open, Daisie," Bryce stated with a small chuckle.

Crap.

Clamping my mouth shut, I stopped my gazing and directed my eyes towards Bryce. He stared with his usual amused expression, sitting casually in his white leather computer chair. Walking towards him, I handed him the cup of his favorite drink — make that our favorite drink.

His blue eyes widened as he smirked.

"About time. I was going to die from being deprived."

I pulled the cup away from his grasp.

"Die? You're a Valentino! You could buy all the hazelnut coffee in the world!"

Bryce stood up from his chair and snagged the cup, leaving me with an absurd expression. As he took in a sip, he shook his head. Bryce laughed softly, watching my face grow into distortion.

"No, it wouldn't be the same. Someone once told me she would buy me this everyday, but where did she run off to?"

Bryce was always the same, no matter what.

Was it weird to say that I liked that?

Clearing my throat, I shrugged.

"Yeah, yeah. Anyway, what did you need me for?"

His smirk slowly disappeared as he continued in a more bitter tone, "They're planning to tear down Legends Garden."

My stomach dropped hearing that. So many memories happened there as it all replayed in my mind. When Bryce caught my now angered face, he nodded.

"The board committee said the place was pointless. They have no taste whatsoever."

Because I cared about the garden just as much as Bryce did, I nodded my head once more and listened.

"The Legends Garden needs to be revamped somehow. And I have a feeling you're the person who could do so."

Not really comprehending his words, I replied slowly, "How am I s-suppose to do that?"

Bryce went on, grinning, "The Garden needs something, you know? Something so the people will appreciate it."

This was a huge task that Bryce was putting on my plate. Last time I checked, I was simply a worker here. Biting my lower lip, I felt unsure.

"Bryce... what if I can't do it?"

"Knowing you, when you care about something, you'll do all that it takes."

Those words.

When my eyes glanced back up at Bryce, the same warm smile was on his face. Why was my heart beating so loud?

After a moment, I agreed with a more positive face, "I'm in."

Bryce gave me a content grin.

"There's another thing," he then murmured.

The delivery boy soon reached down his desk, and I heard some crinkling. Usually it was bad to assume, but I had a hunch on what it would be. Before I knew it, Bryce returned back to his posture, revealing a bouquet of daisies — it was different from the ones Candace took yesterday.

Those blue eyes were on the bouquet before gradually locking them onto mine.

"You didn't deserve to be treated like that, Daisie. These are for you."

I didn't know how to react.

Through my lack of movements, Bryce raised his eyebrows.

"Wait a second, why don't you look surprise?"

Should I say I kind of knew?

No, that wouldn't be right.

Shaking my head, my cheeks still managed to flush out red as I took them from his hands. The white daisies winked in the sunlight making me release a smile at the sight.

I praised with gratitude, "You didn't have to, Bryce. Thank you. They're absolutely beautiful... and I-I am surprised."

There was a satisfied smile growing on Bryce's lips the moment he heard that.

Bryce eventually added, "I actually have one more request."

"What is it?"

I was heating up, growing anxious.

His sky blue eyes had softened, and Bryce heartily remarked, "Don't ever disappear on me again because you're the only one I see."

Chapter 22

No matter what was happening around me, what Bryce said was making my heart flutter in every direction.

And those bouquet of daisies!

Everything about him was taking its toll on me. Here I was, smiling to myself as I walking towards Lockhart's Pantry where Mason and Carly should be.

That was when I realized.

I had to save Legends Garden!

This wasn't what I was expecting, but what made my stomach flip was seeing Mason in the market. Alone. The nine year old who was no where to be seen. Once Mason spotted me, he casually waved until he noticed the shock smacked on my face.

Mason raised an eyebrow, folding his arms.

"What the heck, Maisie. The store isn't that much of a disaster... is it?"

He thought the panic was about the market?

Shaking my head, I frantically walked to the counter and shouted, "Mason, please don't tell me you lost Carly!"

That was when Mason started to laugh his head off. Once he was done being ridiculous, I was impatiently standing there, hoping he didn't abandon her.

Mason replied, "Of course not! She got picked up by her driver. She said for you to not worry about her."

The stress on my heart released, and I sighed with relief.

He seemed amused by my actions.

"You're acting really paranoid. If you're worried about Carly, don't be. She's actually really interesting. Did you know she can say all the presidents in order and backwards? And, she knows all the fifty states in ABC order, even the capital cities! I don't even know that myself!"

Stifling a laugh, I was more relieved to know that Mason and Carly got along. I nodded my head.

"I told you she's different. And I'm not paranoid..."

Soon, my foot started to tap on the ground endlessly. Noticing my movements, Mason scoffed in disbelief.

"Not paranoid? Did Bryce confess his love for you?"

Throwing him a glare, Mason chuckled even though his brown eyes was expressing hope. My younger brother definitely had some imagination. His assumptions was far from what Bryce did.

Actually, the words Bryce said to me before I left —

No. Stop.

It was getting to me again.

"He didn't..." I muttered out, "I have to help him save the garden."

His nose wrinkled in confusion.

"Is that what couples do nowadays? Plant a garden?"

Mason abruptly flinched back behind the counter before I threw the closest object to me right at him.

Grunting, I remarked, "You're not helping, Mason. I'm worried that I won't be able to save the garden!"

"Is 'garden' a metaphor for you and Bryce's relationship?"

That tall punk was stifling a laugh in between. This annoyance had to be pay back for the time Mason was explaining what "heartstrings" was to me.

Letting out an exasperated sigh, I mumbled, leaning towards the counter, "Legends Garden, you big dummy. Apparently, I have to come up with some idea to save it from being demolished."

"Hm… all I could say is, good luck," Mason snickered before I literally threw the bag of chips at him.

"Vanessa, I can't do it! Tomorrow is the day! I haven't came up with anything!" I ranted out on my phone as I was pacing back and forth in my room.

My usually clean room was now cluttered with scrunched up papers, making my hardwood floors non-existent. There were paper balls all over the place which marked all my failed ideas on how to save Legends Garden.

To think, I had a week to prepare.

It was now almost midnight, and I still had nothing to give.

"Maisie, calm down. You can come up with something! Why isn't Bryce helping you? Anyway, what about a fountain?"

Tapping my chin, I sighed.

"He's an ass, that's why. I was thinking of that, but I don't know. It sounds so… typical."

"Still, it's kind of sweet of him to give you the flowers! Yeah, you're right. Hm, a pond?"

My eyes went on the daisies that were now residing in a glass vase on top of my desk. Even though the daisies were beginning to wilt, the flowers always made me smile just by looking at them. Pursing my lips, I tried organizing my room back to normal.

"Van, you're making me not want to get mad at Bryce. Stop that. I tried that idea, but I feel like it isn't enough. This is too much pressure on me!"

"Haha! It is sweet though. You'll make it through, Maisie! Hey, I know this is completely off topic, but I realized ever since summer started we haven't hanged out once together! Let's go to the beach soon!"

Sitting on the corner of my bed, I let out a laugh, getting distracted.

"Wow, that's true. What has become of us? Anyways, the beach sounds perfect!"

Our phone conversation was interrupted when I heard knocking on my door. Cupping the receiver, I called out whoever family member it may be to come in. Turned out to be Pops in his comfortable lounge wear. Once Pops took in the sight of my room, he let out a deep breath, making me giggle brokenly.

Putting my attention back on my phone, I whispered quickly, "Vanessa, I'll call you back. Love you!"

"Please don't do anything crazy, okay Maisie? Good luck, love you!"

Tossing my phone behind me, I quickly got up from my bed and explained, "Pops, I know this looks bad, but my room will look a lot better by tomorrow!"

Pops gave me an amused grin.

"I could have sworn you didn't have any last minute projects that needed to done like in high school."

Laughing at the distant memory, I ran my fingers through my messy hair.

"Um, well, I'm having such a hard time finding what Legend Gardens needs."

That uneasy feeling appeared again, realizing that I was running out of time.

Through my moping, Pops placed his broad hand on my shoulder and encouraged, "As long as you put your mind to it, you'll be able to accomplish the most impossible things in life. Don't over think it, honey."

Kissing my forehead, the notion was a thing Pops would always do when I was younger that calmed me down and helped me figure things out. Every time Dad did this, success would flash my way. Just because I was older now shouldn't mean that it wouldn't work.

I hoped.

After saying good night, I looked back down at the clutter and groaned, "I just wish something would pop in my head."

Only then did I realize my wish was granted.

This was it, everyone.

Time for Maisie Lockhart to make her mark.

Hopefully.

Putting on my best confident face, I came strolling in Legends Hotel in my "professional" attire. Bryce called me earlier this morning saying how I had to dress up because we were going to do the presentation together. I wasn't doing the talking though — I would just be holding the pretty presentation board I made.

Wearing a black high waist skirt with a cream chiffon blouse tucked in along with my trusty black pumps, I felt like a different person. My long chocolate brown hair was curled, bringing the outfit as a whole. Several familiar faces that I usually passed by when I worked would stop and gawk at the sight of me. At first,

I thought they were still thinking about what happened between Candace and me until I realized that they were gazing from head to toe.

Clearing my throat uncomfortably, I swiftly looked away from the attention and made my way towards the seating area where Bryce said he would be at. The thought of us actually working together was quite shocking.

Things sure changed — in a good way.

Moving closer to the chairs, I noticed a figure sitting down that had to be Bryce. Without even thinking, I immediately blurted out his name until my face fell from embarrassment finding that the figure wasn't Bryce, but Logan Valentino.

Logan stood up, revealing himself fully, and I straightened myself from my silly mistake. My cheeks grew hot when he approached me.

Logan said through a sheepish grin, "Sorry, I'm not the one you're looking for."

Shaking my head, I mumbled shyly, "No, it's my fault. Bryce said he would be here?"

His dark blue eyes widened and explained hesitantly, "Bryce didn't tell you? You're presenting in front of the board today. He had something to do and asked me to help you."

Holy crap.

Was it too late to crawl into a dark hole and never come out?

I nearly screeched at the non-present Bryce, "Bryce, I'm going to kill you!"

Logan laughed softly from my actions.

"You're going to do fine. I'm here to help," he then added with a smile, "You look great. Someone might mistaken you as the CEO."

Turning even more red, Logan's sweet compliment still didn't help me from calming down.

Bryce, why are you doing this?

Stupid delivery boy!

Clutching tightly onto my poster board, I glanced at the board and gulped down hard. Now, I wasn't so confident. Soon, Logan peeked over to examine it. Growing embarrassed, I was worried that my idea wasn't that great after all.

Revealing his pearly whites, Logan nodded.

"This is the one."

Heading to the presentation room, I was panicking that Bryce would throw me into the sea like this. I couldn't fail. After Logan's advice, I felt a lot better about my idea.

Glancing around the large room, I stood at the end of the long wooden table where a group of fifteen was staring at me with curious, solemn eyes. I immediately spotted the Valentino's fathers and gave them a friendly smile.

Placing the poster on the stand, I glanced over at my left where Logan was outside the door. We made a signal for him to come in, just in case I ever froze. Logan gave me an encouraging grin, and I returned it before looking back the group.

Clearing my throat, I proposed, "Good morning everyone. Thank you for the your time. I come here today to talk about Legends Garden and how important it is to the hotel."

Pointing at the poster, I continued professionally, "Legends Garden is a natural sanctuary, it's peaceful and gives a welcoming atmosphere to the guests."

Pulling all the confidence I had within me, I added, "But, I have come up with an idea that would make the garden unforgettable."

Removing the covered paper on the middle of the poster board, I revealed a landscaped drawing of my own — art was my hidden forte during high school.

I then smiled proudly at the group of fifteen.

"Have you ever had a moment in your life where you just wanted some reassurance about a dream?"

Their eyes landed on my drawing. Several smiles grew on their faces, wondering where I was going with this.

"Legends Garden will be known for its very own wishing well. It will be emphasized by varieties of flowers I have chosen here and here."

As their eyes glanced from picture to picture, I gulped down after describing the structure and format.

Coming to a close, I added, "I just feel like something like this will leave a huge impact to the public. They would not only come to Legends Garden to admire its beauty, but to also make a wish, giving them hope, and make the hotel a more magical place as well."

After a moment of silence, a woman from the large group complimented, "I really like the idea. It's a new approach, and I have a feeling it'll attract a lot of attention."

Another man commented, "I never thought something so simple would sound so interesting."

Voices were now bouncing off the room with questions and decisions. The suspense was killing me, but my heart was telling me to stay confident.

Standing there nervously, I found Logan with a proud smile from the glass window to ease up my anxiety. My eyes were searching the board members' facial expressions. Some were up for it, saying how this would save more money and benefit the hotel while some were still unsure. There were a few who preferred the supposed golf course idea instead.

After what felt like a lifetime, David's father stood up from his seat and grinned.

"That was a wonderful presentation, Ms. Lockhart."

Nodding my head in thanks, I gave out a tiny smile hoping they would cut to the chase.

"I think you sold us. Congratulations."

Instantly, the room gave me a round of applause, and I didn't believe what I was hearing. Was this real? My stomach untied itself, and my heart returned back to its normal pace.

Letting out a sigh of relief, I just saved Legends Garden!

Several of the board members had stood up from their seats to shake my hand. It was such an accomplished feeling. I could already feel my face flush deep red. When the Valentino's fathers approached me, they all showcased satisfied grins.

Bryce's father complimented as he shook my hand, "My son was right about you."

After the success, I was making my way outside the door to find Logan. He wasn't standing by the door anymore. Instead, his attention was preoccupied as he faced the other direction. Before I could call out to him, my phone rang.

The caller ID was blinking Bryce's name.

Still angry that the delivery boy left me like this, I hissed, "Bryce Valentino, you listen to me —"

"I called, you listen to me. Come to your market after you're done. How did it go?"Bryce finished with a light chuckle.

That was when Logan noticed that I was finally out. Logan's face was grave, and it was the kind of expression I couldn't comprehend.

Briefly looking away, I answered with a light cry, "You're such a jerk, you know that? Why didn't you tell me you weren't coming?"

"Did it go bad?"

"No. They're going with the idea."

"Then why are you mad? I knew you could do it. Go to the market, okay Daisie?"

Confused by his actions, I sighed, "You're killing me, you know that?"

"I kill you with my looks everyday. Go now. Thanks, Daisie."

Before I could even reply back, Bryce had hung up. Stupid delivery boy. When I glanced back up, Logan approached me closer. Despite Logan giving me a smile, his eyes were dark and tainted.

Did something happen?

I broke the ice, "I-I did it, Logan. Thanks for helping me out."

Logan nodded shortly.

"I knew you had it in you," his voice suddenly altered as he stated, "Maisie... you have to stay away from Bryce."

Shocked from his warning, never did I expect Logan to be the one to say that.

Raising my eyebrows, I stammered, "Logan, I can't. Listen, I have to go right now. I'm sorry."

Before I could walk away, Logan grabbed my hand. Behind those midnight blue eyes were begging me to listen. Why was Logan persistent all of sudden? Slowly releasing my hand from his grasp, I bit my lip.

"Logan, if you have something to say, say it right now."

"Just please listen."

I inquired, "Why? He's your cousin, and we're all friends."

Silence didn't fail to grow between us, and I eventually lost patience. Logan's change of attitude perplexed me, but this was the last thing I needed — hearing those words multiple times already. In the end, I fought against my mixed emotions and walked off from the conversation. As I headed to my car, this was the first time that I saw Logan like this.

Was it rude of me to leave?

Letting out a deep breath, I prepared myself for whatever was coming for me at the market. So much already has happened today, I wasn't sure if I was even prepared for more surprises. Dismissing Logan's warning, I parked my car and made my way towards the market.

Glancing around the area, I tried to find Bryce, but that delivery boy was nowhere in sight.

"Daisie!"

Following his voice, my heart seriously fell out at what I ended up seeing.

Chapter 23

S omebody slap me.

This was all a dream, wasn't it?

As I turned around to follow the sound of Bryce's voice, it was almost as if the life had been sucked out of me. No, Bryce Valentino didn't show up with a banner, heart balloons, or a big teddy bear of love.

Instead, this was all I needed to see to make tears pour out of my eyes.

Mason.

My younger brother was driving.

After two years from his tragic accident.

The memories of me trying to get my younger brother behind the wheel again flashed before me. My eyes watched in amazement as Mason was driving Bryce's Ferrari. Bryce was sitting in the passenger seat with the windows rolled down. I noticed the biggest smile on Mason's face as he perfectly drove around the perimeter with concentration and confidence.

Witnessing everything, happiness was just overwhelming me.

I tried wiping the tears away once Mason parked the car on the curb, and the two got out. Mason tossed the keys to Bryce as he thanked him. I never saw the kid look so comfortable before.

Bryce patted Mason's back for a successful test drive and headed their way towards me. Sniffling, I was frozen for a while until I just wanted to run to that — not so little — rascal and start bawling like a proud fan.

Where was Mom and Pops? They needed — no, scratch that — they had to see this!

Bryce had his blue eyes on me with a pleasant grin on his face.

Had Bryce been helping Mason this whole time?

Giving Mason a high five, tears streaked down my cheeks as I congratulated, "I thought I was dreaming for a moment. You're driving, Mason! I'm so happy!"

Mason snorted a laugh.

"Obviously, you're crying like a weirdo right now. It's a little embarrassing."

Before I knew it, Mason pulled me into a hug and whispered through the embrace, "I'm sorry for being so stubborn these past two years. You really did help me and Bryce made me realize it."

Mason, being the sweet brother he could be, even wiped a few tears away.

Turned out that Bryce was helping Mason get back on the road ever since he found out the night of Candace's welcoming party. It surprised me because I always thought that it would be impossible. All these questions started to flutter around me, wondering how in the world Bryce was able to do this.

When I asked, my younger brother simply shrugged and grinned.

"Bryce told me to let go of the past because this is now, and the future is waiting for me. I had to let go of my fears because that's what is drowning me. The motivational speech Bryce said was much more epic, but it was along those lines. Haha! And you know, since he trusted me in the hands of his car, I kind of had to do it."

I joked through a cheesy smile, "So my car just wasn't good enough for you, huh?"

Mason stuck his tongue out, and we shared a laugh.

When I turned my attention to Bryce, he had such a gentle expression. It was all because of Bryce Valentino. The delivery boy didn't have to do anything for me or give me anything directly to make me feel genuine happiness.

Walking towards him, I couldn't help but ask, "Bryce, why? Why did you do this?"

Bryce replied, smiling, "Because I know how it feels to be in that kind of position. Mason's still young and growing, and he shouldn't live his life afraid of driving. So with my incredible skills, I helped him."

He chuckled at his last words, causing me to join in.

Lowering my head, I mumbled, "You didn't have to though."

Soon, I felt the tips of Bryce's fingers lift my chin back up just so I could directly gaze at me. I felt my face growing hot as I tried to demand my eyes to look away.

His voice churned as his sky blue eyes brightened.

"I did it because I wanted to. You and I are the same, you know that? When you care about something or someone, you'll do anything in your power to make things work."

As if my heart couldn't stop beating any quicker!

These damn heartstrings.

Gently moving my head away from his fingers, I laughed quietly.

"And, because I also care about you, how about I get you a towel to wipe your face? I don't think a tissue is enough, your snot is getting everywhere."

Bryce sounded so serious yet was holding in a laugh.

Why was I not surprised?

Shooting him a look, I quickly wiped my nose with the sleeve of my cardigan and huffed.

Bryce chimed through his grinning, "I'm joking! So, are you surprised?"

Letting his taunt go, I nodded.

"Definitely. You really got me there."

Before I knew it, I found myself hugging Bryce.

I didn't know what took over me, but I was hugging that delivery boy.

Feeling the shot of shock run up Bryce's spine, I could tell that he was just as surprised. I had to thank the delivery boy for doing this, and I guess my actions got the best of me. Seeing Mason drive after all his struggles just meant everything to me. Slowly, Bryce's arms eventually tightened around me too.

Through the hug, I beamed, "Thank you, Bryce."

When we pulled away, I was probably seeing things, but there was a tint of red appearing on Bryce's cheeks, making me giggle at the sight. Bryce cleared his throat and swiftly glanced off momentarily.

Once Bryce seemed to have regained himself, he murmured, "It really is nothing. So, about the presentation —"

That was right, I couldn't forget the fact this shady Valentino left me like a fish lost in sea.

But, things all worked out in the end, right?

I faked a mad face.

"Oh, and thanks for leaving me like that."

Bryce smirked.

"It was worth it, right? Now, you can go around saying that you're the mastermind behind it. And Mason is a new person now. Oh yeah, was Logan any help?"

Logan.

The sudden memory of our conversation hit me again.

"Maisie… you have to stay away from Bryce."

Logan's words soon echoed all over in my head. Remembering how much his eyes were pleading me to listen made me wonder what was wrong. Why couldn't he answer my question? But then, I wondered —

Tilting my head, Bryce was now curious, noticing my abrupt silence.

I asked for an opinion, "Bryce, what do you do if you don't feel the same way another person does?"

Hearing this, Bryce's face fell into distortion, and his dark eyebrows furrowed together. I noticed him gulping, probably trying to find words to respond.

His blue eyes dropped to the floor until he nearly shouted at me, "Well then, I guess you can't do anything about it but to reject that person!"

No need to shout. It was harsh how Bryce said it.

Then again, I was just assuming Logan's motives.

Sighing, I nodded.

"You're right, but I don't know just yet."

A frown then appeared on Bryce's lips.

"You having mood swings or something, Daisie?"

"Look who's talking, Mr. I-Shout-My-Lungs-Out," I retorted back at him.

"That doesn't even make sense!" Bryce countered with a short laugh, making me look like an idiot.

The two of us stared blankly at each other for a moment until Mason jumped in. Mason slammed both his hands on our shoulders, letting out a broken laugh.

Mason chimed, glancing at our puzzled expressions, "Okay, one moment you two are hugging, the next I see you two looking like you're about to tear each others' faces off. Hey, why don't we show Mom and Pops me driving?"

Letting the subject drop, I shook my head.

"Sorry, this is stupid. You're right, we should be celebrating."

Bryce eventually nodded in agreement, his eyes wandered left to right.

"Yeah. For you and Mason."

Seeing the sudden resolved situation, Mason took a step back and folded his arms. My younger brother shook his head side to side before he grinned.

"Wow, you two are seriously confusing."

"I'm sorry if this isn't anything special," Mom expressed with a sweet smile on her face as she placed one of her hearty home cooked entrees onto the dinner table.

Bryce returned with a grin, his eyes probing the dish.

"No, I'm looking forward to try it."

As if the day couldn't get any weirder, Bryce Valentino was having dinner with the Lockhart family.

Mom and Pops were just as joyful and speechless seeing Mason drive. I was still pretty stunned even till now. My parents were even more shocked finding out that it was through the help of Bryce. In thanks and in congratulations for this very accomplished day, we invited the Valentino to have dinner with us.

To be honest, I was feeling slightly awkward having him here and sitting next to me in the dinner table. After our short, uncalled for argument, things got a little tensed between us. What made me wonder was why Bryce got all worked up by my question. I just wanted his opinion.

Mason pointed at the steaming seasoned chicken and promoted, "Bryce, you'll love this."

Pops, who was sitting in the head chair, looked over at me and hinted, "Maisie, what are you doing just sitting there? Why don't you offer food to our guest?"

Shaking my thoughts away, I blinked momentarily and found Bryce gazing my direction with a small amused grin on his face. Taking his plate, I plopped a little bit of everything onto it.

I expressed hesitantly, "I hope you like it."

"I'm sure I will," Bryce answered happily, grabbing his fork and knife.

All of us soon got our servings and began eating. As usual, Mom's cooking never failed to satisfy me — no bias intended. I did hope she would teach me her recipes soon. The tenderness of the chicken nearly melted in my mouth, and the pasta was perfectly made with her made-from-scratch sauce.

"This is amazing!" The four of us heard Bryce blurt out.

Surprised, I glimpsed over to my left and found Bryce chomping away at his plate of food.

I never saw him look so happy... eating.

Mason smirked, saying how he told him so. Mom and Pops both glanced at each other before looking back at Bryce with satisfied grins on their faces. And me? I was twitching into a smile seeing Bryce like a little kid, eating the food we enjoy on a daily basis.

Mom then spoke up, "I'm very happy you like it."

After wiping his lips clean properly, Bryce nodded his head.

"This is perfect," he then revealed after a sheepish laugh, "Actually, it's been forever since I ate a home cooked meal."

This left us all with stunned expressions.

Pops questioned in a gentle tone, "You don't eat dinner with your family, Mr. Valentino?"

Bryce answered through a polite smile, "Feel free to call me Bryce, Mr. Lockhart. Well, my parents are always busy with Phoenix Empire, we rarely eat together. And if we do, it's usually served to us. So, something like this is really refreshing."

I watched as his icy blue eyes dropped onto the plate momentarily before he lifted his head up with a more charming grin.

Bryce added, "It's okay though, this kind of opportunity means a lot to me."

Suddenly, Bryce switched the topic, "So, I'm sure you heard about Maisie, right? Without her, Legends Garden wouldn't be here anymore. Thank you, Maisie."

All eyes were on me now, and my parents had such proud smiles on their faces. Mason was pumping his fist in the air calling this the "best day ever". Despite me stifling a laugh, it didn't change the fact that I felt an aura of sadness from Bryce that moment. When I turned my attention to him, he grinned at me warmly, and I smiled back.

As we finished up dinner, I was helping Mom clean up the table. The two of us were both by the kitchen sink. Scrubbing the dishes clean, there were many things happening this day. Too many.

Most of all, it was Logan's warning that was circling around my mind.

Why should I stay away from Bryce?

Mom soon garnered my attention, "Bryce is really a sweet boy, honey."

Coming back to reality, I finally responded, "He is, Mom."

"Something on your mind, Maisie?"

When I shook my head indicating that it was nothing, Mom took a good look at me before saying she would take care of cleaning. Even though I insisted on helping her, she was already pushing me out to the living room where Bryce, Mason and Pops were. The three were taking about something on the sports channel.

Once Bryce caught sight of me, he stood up and politely cleared his throat.

"Guess I should be going, huh?"

Biting my lower lip, I shrugged.

"You don't have to."

Bryce shook his head, his eyes tinted apologetically.

"Actually, I would love to stay, but I have a meeting to prepare for early tomorrow."

After thanking my family for having him for dinner, Bryce soon said his goodbyes to my parents and Mason before the two of us were standing outside the front porch. The only light was coming off from the bright moon.

Closing the door shut behind me, I said sincerely, "Thanks for joining us today, Bryce. And for helping Mason, you don't know how much that means to us."

Bryce replied with a small grin, "You don't have to thank me for what I did. I helped Mason because I wanted to. Having dinner with your family was a great experience."

"About that, when you said that you don't eat —"

He cut me off, "You don't have to worry about a silly thing like that. I enjoy eating with the Lockhart family more. Anyway, I need to be the one thanking you. I admit I wasn't much help with the Legends Garden project, but it's because, uh, never mind. I knew you could do it."

Confused from his change of thought, I stood there until Bryce pointed out, "Even though I wasn't there, I knew the board would be impressed by you, Daisie."

Speechless, I quickly stammered, "It's probably because of my professional clothes, huh?"

I hoped that my comment would lighten our conversation. My hopes were granted when Bryce started to chuckle.

He winked.

"If you say so."

"Bryce, you're a really good person," I involuntarily confessed.

There was something in those blue eyes that twinkled hearing that.

However, in the end, Bryce quietly replied, "But, I'm not the one, right?"

Thinking I heard wrong, Bryce was already waving goodbye as he headed to his car.

"I'll see you later, Daisie. Good night."

"Not the one"?

Was this delivery boy kidding me?

Chapter 24

That had to be a mistake.

I probably heard wrong, that was all.

These thoughts were running along my head continuously as I walked inside Legends Hotel this afternoon. Going through the revolving glass doors, I adjusted my bag against my shoulder and was suddenly greeted by the voice of —

"Well, if it isn't Maisie Lockhart."

She was the last face I wanted to see.

Lifting my head up, my eyes caught sight of Candace and the Valentino boys.

Glancing past Candace, I noticed Bryce, and his eyes briefly looked away. Logan seemed more reserved than usual and was glancing the other direction. Could this get any more awkward? The only one who waved was David, and I returned with a weak smile. Candace flipped her blonde hair with her thin fingers and I sighed since I was not in the mood to hear whatever was going to come out of her mouth.

"Maisie, I heard that they're going to follow through with your proposal," Candace spat out.

Nodding, I answered bluntly, "You heard right, Candace."

She rolled her eyes.

"It's a stupid idea. I can't believe they didn't go with the golf course."

Clearing his throat, David cautioned, "Candace..."

Candace glanced over at David and scoffed, letting go of the topic.

Logan finally spoke up, "Is your shift starting soon, Maisie?"

Surprised, I slowly nodded my head.

He then offered, "I'll walk with you there."

All of a sudden, Bryce interjected, "No. I can take Maisie."

Just when the atmosphere couldn't have gotten any more tense, I stood there, taking in the glares Bryce and Logan were throwing at one another. Candace's blue-green eyes widened, and she scoffed again from their indirect argument.

About to say that I was perfectly capable of going there myself, David quickly swerved their attention, "How about I take Maisie to work? Let's go, Maisie."

Sighing in relief, I followed David for being so civil as he gave me a small smile. I didn't want to look back at the three's reactions. This wasn't turning out good at all.

Walking inside the elevator, I had a hard time looking at David in the eyes. My attention was stuck on the floor the whole time. When David called out to me, I hesitantly gazed up. David's dark blue eyes appeared so solemn.

He questioned, "You probably noticed, but things aren't going so well between Bryce and Logan. Do you know why?"

Shaking my head, I didn't know what to say.

As David pursed his lips, he continued, "It's been like this for a while, ever since, well, Bryce's birthday."

That long?

Feeling my eyes widened, I raised an eyebrow.

"You don't think it's because —"

Stopping myself, I couldn't finish my sentence.

David shrugged.

"Let's just say, I've never seen the two like this before."

All of a sudden, the elevator doors slid open, revealing the exquisite Symphony's Fine Dining. David motioned his arm towards the door, smiling softly. Giving him an apologetic look, I pulled my hair behind my ear, ready to head out until he stopped me.

His words echoed in my ears.

"Do what makes you happy, Maisie."

"I'm so excited to go to the beach today! Call me back!"

Missing Vanessa's phone call earlier, I closed the voicemail and tossed my phone back onto my bed. I was busy packing up for the beach trip we were going to have. Once I was finished, I planned to return her call.

Best friend bonding — this was what I needed.

Rummaging through the mess of things in the bottom of my bed to find the sunblock, my phone started ringing again. Without paying attention to whoever it may be, I picked it up and greeted with my usual hello.

"Daisie, you're not going to the beach today."

What the hell.

Bryce?

Glancing at my cellphone screen, it was indeed Bryce.

Placing the phone back to my ear, I finally replied, "How did you know I was going to the beach today?"

"Because I just do. Anyway, why are you going to the beach? We have a water park already."

Bryce was referring to the newly built Legends water park that finally opened on Friday at the hotel. Remember that it was still in process the first time Bryce gave me a tour of the hotel? The water park was outstanding with its attractions and huge slides. It was the perfect place to cool off from the summer sun. Right when the red ribbon was cut, the park was mad packed already.

Sighing, I explained, "Mason is going to be there. You gave him and his friends passes, remember?"

"Are you afraid that Alec will see you in a swim suit?" Bryce teased on the other line.

Scoffing, I held in a laugh.

"No! I could care less. Why are you so worried about me?"

"Daisie, pack like you're going on a five day trip."

"What?"

"I'll show you what a real beach looks like. A driver is going to pick you up at 12."

"Huh?"

My mind wasn't comprehending anything. Suddenly, my ear was soon welcomed by the dial tone. That delivery boy hung up on me! Again.

Not taking Bryce's words seriously, I still ended up looking at the time on my phone. It was almost twelve. How was I going to tell this to my parents? Scrolling through my contacts, I quickly dialed Vanessa's number.

When she picked up, I ranted out, "I don't know what the hell is going on but Bryce said I'm going on a five day trip!"

Vanessa burst out in laughter.

"Yeah, about that... it turns out they're taking us to their private island for a few days. Your parents already know."

"Vanessa... you serious?"

My voice shook with doubt.

Why was I not aware of my own plans?

"Yes Maisie! Now go get ready. It's going to be fun!"

Leave it to the Valentino's to make a simple beach trip into a vacation to paradise.

"Would you like a refill of your drink, Ms. Lockhart?"

The sweet voice of the stewardess rang in my head, reminding me that this was reality.

Glancing up at her, I gave her a small nod before letting out a sigh.

Where was I, you ask? I was riding in the Valentino's private jet to their private island. I had a hard time believing all of this, but apparently, my parents knew all along. I still remembered their smiling faces as they stood outside the door, waving me goodbye, saying to have a good trip.

This was happening all too soon.

I felt like I just got kidnapped — well, a good kind of kidnap.

The Valentino jet line was absolutely amazing. The comfortable, large seats that came with a personal foot rest, their stewardess who would constantly make sure you were always satisfied, the flat screen TVs that were scattered upon the plane — just everything about it made you feel at home. Their private jet also had beds you could sleep on and a miniature kitchen of its own. Even the bathroom looked nice! The experience was better than first class, but it wasn't like I ever rode first class to begin with.

As much as I wanted to rave about my ride here, there was one thing wrong.

Candace Reynolds was here.

Right now, her presence wasn't a problem because the annoying model was snoring her life away with that pink sleeping mask of hers on.

Breaking away my thoughts, my phone vibrated against the pull-down table. Picking it up, it was a text from Carly.

This is your chance! Have fun on your trip, Lockhart!

I couldn't help but break into a smile reading her little message.

"They've been staring at you this whole time, Maisie," the familiar voice of Vanessa whispered, garnering my attention.

Lifting my eyes up from the screen, I realized Vanessa was talking about Bryce and Logan. However, Bryce was now preoccupied looking outside the window with earphones plugged into his ears while Logan had his eyes shut closed.

That wasn't obvious at all.

Putting my phone down, I shook my head and pretended, "No, they're not."

Vanessa raised her eyebrow with curiosity.

"Seriously? Even David noticed. You texting someone I don't know?"

There was a sly grin growing on her face.

Sticking my tongue out, I then confessed, "No, Vanessa. Besides I have other things to tell you."

She snapped her fingers and assumed, "I knew it, there is someone!"

Her voice was loud enough to grab the three Valentino's attention towards us. Bryce and Logan seemed slightly perplexed while David was watching Vanessa with an amused expression.

Placing my index finger over my lips, I complained, "It's just Carly. And the other things I have to tell you... it's about..."

When my voice drifted off, she eventually caught on. Blowing a kiss, Vanessa then headed over to David, leaving me alone with my thoughts again. My attention was gradually pulled away from the window where I overlooked the clouds that was like cotton candy once Bryce took the seat across from me. The three Valentino's looked so casual for once, wearing simple screen t-shirts and nicely fit jeans.

Clearing my throat, I thanked him, "Hey. Thanks for taking us."

Bryce shrugged comfortably with a small grin.

"Don't thank me yet until you're there having fun."

Adjusting my position in the seat, I questioned, "This is so random though. Why?"

"We all need a vacation, right?"

This caused me to nod in agreement even though having Candace here wouldn't really make it a "vacation". I was already satisfied with the idea of having a trip to a nearby beach — not a grand scale vacation to their own tropical island.

Dropping the quiet atmosphere, I finally cut to the chase, "Bryce, I've noticed you've been acting different... around me. Is something the matter?"

After a moment, Bryce blinked his icy blue eyes before he answered sincerely, "Nope. You're still Daisie, and I'm still the delivery boy."

As my cheeks flushed out red, Bryce gave me a short nod before walking back to his seat. Even though I wanted a more straightforward answer, I was fine with that at the moment.

Once an hour or two passed, my eyes fluttered open, hearing the voice of the pilot.

"Hello Valentino's and welcomed guests. This is the captain speaking. We are now arriving at our destination. Please fasten your seat belts. I hope you enjoyed your stay, thank you for riding with us."

Before I knew it, I was stepping out of the jet and was welcomed by the island's beauty. My mouth nearly dropped from astonishment taking everything in.

Maisie Lockhart was on a tropical island, everyone.

The sun was shining at its best, making the clear ocean waters glitter, and the waves dance. The shore — how excited I was to let my feet touch that white, soft looking sand. The Valentino Island was a dream come true. My eyes scanned the mountains of tropical trees and plants and the large gazebo on one of the hills. It was all a picture perfect scenery. I had to pinch myself to make sure this really was real.

Then again, when it came to the Valentino family, the best was always expected.

"We used to go here all the time when we were younger. It was our great escape."

Jumping slightly from the sudden voice, it was Logan behind me. Turning around, I found Logan smiling for the first time in a while, and I managed to smile back at him.

Complimenting the place, I beamed, "It's perfect. I can't believe this is all your family's."

"Maisie, here's your bag," a voice entered our conversation.

When Logan and I broke off glances, we found Bryce holding my luggage. Immediately heading over to him, I thanked Bryce but was surprised at the same time for him doing so.

"Bryceyyy! Help me with my bags!" Candace screeched on the top of her lungs.

Now that everyone was huddled together, we all turned and spotted Candace waving her hands with her six huge luggage bags outside the plane. Just one of her luggage bags made up two of ours.

She had to be kidding me.

Vanessa gave out a stale remark, "She's acting like she's moving here."

Bryce mumbled bitterly, "That's Candace for you."

"Hey! You guys are finally here!" A voice called out to our attention.

Our eyes were now fixated at a boy, who looked slightly older than us, making his way down the man-made stone stairs embedded onto the island. When the guy was close, I noticed he had very short chestnut brown hair and expressed kind blue eyes.

Immediately, the three Valentino's accompanied the mystery guy. They all looked close as they greeted him. The guy acted like their older brother even though he was a bit shorter than the three.

"You three have seriously grown from the last time I remember. Welcome back!"

Soon, his blue eyes glanced off finding two more faces — Vanessa and me.

David smiled and got us acquainted, "This is our good friend, Zackary Romano. His parents help take care of the island. Zack, this is Maisie Lockhart and my girlfriend, Vanessa Montgomery."

Instead of taking our hands for a handshake, Zackary kissed it gently, making us release a giggle.

What a charmer.

Logan suddenly reminded, "Aren't you getting married to Kelsey soon?"

It was revealed that Zackary Romano was engaged to his high school sweetheart, Kelsey Owens. The two currently lived together in Vancouver, but since he heard news about us coming here, he had to come reunite.

Once he finished explaining, he chuckled.

"Just showing my gentlemen ways. Call me Zack. Anyway, are these kids taking good care of you two?"

I immediately noticed how the three Valentino's all broke out in complaints at Zack's words which made Vanessa and me laugh.

Vanessa gushed, "I wouldn't have asked for a better boyfriend."

Zack threw on a proud smile, patting David's head.

"Good. I taught you well, young cricket."

Bryce coughed, "You're only four years older than us, Zack. You act like a proud father."

"Zacky! Do you remember me?"

Oh yeah, I forgot she was here.

Candace was struggling, trying to pull her bags along with her. Vanessa and I did our best ceasing our laughter in front of her. Zack took a good look at Candace and soon gulped down.

He laughed hesitantly, scratching his head.

"Oh yeah, you're that Reynolds kid. You're… still the same."

She batted her eyes.

"Still the same? Aren't I beautiful now?"

Zack pursed his lips and thought about it, "Uh, sure. Anyway, why don't we all take your stuff back to the villa?"

Candace smiled, showing those bright teeth.

"How sweet of you, Zacky! Here are my bags."

Raising his eyebrows, Zack repeated more clearly, "Reynolds, I was, uh, talking about everyone."

Candace scoffed in disbelief, pouting her lips.

Would it be okay to just burst into laughter right now?

AsZack turned his attention to our whole group, he grinned.

"Well kids, let's all have fun, okay? Welcome back, and welcome ladies to Valentino Island."

Chapter 25

"I really wish you guys were here to see all of this," I gleamed through the phone receiver, speaking with my family.

It had been a day since our arrival here on Valentino Island, and I told them about all the adventures.

After meeting Zack's generous parents, Zack gave us a tour of the island — even though the Valentino's knew the place by heart — and it was just so beautiful. I couldn't help but whip out my camera and take pictures of the scenery. Their island even had a golf course that circled around the perimeter. Too bad I was horrible at golf.

Nonetheless, the weather was perfect ever since.

My favorite part of yesterday was the beach. The white, luscious sand tickled my feet as Vanessa and I ran around, making up for our canceled beach trip. I guess I couldn't complain now. I was kind of glad to be here. We didn't have to worry about crowded beaches or crowded anything.

The crystal, clear waters left me with amazement. There was even a nearby coral reef which was stunning when Zack took us climbing up a large rock by the shore, getting a perfect view of it.

Mason was on the line and playfully bragged, "Well, the water park was so much fun! We're going again today!"

I countered back jokingly, "Yeah. Okay, Mason. I really miss you guys though."

Pops then spoke since I was on speaker, "We miss you too, honey. You better take care over there."

"Pops, you and Mom were the ones who knew before I did. Don't worry, everyone is treating me well," I answered with a smile even though they wouldn't be able to see it.

All of a sudden, there was knocking on the door. I was currently sitting on the love seat that was placed in my designated room at the Valentino's villa. Their villa was located right in the middle of the island. It was gorgeous and showcased a Tuscan feel in the inside.

The guest room I was occupying was three times bigger than my actual room, and I secretly ran around with all the free space. The bed and furniture was very Victorian. The atmosphere of the room made it feel like I wasn't in a tropical island at all.

Telling whoever to come in, it ended up being Zack's mother, Mrs. Romano. She was very friendly and treated us like her own. Her sweet blue eyes that Zack inherited shined from the sunlight of the balcony door across as she took a step in.

Straightening my position, I grinned.

"Did you need me, Mrs. Romano?"

"I'm sorry to disturb you, Miss Maisie, but Miss Vanessa has been looking for you. She's at the beach."

I laughed lightly.

"You weren't, Mrs. Romano. Okay, I'll be out in a bit. Thank you."

Mrs. Romano smiled in return before exiting out my room.

Placing the phone back to my ear, I spoke, "Vanessa's looking for me. I guess we're all going to get the day started. I'll call back again, okay? Take care, I love you guys."

After saying goodbye to my family, I placed the phone back to its charger and searched through my luggage for something to wear. Settling with a floral summer blouse and denim shorts, I slid my feet into my pair of strapped sandals and made my way out to Vanessa.

Walking down the stair steps, I wondered where everyone else was. So far, the visit here was satisfying as a group. Candace wasn't as annoying as I thought she would be despite her attempts to cling onto Bryce with every chance she got. The only ones I was slightly unsure of was Logan and Bryce. Both were keeping their distance, but at the same time, they were trying to talk to me.

Did that even make sense?

With the way they were acting, it didn't even make sense to me either.

Glancing around, no one seemed to be at the villa. I soon spotted Vanessa's figure as she was walking along the shoreline from the window. Why was she all alone? Well, it was still early in the morning. Maybe everyone else was still asleep.

Heading out the doors, I made my way to the beach. The temperate winds breezed towards me. The breeze was so refreshing to escape from the suffocating cityscape. For once, it was like I was surrounded by the same atmosphere Legends Garden gave off. Waving my hands, I called for Vanessa's attention. She quickly turned around as her purple summer dress followed behind her.

Vanessa grinned brightly at the sight of me. We both met up half way, and the sand was starting to seep through my sandals — I should have resorted to flip flops.

Vanessa hugged me tightly as she beamed, "Maisie! It happened!"

She was always lively, being the morning person I knew, but this time it was different.

"Wait, what happened?"

I sounded more scared than excited. Once we pulled off from my hug, it was like déja vu again. Vanessa was being her overly happy self, and then, it all made sense.

My mouth dropped, and I concluded, "You and David finally kissed?!"

Her cheeks flushed.

"Yes! Yes! We kissed last night! We were together at the gazebo, and it was so romantic. At that moment, I just knew and it was..."

Vanessa clapped her hands, her eyes glittering with joy.

"So perfect."

Soon after, Vanessa started squealing like a school girl which left me amused. It finally happened! Through all Vanessa's sixteen boyfriends, David Valentino was the one who rightfully took her first kiss. I wasn't complaining. They were — how to put this? — made for each other.

Joining Vanessa, I was smiling like there was no tomorrow. What made things better was knowing that David left this effect on Vanessa. That kind of effect where you knew that they were both happy no matter what.

I said through a giggle, "About time!"

Vanessa stuck her tongue out and rejoiced, "David's old fashion, but I absolutely love it! Now, Maisie, let's talk about you."

Oh no. I just thought this talk was only about her first kiss.

Suddenly gulping, I reminded her that there was nothing to talk about. Sure, I caught her up with all the happenings between Bryce and Logan. However, Vanessa came up with this crazy result that the two were actually fighting over me. It was confusing though because I was getting so many mixed signals.

Vanessa folded her arms.

"You tell me which one you choose right now."

I let out a light complaint, looking out to the ocean, "Vanessa, they're not two cupcakes I happen to be indecisive over at a bakery. They're both human with feelings, and I-I don't know. Wouldn't it be easier for us to stay friends?"

Then again, I'd be lying to myself.

Vanessa let out a sigh and explained, "Sorry Maisie, but it doesn't work like that. Either way, the two are going to stay like that until you decide."

As much as I didn't want to agree, she was right. Vanessa experienced all types of love.

But me? Nothing.

Before I could answer, a voice shouted from behind, "Hey, we've been looking for you two! You guys ready for some jet skis?"

When Vanessa and I turned around, the voice belonged to Zack. Looked like he came in the right time. He was accompanied by the Valentino's and Candace, who looked like she was still half asleep. As a response, we both gave them smiles and a thumbs up.

Making our way towards them, I mumbled towards Vanessa, "I just can't bear to see anyone hurt."

Vanessa replied softly, "And I can't bear to see you unhappy either."

After a day of exploring the ocean and soaking in the summer sun, we were all circling around the outdoor table of the patio for some dinner. Honestly, I was scared about jet skiing, but I eventually got a hang of it. Candace fell, and even though it was hilarious seeing her wipe out, I helped her. She actually thanked me because of it.

Weird, right?

Once we finished, we had delicious lunch — lobster macaroni & cheese and sirloin steak — made by Mr. and Mrs. Romano. Zack then busted out some scuba diving equipment, and we all jumped in the waters. Seeing the coral reef up close was going to stay a worthwhile memory. I had to give it to Zack. He was really good at entertaining.

Now that we were sitting around the table with the Tiki torches being our light source, I couldn't help but wonder where Bryce, Logan and Zack were. They've been gone for an hour or two, leaving the four of us dumbfounded. Candace was picking at the fruits that were set in the table, but I didn't want to start a conversation with her. So, I glanced over at Vanessa and David, and the two were busy in their own little world.

Tapping my fingers against the table, I asked as a whole, "So, what did you guys like about today?"

Candace complained, "Let's see. I almost died, and I almost got attacked by a bunch of fish. Nothing!"

We all held in our laughs.

Vanessa answered with all seriousness, "I could have sworn those fishes had a thing for you, Candy."

She emphasized Candace's nickname, making Candace shoot a glare at her.

David lightened the mood, "How about you, Maisie? You seem to be enjoying yourself today."

Nodding my head, I confessed, "Today was fun. I guess we could say, we all needed this."

"Really? Because I could do this any day," Candace bragged nonchalantly, chewing on a grape.

From the corner of my eye, I noticed Vanessa mocking her every word silently, and I chuckled to myself. All of a sudden, Zack emerged out of nowhere, causing us girls to jump from surprise.

He grinned mischievously.

"How about we play a little game?"

Candace, who was now busy with her nails, asked in an uninterested tone, "What's this game about?"

Zack smirked, glancing at each of us, "Food. Now, who would turn that down?"

"I can't. I have to watch my figure," Candace stated.

The look in Zack's expression seemed to have grown annoyance, but he shook it off.

Keeping that host-like attitude, Zack revealed, "Doesn't matter to me. This game consists of two of my lucky contestants. Bryce and Logan Valentino."

Hearing this, all our eyes shot up with curiosity. Seeing how he had everyone's undivided attention, Zack chuckled.

"A-ha, you heard right! I am going to serve you several dishes made by the two and you have to pick which you think is the best. Sounds good?"

Candace's blue-green eyes lit up and she roared, "I'll eat anything my Brycey makes!"

Zack let out an exasperated sigh before continuing, "Anyway, come on out, my young crickets and parents!"

Gulping down, my eyes quickly went to the sliding doors from the villa. Soon, Zack's parents appeared with plates on their hands. This was so we wouldn't know who made which. Eventually, Bryce and Logan followed out. I had a thought that the sudden disappearances were because of this. Looking over at Vanessa, she gave me a wink, and I gave her a measly smile.

Bryce and Logan both held solemn faces, and I could easily see that they were both nervous. I was quite positive they were great cooks. The Valentino's were practically good at everything from what I've noticed. Suddenly, Bryce stole a glance from me before quickly looking off the other direction. Mr. and Mrs. Romano soon placed the plates in front of us. They both looked as excited as Zack with this game.

Zack motioned his arm and announced, "Okay, eat away!"

As we poked through the seafood, chicken, stuffed potatoes, seasoned vegetables, and all sorts of tasty delights presented before my eyes, there was one was way more better tasting than the other.

In fact, as I chewed onto the chicken, it was so savory that I craved for more. The other was bland.

Candace, who tried both the seasoned crab and stuffed potatoes, ended up spitting one of them out.

"Um, who made this? It tastes horrible."

Instantly, our eyes went up at the two. My stomach dropped once Bryce's face fell hearing that. Zack let out a broken laugh, looking at the rest of our reactions. Vanessa and David were both comparing their dishes.

Vanessa murmured quietly, "Mine doesn't taste like anything."

David was slicing a piece of the chicken and taking in some vegetables.

"Really? This is absolutely delicious!"

I then caught Logan twitch into a smile. It eventually hit us that Logan was the exceptional cook while Bryce, on the other hand, needed some more work.

Candace's eyes widened in shock.

"Brycey, you can't cook?! What about our future family?"

Aggravated with the outcome, Bryce soon stormed off into the darkness. All of us were left in silence, and Zack looked guilty from the negative responses. Placing my fork down, I didn't want to see Bryce — or anyone — in a bad mood. This was supposed to be a vacation, right?

Getting up from my seat, I excused myself and followed after him. I eventually found Bryce in the villa's courtyard. His attention was fixated on the ocean. The light from the moon made the waters glow sadly.

Calling out to the delivery boy, he turned around, and I was greeted with an irritated expression. Trying to comfort him, I smiled.

"Hey, what you made wasn't that bad."

"It's bad. You don't have to lie," Bryce remarked coldly.

Moving closer, I shrugged.

"Bryce, we're not perfect at everything, you know."

"It's embarrassing though. I knew I shouldn't have listened to what Zack said. God, I'm an idiot," Bryce ranted out, running his fingers through his black hair.

Tilting my head, I inquired, "What are you talking about?"

Bryce blurted out, shocking me, "Everything! What was I thinking? I can't fucking cook to save my life and — and —"

He quickly stopped himself and glanced away to the ocean. For once, I was witnessing a vulnerable side of Bryce. He wasn't the confident Valentino I always seemed to encounter everyday.

I gently insisted, "Something's been bothering you, Bryce. You can tell me."

His icy blue eyes jumped back at me and he scoffed lightly.

"Nothing has been bothering me," after a moment, Bryce sighed, "do you really not see me the same way?"

Blinking my eyes, my mouth dropped, realizing what he said.

I stammered, "I-I wasn't talking about you!"

Bryce scrunched his eyebrows together and clarified again, "What?"

"You thought I was talking about you? I was asking for your opinion!" I managed to shout out.

Gulping down, Bryce exclaimed, "Opinion? You made it sound like — couldn't you have been more specific?"

"You should have asked me! No wonder you've been acting so damn weird."

"Weird? I'm the weird one? Look who's talking!"

"Excuse me? It's you!" I shouted back.

"No. It's you!"

"No, you!"

"It's you, Daisie."

"Good grief, could you two just kiss already!" A distant voice screamed from the dark.

We finally both shut up, searching for that voice.

I murmured, "Was... that Zack?"

When I turned back at Bryce, he appeared to be cursing under his breath, making me laugh quietly. Clearing his throat, Bryce tried to rid the embarrassment in his face.

"Do me a favor. Tell me what you really meant."

Biting my lower lip, my eyes wandered as I spoke, "It doesn't matter who I was talking about, but it's not you, Bryce."

Suddenly, my voice turned up a notch.

"Wait... did you try cooking to impress me?"

His glacial blue eyes blinked until he tried swerving his motives, "No! Of course not!"

Bryce lowered his head, and I wanted to laugh at how the delivery boy was acting.

Suddenly, Bryce barked out, "Daisie, you owe me. For tricking me and making me feel like an idiot."

Smirking, it was entertaining seeing how the tables finally turned.

I folded my arms and offered confidently, "Fine, how about I help you become a better cook?"

Bryce eventually nodded in agreement before he grinned faintly.

"And for making me feel like an idiot, you have to close your eyes."

Pursing my lips, I felt my cheeks heating up, "Why?"

"Just do it, okay?"

Grunting, I ended up closing my eyes. My heart thumped, wondering what in the world Bryce was planning to do.

"No peeking, you got that?"

I heard his voice strum against my eardrums. Shutting my eyes tighter, I nodded my head several times, hoping Bryce would hurry up. Was he going to whack me in the head as punishment?

Then, the impossible happened.

My whole body shook with surprise the moment I felt Bryce's lips press against my cheek.

Bryce Valentino kissed me!

Immediately, my eyes opened only to find Bryce's handsome face an inch away. These heartstrings! I was so close to fainting, and I probably looked like a space cadet from that simple kiss on a cheek. A smile appeared on Bryce's lips. His white, straight teeth revealed, knowing that he had me breathless this very moment.

Bryce assured me, "I won't take your first kiss until I know you're completely happy to be with me. But, I need to tell you that you've been tugging my heartstrings for a long time, Daisie."

Chapter 26

The voice in my mind screamed, "He kissed you! Even if it's just on the cheek, snap out of it, Maisie!"

Bryce Valentino had me weak in the knees.

When Bryce and I headed back, everybody was all scattered back in the villa. We were fortunate to not have to worry about explaining ourselves. Once I found Vanessa, we both drowned ourselves with glee and laughter. It was so embarrassing, but I couldn't help it.

Who could possibly contain this happiness?

That moment replayed in my mind over and over again.

Something like this already had my heart tossed in many directions — imagine a real kiss?

"But you've been tugging my heartstrings for a long time, Daisie."

When I asked where Bryce got that from, he just gave me a sly grin and shrugged in reply. The first thing that came to mind was Mason. It appeared like the two got closer than I thought.

Smiling, I realized just having this kind of reassurance was all that I needed.

It was now late at night, and I needed to take a stroll outside alone. To "recover", I guessed.

Walking along the grasslands of the golf course, I let out a happy sigh and just wanted to scream on the top of my lungs. However, I only giggled and got a hold of myself. The island winds were nonexistent. It was so peaceful, minus the chirping of the crickets.

From afar, I noticed a figure in the golf course as well. It was one in the morning, who could that be?

Listening to my curious mind, I headed towards the silhouette that was casted from the moonlight. My eyes nearly jumped out when I discovered who it was.

It was Candace.

She was playing golf, swinging the golf club seriously. What surprised me was how she actually looked like she knew what she was doing. As I took a few more steps, my ears caught her sniffling.

Candace was crying.

Biting my lower lip, I eventually called out her name. Following the sound of my voice, her blue-green eyes widened in shock. From the moonlight, it revealed puffy eyes and trembling lips. Before I could say anything, Candace threw the golf club and ran the opposite direction. Even if I tried to catch up, she was long gone which left me in wonder.

The next morning, I was woken up by the sounds of constant knocking at my door.

Why was it still dark?

Rubbing my eyes, I glanced at the clock. It was only 5 a.m. I could have sworn we all fell asleep past midnight. Lazily dragging myself off the comfy bed, I stopped moving any further when a note and pen was sliding under the cracks of the door.

Picking up the small index card, I turned it over and found familiar handwriting:

Did you tell anyone about what you saw?

Recognizing the handwriting, I called out, "Candace, is that you?"

Instead of a voice replying, there was kicking at the door. Sighing, I picked up the pen and wrote down my answer, feeling the essence of middle school again. Moments later, the paper slid back to me.

Yes, it's Candace. Who did you tell?

If she was talking about when I saw her playing some intense golf, she was crazy. Why would anyone care about her being good at golf? She did run off crying though.

Writing back, I returned the message. This whole situation was getting awkward. Soon, the paper came back to me.

Okay, good. We need to talk.

Not wanting to play messenger anymore, I answered, "Fine. Right now?"

But, no. She began kicking at the door again. Shaking my head, I couldn't believe Candace was annoying me this early in the morning.

After exchanging a few more messages, she finally wrote:

That same place in one hour. You better be there!

I came up with a conclusion soon after. The Valentino's and Reynolds' were definitely an interesting sort of families.

Throwing on a white hoodie and shorts, I was still half asleep as I made my way towards the spot of the golf course where I first found Candace. The sun was slowly rising which made me wish I came out earlier to watch the full sunrise. The shades of orange to purple filled the sky and fluffy clouds beautifully.

As expected, Candace was there, swinging the golf club professionally as it launched the golf ball to its designated location. It amazed me seeing Candace look so concentrated. This whole time, it didn't phase me to wonder what she wanted to talk about.

I was too tired — and dizzy from Bryce's kiss.

When she noticed me heading up the grassy hill, she dropped the golf club to her side. Folding my arms from the slight breeze, I raised my eyebrows.

"Candace, it's so early in the morning. What's up?"

Her voice projected with such seriousness.

"You have to promise me you will never, ever tell this to anyone."

"I'm here, aren't I?" I countered gently.

Candace played with her ponytail as she mumbled, "I couldn't sleep at all because of this. You're probably wondering why I'm playing golf."

Pursing my lips, I gave her a honest reply, "Well, no. What I'm thinking about is why you were crying."

Suddenly, Candace bit her lower lip as her eyes wandered off.

What was going on?

Finally, Candace spat out, "It's so easy for you, Maisie! You get everything you want, the way you want it."

Taken back, I furrowed my eyebrows in confusion. Candace Reynolds was a rising model coming from a top family. She was rich, pretty, and probably has a lot of friends too.

What more does she want?

I reminded, "Candace, have you taken a look at yourself?"

Candace shook her head and shouted, "You don't get it, do you? I'm jealous of you! The more I'm with you, I can't help but bury myself with jealously. You're always so happy with having so little. You have people that adore you even though you're just you. You don't have loads of money, but people would still love to be around you. You're naturally pretty inside and out, and you get to do whatever you want."

As Candance was throwing that at me, I noticed the tears that were welling up in her eyes.

I let out a sigh.

"Candace, you have nothing to be jealous over. With everything you have already, you can achieve anything you wish for. Like being a model, doing all these fun things whenever you want, you have a life of luxury."

"That's not the point, Maisie! When I was younger they had this life plan for me, that I would become a model and marry Bryce. They forced it to be my dream. At the time, it was set in stone in my eyes. But, it's all wrong! It's all wrong!"

The tears began to fall down as she ranted, "I can't even play golf or have anyone like me because of who I am. I'm just so disgusted with myself. I'm so sick of it."

My stomach twisted itself the entire time, seeing Candace pour her heart out to me — on such a random occasion. The more she talked, I realized that there was more to Candace. This was what has been happening behind the scenes in her life. Despite everything she had done, it made my heart ache seeing her break down like that.

Candace tightly clutched the golf club, her eyes staring hard at the ground.

"It's just so easy for you, Maisie. You don't even know."

Hearing that, my hand reached out to touch her shoulder. Her shaken eyes made their way up at me.

I explained, "Candace, I don't have an easy life, but, I know what you should do. You need to tell your family what you really wish for. The little thing called compromise will make everything easier for you. We can't have everything we want... I noticed that's just the way life works. However, that doesn't mean you should give up."

"You're a beautiful person, Candace, I can see that, not just with your looks, but there's someone inside of you that's waiting to truly come out. I think... it's time to finally let her out in the world."

After taking in my words, Candace pulled me into a surprise hug. I could feel her uneven breathing as she cried freely into my shoulder. When Candace was finally at ease, we faced each other again. She wiped her nose as her cheeks were sticky with tears and traces of snot ran down.

For once, Candace didn't let her appearance get the best of her.

Candace responded with shadowed eyes, "Thank you, Maisie. You're right, you're totally right."

She apologized, "I'm sorry for everything. I didn't mean to say all those things to you, or do all those things to you. You don't have to forgive me because I don't deserve it, but just know that I'm really sorry."

She smiled before she let out a laugh, admiring the golf course before us.

"It's funny, right? A model that loves to play golf. Who would pay attention to her? You know, I play golf because I feel like I can be me. There's nothing in my way — no competition, no fighting, no one telling me what to do, nothing."

"Well, if you ask me, it's pretty awesome that you're actually different," I grinned, exchanging a genuine compliment.

Candace sniffled, glancing back at me.

"I'm going to tell my parents the truth that I want to play golf and maybe go back to school while I'm still young," she then revealed, "you want to know another reason why I'm so jealous of you, Maisie?"

Gulping down, I was unsure with what I was about to hear.

"You're the first person to make Bryce smile like that," when Candace noticed my look of disbelief, her eyes expressed sincerity, "it's true. If I wasn't the little kid I was back then, maybe Bryce wouldn't be so bitter towards other people. But, I can see that you opened his eyes."

For the first time, I saw Candace smile authentically as if we were friends. As I returned the smile, I couldn't help but feel embarrassed.

She added, "He really cares about you. Ever since I got here, all Bryce did was worry about you throughout everything. I'm sorry. I shouldn't have judged you so quickly. Aunt Monica was really wrong about you, it looks like she doesn't even know you either."

Surprised, I didn't know what to say about Bryce's mother — I never had the courage to confront her. Hearing about Bryce though was making my heart melt endlessly.

But, this conversation wasn't about me — it was about Candace.

Looking up at Candace, I stated, "We went through a lot Candace, but it doesn't mean we won't be friends in the future. I just want to see you happy with yourself first."

As my eyes wandered around the green scenery, I casually mentioned, "I also think Carly's been waiting for her older sister to be there for her."

Hearing a light gasp from Candace, I gazed back at her and noticed how her eyes started to tremble again. Her lips pulled into a smile as she giggled quietly from embarrassment.

"I haven't been a great person at all. I'm going to take things one step at a time."

Joining her laughter, I then offered my hand out between us.

"And I'll be here cheering you on. Come to think of it, we never introduced ourselves properly," I smiled before continuing, "hi, I'm Maisie Lockhart."

Taking my hand, Candace beamed as the tears began to fall down her face, "Nice to meet you, I'm Candace Reynolds."

"You want me to — What? No!"

I knew he was going to say that.

Grinning, I insisted, "Bryce, come on. Make amends with Candace."

Bryce fully faced me, giving me a stare like I had lost my mind. Actually, I didn't blame him for being so shocked.

Everything was happening like a whirlwind ever since we stepped foot on Valentino Island. We were walking together along the shoreline as the sun reached its high point. Our feet were welcomed by the calm waves of the clear, blue ocean. Because I was up so early this morning, I was fighting the tiredness. However, seeing Bryce like this kept me entertained.

Wearing a simple white tee and board shorts, Bryce ran his fingers through his hair and looked irritated.

"If I had a choice, I wouldn't speak to Candace again."

"Just talk to her... like a civil person. Trust me," I implied with honest eyes.

The whole time Bryce was confused with my sudden persistence, but he eventually agreed, leaving me with a content smile. I wanted to make sure by the time we leave this island, everyone would be okay.

Nodding my head, I teased, "And, tell her that you always thought she was a beautiful person. Honestly."

He groaned, rolling his icy blue eyes, "Now, you're just pulling my leg, Daisie."

As I laughed from amusement, Bryce had a small smirk on his face. Pulling my laughter to a stop, he suddenly moved closer and grabbed my hand. Squinting my eyes, my heart was racing with whatever Bryce was going to do.

Finally, Bryce winked.

"Why do you have dark circles under your eyes? You couldn't sleep last night because of the kiss?"

This time, Bryce got me.

In return, I pulled away from his grasp and kicked the ocean waters to splash up against him. Cupping some water in my hands, I tossed it towards Bryce. The water drenched down the delivery boy's face, causing me to start laughing again. Bryce blinked numerous times, keeping a still position.

When I thought I won, he fought back and splashed some water back at me in return. Since I was busy laughing to my heart's content, the water went into my mouth. Salt water was absolutely disgusting. Even though Bryce was bursting with joy now, I couldn't help but join him.

We were just a pair of laughing idiots.

Once night hit, another day on Valentino Island was coming to a close. When we all finished dinner — minus Candace who literally slept in the whole day — I was walking around the villa after helping Mrs. Romano with the dishes.

Passing by the patio, my attention was pulled when I heard my name being called.

Heading back to the sliding doors, I jumped in surprise when I clearly saw Logan. Was my eyesight getting worse or what? Fully sliding the doors open, I gave him a friendly smile.

He was sitting in the one of the bamboo chairs and asked casually, "Mind if we talk?"

If there was one person I needed to talk to about things left unsaid, it had to be Logan Valentino.

Chapter 27

"I'm going to tell you a story," Logan announced as I took the chair across from him.

Even though no words came out of my mouth in reply, Logan still continued, "Once upon a time, there were three teenager boys venturing off the city of Paris, France. They didn't know where they were going at the time. The eldest suggested that the three should call someone to pick them up, but the youngest found joy and insisted to keep going. The middle didn't mind. He was eager for some adventure in an unfamiliar city."

"As the three continued on, the youngest pointed out a fortune teller shop from across the street. He told the two that they should test their luck and get readings. So they did. It was stupid in their eyes, but they wanted to do something stupid at the time. One by one, the fortune teller told them what would come in the near future. The middle simply thought it was all lies, and the fortune teller was just repeating the same things to different customers."

"That was until the fortune teller predicted the youngest one's future. The fortune teller asked the youngest if he loved drinking hazelnut coffee. The three all looked at each other in confusion from her question, but the youngest nodded his head. It was indeed true. The fortune teller grew a smirk on her lips and announced that in a point of his life, he would fall in love with a girl who loves hazelnut coffee as much as he does. The three teenagers all bursted into laughter, not believing the silly words of the fortune teller."

"The youngest had tears in his eyes from laughing so hard and told the fortune teller that she needed to get help. The eldest and middle had enough of her games, so they all stood up from the raggedy chairs and walked out of the shop, still laughing with one another. However, the middle caught something that the two didn't hear. The fortune teller muttered under her breathe that it would happen, and nothing or no one would be able to change that."

"Seven years passed, and that same moment replayed in the middle's mind when he met a girl who liked hazelnut coffee. The middle even thought of doing something silly and pretend to like the drink he never appreciated like the youngest. The middle grew scared that it was all too late because it seemed like the fortune teller was right. The middle didn't want to believe that the youngest found that girl first before him, and he didn't want to believe that she would be the one the fortune teller predicted."

As Logan ended his story, a small grin grew on his lips when he saw my reaction.

Logan chuckled out, "It's a bittersweet tale, isn't it?"

Taking this whole story in, I soon realized that Logan was talking about him and his cousins. The eldest was David, the middle was Logan, and the youngest was Bryce. When the fortune teller predicted Bryce's future about finding someone who liked hazelnut coffee as much as he did, and the girl —

I stopped.

A tiny laugh of disbelief escaped from me as I widened my eyes. "You're kidding me?"

Sure, I was expecting a more serious talk, but this story Logan just told me had me even more curious.

"I... actually asked Vanessa earlier that day what drink you liked just so I would be prepared when we met up. When I drank it with you though, it tasted decent. But Maisie, I can't tell you the reason why right now."

Was this the reason why Logan pretended to like hazelnut coffee around me?

Shrugging in return, Logan's dark blue eyes roamed.

"I probably am, I'm probably not. What do you think, Maisie?"

Tapping my fingers on the arms of the chair, I stammered, "I mean, if that really happened, that's an extremely weird lady you three met. You don't honestly think she was telling the truth, right?"

Logan soon settled his eyes back to me, letting out a sigh.

"I know what I think. The question is, do you think she was telling the truth?"

With the direction this conversation was going, Logan was having me indirectly cornered.

My eyes fell to my lap, and I firmly spoke, "She probably tells that to anyone who likes something. I'm sure there's other hazelnut coffee lovers out there too."

"You could say that, but if you look at it right now, maybe the fortune teller was right," Logan replied in a low murmur.

Glancing back at Logan, this was his way of telling me that I was hurting him. The notion was killing me.

Looking at him in the eyes, I gave him a sincere apology, "Logan, you're an amazing person, and I see you as one of my closest friends. But, I just — I'm really sorry, I really am."

After a moment of silence, Logan replied, "It's okay..."

He was lying. His midnight blue eyes were betraying him at this very moment.

"I just realized how stupid I sound right now. The world is starting to spin on me," Logan quietly revealed, his hand reaching for his head.

Fixing my position on the seat, I inched closer and asked, "Logan, are you okay?"

That was when I noticed that Logan was experiencing pain... and the smell of alcohol. Logan tightly clutched onto his head and hissed.

My voice rang.

"Hey, what's wrong?"

He shook his head and insisted, "I'm okay, Maisie, I just had a little to drink."

"No, you're not okay! Wait, you're drunk?" I unintentionally exclaimed.

Logan gritted his teeth together.

"A little. I don't take alcohol that well."

Before I could say anything, Logan collapsed on me.

Quickly, I pulled him back to his chair and started to panic. Logan passed out! Doesn't this remind you of the time Bryce passed out sick on me? At least this time, I was much more smarter and called for everyone's attention as I rushed back inside the villa, shouting for help. In the back of my mind, I couldn't help but pound myself with guilt seeing Logan like this.

It was all my fault, right?

"What the — I just had to use the bathroom, and now he's gone!"

Zack was peering over his mother's shoulders as Logan was placed snugly in the bed of his designated room.

Mrs. Romano wasn't pleased with the outcome of Zack and Logan's little drinking charade.

She shook her head, placing her hands on her hips as she scolded, "Zackary Romano, I could have sworn I taught you to be more responsible. You're twenty-five yet you're being careless. I will definitely tell Kelsey about this."

Zack's voice shifted seriously towards his mother.

"Come on Mom, I'm not going to hear the end of it from Kelsey. I told her that I wouldn't do any of that stuff, but we just wanted to have a little fun. Logan needed to ease himself up."

Mrs. Romano's blue eyes were still expressing disapproval.

"And, look at what has become of Sir Logan. Zackary, I understand the boy's twenty-one, but you of all people know this isn't always the right way of having fun."

The whole time, I felt my body grow cold, seeing Logan in his deep slumber. When Logan passed out, Bryce and David helped support him up the stairs, and they both looked at me with the most confused expressions. Hearing what Zack said didn't make things any better. Zack eventually nodded his head, acknowledging his faults and took full responsibility.

Mrs. Romano then told us that Logan needed his rest and how we should all get some rest too. Before exiting out of the room, Mrs. Romano pulled Zack's ear lightly in a half joking matter which caused us to cease our laughs.

Zack laughed brokenly when he turned back to us.

"Sorry you had to see that, kiddos, but yeah, it's late. Get some sleep".

David folded his arms and teased, "Being responsible, huh?"

"Hey now, Logan looked down this whole day, and I thought a drink or two would cheer him up," Zack returned as he waved his hands in defense.

We all heard Vanessa announce, "You practically killed him."

"Hey, don't poke him!" David playfully warned Vanessa as she was poking Logan's cheek like a science specimen.

Vanessa looked back at us in entertainment and laughed. Zack groaned after his chuckling.

"Alright, alright. I think my mom already got it in my head. Let's give the guy some rest."

Zack walked towards the door, opening it as he used his right arm to usher us out. Looking back at Logan one more time, I couldn't help but release an upset sigh. Turning back straight ahead, I found Bryce observing me this whole time. As Bryce gently placed his hand behind my back, we both walked outside the hallway together. I exchanged glances with Zack, and his blue eyes flickered with knowledge and sympathy.

He knew everything.

Once Zack closed the door, he questioned all of us, "Oh yeah, where has Reynolds been?"

That was when everybody nodded their heads, finally realizing that she wasn't with us this whole day.

I replied, "She decided to sleep in."

Vanessa flashed me a 'how do you know' grin, and I quickly shot her an 'I'll explain all later' look.

After years of friendship, shares of simple glances were an easy way of communicating with one another.

Yawning lightly, Vanessa then decided she was heading to bed. Being the kind boyfriend he was, David offered to escort her even though it was just a few doors down. What an amusing couple. This was Zack's signal to call it a night too. As the three said good night to Bryce and me, we both gave them smiles,and then, it was down to two.

It wasn't my intention to look bothered, but Bryce immediately caught on. His voice bought my mind in the right state.

"You want to talk about it?"

Sighing, I dropped my tensed shoulders.

"Logan just told me something,and I feel like it's my fault."

Bryce scoffed out, "What did he do?"

My eyes looked up at Bryce, and he was getting the wrong signs again. Logan wasn't the bad guy.

As I shook my head, I explained, "I don't know if you remember, but Logan told me a story when you three were younger. You met some fortune teller that told you you'd fall in love with a girl who likes hazelnut coffee."

When Bryce listened to my explanation, his eyebrows slowly raised in surprise. Did he remember? Instead, Bryce released a laugh.

"Wow, was Logan that drunk? He'll be back to normal tomorrow. Anyway, let's call it a night, Daisie. You look tired as hell right now."

There was something in Bryce's blue eyes and tone of voice that made me question what he really said. It was like Bryce really did remember, but he pretended not to.

Because like me, Bryce knew that us being together was hurting his cousin too.

As soon as I woke up the next morning, I prepped myself up for the day and immediately waited outside for Logan. Anxiety was taking over me. I couldn't sleep or think clearly because of Logan. Leaning against the wall, I was tapping my fingers against the villa's main doors, wondering if Logan was already awake and with everyone else.

Instead, I literally jumped when something or someone whisked against my side. Logan was walking along, fixing his mildly damp hair with his fingers. He didn't realize I was there.

Taking a deep breath, I called out his name confidently. The moment Logan heard me, his entire body stiffened into place. He eventually motioned his full attention to me.

I couldn't read his facial expression. If he was annoyed, mad, upset — I couldn't tell. Logan's eyes were simply blank even though he had a closed smile upon his lips.

"Hey..."

My voice was weaker and accidentally scared.

Logan gave me a short nod and greeted me back, not saying anything else.

Okay, I started the conversation. I had to say something!

My eyes roamed the island's surroundings, not daring to look at Logan directly.

"How are you feeling?"

All of a sudden, there was a trace of soft laughter from Logan. When I found confidence to fix my sight at him, my lips fell as I wondered why he laughed.

Logan grinned lightly.

"I'm sorry for laughing. You're just being really awkward right now, Maisie. If anything, I should be the one embarrassed that you had to see me like that."

"I'm sorry."

Why was I being so uneasy?

He raised both eyebrows and questioned, "Sorry for what exactly?"

Letting out a sigh, I explained through a mumble, "For last night — for being awkward — for everything."

"You have nothing to apologize for. I guess it's my fault for not acting sooner, right? Even if I did try, I guess it wasn't enough."

Logan looked away momentarily but soon gave me a comforting smile. My lips couldn't help but drop into a frown again hearing that.

"Logan, I'm sor —"

Lifting his hand up, Logan interrupted, "I don't want you to apologize to me, Maisie. It's all right."

Observing Logan's body language, it appeared like he was serious about what he said. Still. My gut was telling me that he couldn't forgive me. My eyes fell to the floor, and I felt failure. It just seemed like things wouldn't be the same anymore between us.

Why was I being so pessimistic?

Challenging the negativity in my head, I had to make sure everything would be okay before we left this island.

Staring at Logan directly in the eyes, I gulped down before stating in a sincere tone, "Logan, I just don't want anything to change between us."

After what felt like forever, Logan finally responded by nodding his head.

Following after, he replied in a stern tone, "Nothing will change unless we make it change."

"You're right," I replied, "can I ask you something though? It's been bothering me for the longest time."

Logan's dark blue eyes deepened in reply before he nodded once more.

I stammered, "Why... are you telling me to stay away from Bryce? The moment I walked out of the doors after the presentation, you appeared different."

The voice in my head scolded, "Seriously, Maisie? You think this will help your current situation with Logan?"

His jaw clenched before Logan responded, "I just... thought he wouldn't be good for you, that's all. I have no right to tell you what to do. It's your choice."

Taken back from his answer, I furrowed my eyebrows together in confusion.

"And why's that?"

Logan's eyes drifted down to the ground until he finally spoke up, "Because it's obvious, isn't it? Or you still can't see it, Maisie?"

Suddenly, he switched the topic, "Maisie, just forget about what I said, okay? If you're happy, then that's okay with me."

Blinking my eyes, Logan's words and actions were troubling me. Behind those dark blue eyes were telling me that Logan — himself — couldn't forget about it. What was I going to do? Just looking at Logan right now, the way he tried to hold a strong front was so clear to me. I knew what he meant, but there was nothing that could come out of my mouth. I hated this feeling and being stuck in this position. Logan would make me feel frustrated one moment, and guilty the next.

When I didn't reply, Logan smiled in an encouraging effort and suggested, "Don't worry about me. Your happiness matters too, remember that."

Logan went on like nothing happened.

"Let's go meet up with the rest. It's our last day here before we leave in the morning. We should make the best of it, Maisie."

Even if everything did seem resolved between us, my heart was dying to etch it in my brain that it was all fabricated.

Throughout the day, it was like everything was back to normal — like the first time I met the Valentino's.

The Valentino boys looked closer than these past few weeks combined. Bryce and Logan were getting along, even joking with one another after so long which was storming a thought tornado in my head. Even though witnessing something like this should be relaxing, it was tensing me up even more.

Despite my doubts, I did have a good time during our last moments at the island. All of us spent the day swimming in the crystal clear waters and climbing up the tropical lush mountains because city life would never look like this.

I couldn't help but laugh when Vanessa told me that Candace probably got hit hard in the head by a coconut, and that was why Candace was being unusually nice the moment she woke up today. Everybody was shocked to see the renewed Candace in action. I was happy to see that she was opening up.

Of course, she still had that essence of "Candace" in her when it came to being glamourous.

The moment I found Bryce and Candace having a regular conversation for once, I broke into a smile when I saw how ecstatic Candace's large blue-green eyes lit up when Bryce said that it was pretty cool that she liked golf.

All my worries seemed to have disappeared when all of us were standing or sitting together in the beach, watching the sunset.

This made me wish that we were stuck in this moment. Everything seemed perfect. It was absolutely beautiful, watching the golden sphere slowly cast away as it offered the moon its turn to shine. The shades of deep oranges, red and yellows stretched across the sky, painting an astonishing canvas.

My heartstrings were tugged when Bryce surprisingly grabbed my hand and smiled warmly at me as we took in the beauty. Flushing out red, I sheepishly looked down before gazing back up at him, smiling back.

Zack had his hand against his forehead, looking out at the sea as he announced proudly, "Take this in, kids. These kind of moments won't be lived again."

Chapter 28

arly grinned ear to ear as she jumped up and down.

"Lockhart, does this mean that you and Bryce are officially together now? Like boyfriend and girlfriend!"

How was I supposed to answer this?

Glancing around the currently busy market, I replied with an honest tone, "Carly, I actually don't know."

The little girl scrunched her nose, letting out a complaint, "You don't know? He kissed you! Bryce didn't ask you to be his girlfriend after that?"

It had been two days since our return from the Valentino's vacation.

Saying goodbye to the Romano's and Zack was something I hated to do, but we assured them that we would see each other again. Zack even invited Vanessa and me to his wedding. Ever since our arrival back, thing was somewhat normal again.

Except the fact that everyone's eyes were on Bryce and me about our "statuses".

Before I could find words to reply, I heard Carly scream, "Hey! If you're not going to buy it, put it back!"

Holy crap.

The shady high school kid shook from the little girl's outburst, placing the candy back in the aisle. He flushed from embarrassment, seeing how he was clearly caught, before escorting himself out of the market.

Maybe Carly should keep an eye on the store. She was doing a better job than me.

That was a bad thing, right?

Carly shook her head side to side, folding her arms.

"It scares me that that's the future before me. Reminds me of Mason and his friends. They were acting ridiculous at the water park."

Amused, I inquired through a chuckle, "You were there with them?"

Carly nodded.

Her blue-green eyes were dull as she recalled back to that moment, "Not really. I just happened to see them, and they were acting like a bunch of giggling girls prancing around the place. I was embarrassed to even approach him."

Hearing that made me burst into laughter. Never did I expect a nine year old to make me laugh like that.

Carly Reynolds was an exception.

I couldn't wait to see the look on Mason's face when I told him about this.

She waved her hand around and returned back on topic, "You never answered my question, Lockhart. Did Bryce ask you to be his girlfriend?"

Bryce told me that I had been tugging his heartstrings — did that count?

As she waited for a response, I finally concluded, "Bryce didn't say those exact words."

Carly frowned.

"Seriously? I'm going to talk to him."

Her response reminded me when I told Vanessa. Vanessa even stated that what Bryce did wasn't good enough. Were they expecting a parade of some sort? Then again, I was left confused too because Bryce wasn't so straightforward about it either.

Shaking my head, I replied hesitantly, "You don't have to. Time is all... is takes, right?"

"You don't even sound confident with your answer, Lockhart!" Carly scolded with a teasing laugh.

Joining her laughter, I couldn't help but sigh afterward.

Were we — what people call "official" — or just seeing each other?

Snapping out of my thoughts, I soon noticed that Carly was taking charge of the cashier. The little girl was ringing some customers up for me. It amazed that she had the knowledge to do that. There were many things to figure out about Carly. Our usual customers all asked who the cute girl was, and Carly replied that she was an apprentice.

Everyone adored her natural charm.

When the rush died down, Carly quickly questioned, "Are you going to be done any time soon?"

Blinking my eyes, I answered, "Mason should be here in an hour."

Carly then asked for my cellphone as soon as she heard that. Carefully handing my phone to the Carly, she was pushing buttons and eventually placed the phone by her ear.

It was only a matter of seconds before her childish yet strong voice projected, "Hey prancing pony, come to the market right now."

I took a guess that "prancing pony" was none other than my eighteen year old brother, Mason.

You know that awkward moment when you and that certain person happened to walk into each other unexpectedly?

Yeah, that.

Right when Carly and I were walking into Legends, Bryce was there by the revolving doors, about to walk out the opposite direction. We both exchanged surprised glances and stopped moving until the revolving doors hit my back. The force caused me to move forward unwillingly. Bryce was holding in a laugh as he witnessed the entire thing.

Straightening myself up, I attempted to play it smooth.

"That was all intentional."

Bryce smirked.

"Right. Anyway, what are you doing here, Daisie? You told me you were at the market."

"I had to drop —"

When I glanced over to my right where I expected Carly to be standing, she wasn't there anymore. What the hell? Becoming a little delirious, I looked on both my sides, and she was nowhere to be seen.

I wondered out loud as I raised my eyebrows, "Where did she go?"

That was when Bryce started to chuckle.

"You're really not being obvious at all. It's okay to tell me that you missed me and that you just had to see me."

There was the confident delivery boy we all knew.

My eyes widened, and I shouted with assurance, "Bryce! She was right here. Am I losing my mind?"

Bryce playfully answered through a shrug, "You're always that crazy Daisie. It doesn't matter. Carly is able to take care of herself."

He then joked, "If she really was with you in the first place."

Exhaling sharply, I retorted back, "She was here! Why does she always disappear on me?"

While I was literally losing my mind, Bryce was staring at me with an entertained expression on his face. He probably got a kick out of it, thinking this was cable. The scene was very humiliating. Taking a deep breath, I knew I wasn't going crazy, and this had to be one of Carly's method in getting us to talk.

Remember when Carly just disappeared as we were searching for her "missing" bow at Legends Garden during Candace's welcoming party?

Bryce's taunting voice poked my thoughts away.

"You done over there?"

Placing my hand on my hips, I stated in a firm tone, "Believe whatever you want. I know I'm completely sane. Anyway, were you going somewhere?"

Bryce replied through a nod, "I was going to see you."

Blinking my eyes, I slowly fixated my attention back to him as he looked at me with honest glacial blue eyes. I hated when the things he said got to me like this. My heart thumped when I asked why.

"We have things to talk about. I'm sure you know," he claimed sincerely.

Bryce then motioned me to follow him. He grinned as we walked side by side.

"You must be that attracted to me to naturally come when I need you."

At the same time, I gave Bryce a slight shove as he laughed.

"We're working on the Legends Garden project in a week," Bryce announced as we were strolling in the actual garden itself.

My eyes widened at how quickly they would start. In my mind, I thought it would be in a couple months. Bryce pointed out the spot where the wishing well would be placed. He gave me a proud smile, reminding me that it was my work.

Feeling embarrassment take over, I smiled weakly.

"You don't think the idea is stupid, right?"

Bryce gave me a bewildered look and scoffed out, "Why would I? You can't find any wishing wells anywhere near here. I haven't even seen one in my life actually."

Hearing that made me feel more confident, but I stammered out, "It's just — why did you even ask me to do it? I'm sure you and your family could have hired some professional."

"I personally don't give a crap who's professional or not. And since you asked, I wanted you to do it, that's why," Bryce stated a matter a fact.

Suddenly, a smile appeared on his lips as he momentarily looked away.

"And I wanted Legends Garden —"

His voice trailed off to a point where I couldn't hear his last words.

"What's that?"

"You're going to laugh," Bryce plainly replied.

"You laugh at me practically every time we're together," I mentioned with a clever grin even though that was nothing to be proud of.

Releasing a sigh, Bryce's sky blue eyes soon stared deeply into mine.

"It's mainly because I know how much you love this place... and I wanted Legends Garden to have a part of you in it."

The delivery boy did it again.

These heartstrings of mine were tugged as my cheeks flushed red. Trying to hide the embarrassment, I glanced directly at the ground and started to laugh quietly.

I soon heard Bryce say, "I told you so."

Gazing back up at him, I beamed, "I'm glad you did though."

The two of us shared smiles before walking on. Breaking the silence, I continued our conversation.

"Bryce... what exactly are we?"

"Human beings," he answered through a light laugh.

Way to ruin the moment.

"No, I'm serious."

"I'm serious too, unless you're telling me I like an alien."

"What?"

"You heard me."

Bryce winked, another chuckle followed after.

"Bryce!"

Bryce smirked when the two of us stopped walking to face each other once more. Despite his amused expression, Bryce's eyes were held solemn.

"I'm kidding. Of course I know you're not an alien. You're Daisie, and I'm the delivery boy. Let's make this a math equation then. If you add those two together, it equals that the two like each other, but one of them is still acting like an unknown variable over here."

"That person is obviously you," I responded with a taunting grin.

Bryce rolled his eyes playfully and nodded.

"Oh yeah, definitely. After I gave that person all the clues, she still never got it."

"Uh huh, right. It's because that other person was never forward about it in the first place," I retorted, holding in a giggle.

"It's kind of sad how that person can't take a hint though. I guess that's how daisies are," Bryce jokingly countered.

Even though I was trying express anger, my lips were fighting itself to smile. Bryce noticed my mixed expression, and his soothing voice strummed.

"You're funny when you make that face, but I'm just kidding. You get it now though, right? Other than us being human beings."

As I nodded my head, laughing, Bryce surprised me when he grabbed my hand.

He announced through a charming grin, making my heart beat faster, "Good. Now I could properly hold your hand."

Walking hand in hand through the maze in Legends Garden, Bryce muttered, "There's another thing we have to talk about actually."

Judging by the shift in tone, it sounded like bad news. I gulped down but eventually replied to go on.

Bryce continued on, "I'm going to be gone for the next three weeks."

Thinking he was pulling a joke with me, I stopped on my heels again and waited for Bryce to burst out laughing.

But nothing.

I raised my eyebrows and clarified the doubt from my ears, "You're serious? Why?"

He pursed his lips and nodded slowly.

"I have some business arrangements that need to be done out of the country. Phoenix Empire is planning to expand through Europe and hopefully Asia. It's only going to be three weeks."

My ears had a hard time taking that in. Three weeks? I wasn't expecting this kind of news.

I carefully repeated, "You're not going to be here?"

Bryce nodded his head again, and I couldn't stop my facial expression from falling. He sighed.

"I'm sorry. But, you'll be there when I leave, right?"

"Of course."

I forced on a smile, still affected by the news.

"By the way, you're going to be in charge of the Legends Garden project."

"Bryce!"

My eyes widened. His blue eyes blinked, holding a sincere expression.

"I know I keep throwing things at you, but that's just the way I am," Bryce chuckled at his last words before saying, "anyway, you're not going to work at the restaurant anymore. From now on, you're going to be in charge of the project, and you have to make sure everything and everyone is doing a good job. Besides it's your design, you'll know what's right from wrong. If anyone is giving you problems, tell me, and I'll fire their ass."

I gasped, "You can't be serious."

"Of course I'll fire them. I'm going to be a CEO soon, I have a right to," Bryce completely missed my point.

I explained thoroughly, "I know that, but that's not what I mean. I can't do it. I-I'm not even fit for that kind of job."

Bryce tried to get it in my head.

"Maisie, you need to be more confident about yourself. You can be successful in your own ways. You'll be fine. Also, if you need any help, there's David and Logan too."

Shocked, this was the first time Bryce actually said my real name towards me. Ironic, wasn't it? His encouraging words did work on me in some ways. The delivery boy was right. When I nodded my head, the uncertainty was still present but not as bad as before.

"Promise me something," Bryce requested, his hand tightening lightly around mine.

As I gazed up at Bryce, he continued with that warm smile on his face.

"That you won't be scared. And when I come back, I want you to be the first person I see."

I didn't have to think twice about making that promise.

Chapter 29

"**M**s. Lockhart, how is this?"

"Is this fine with you, Ms. Lockhart?"

"Ms. Lockhart, we need your approval before starting."

For the past three weeks, these were the questions and words I heard every single day.

I was in charge of the Legends Garden project. Yes, me. Every time I woke up in the morning before heading to the construction sight, I couldn't believe that I was the one people would look up to. To be honest, I was satisfied with what I have — so something like this was hard to get used to.

Did I get use to it yet?

Not so much.

I was still and always going to be Maisie Lockhart.

These three weeks without Bryce was definitely different. I couldn't help but worry about his behalf, but we would keep in touch whenever we could. The only time I saw or heard Bryce would be when there were several news coverage talking about Phoenix Empire's expansion or when Bryce has time to call.

It was only three weeks, right? Yet, no matter how many times I told myself that, the days would drag and become endless.

I couldn't lie. I missed that delivery boy. His sarcastic humor, his smile, his presence — not having Bryce here felt off.

It had been bittersweet ever since Bryce left. Not only did Bryce leave for his business trip, but things got pretty depressing when Carly and Candace had to go back to their London home last weekend.

Carly was crying before boarding onto the plane, and I hated to see the little girl like that. Even though I told her that we would see each other soon, she didn't want to go. I didn't want her to leave either. We grew a bond like sisters. Candace, being a renewed person, told me that she would tell her parents what she truly wanted, and I wished her the very best in hopes to see her again as well. I guessed we could all say that everyone was leaving.

And, it became quite empty because of it.

Nonetheless, Logan and David both were helping me whenever they can which I was thankful for. Like I said previously, I have no experience on how to bring my wishing well idea to life. At the same time, I grew closer to them. Overall, it was an interesting experience. Legends Garden looked like a mess right now, but Logan told me in due time, it would look beautiful.

I did hope he was right.

Throughout these weeks, Logan and I weren't — you could say — awkward anymore. We would eat out together every now and then, and that old friendship was coming back alive once again.

"Maisie, you've been staring at your coffee mug for the longest time now."

Vanessa's voice caught my absent-mind.

We were both sitting together in Brightside Café by the window — our favorite spot in the café. Glancing back up at her, she was staring at me with widened green eyes, and I laughed at my actions. Or lack of.

Soon after, she joined my laughter. Vanessa gave me a bright smile and winked.

"You're probably daydreaming about Bryce, huh? Well, say good-bye to those daydreams because in a few hours, he's coming back!"

I wasn't daydreaming, honestly, but Vanessa was right in some-way.

It was finally the day I had been waiting for.

The delivery boy was arriving back from his business trip!

Giving her a look, I chuckled softly, stirring the coffee.

"I wasn't, Van."

As a response, Vanessa rolled her eyes playfully, not taking my word for it. Still, the thought made happiness spread throughout me like a virus. I was just waiting for 6 o'clock to hit so I could head over to the airport. We would all be spending the last weeks of summer together.

I loved the sound of that.

Vanessa and I spent the afternoon together, doing some window shopping in a nearby promenade to kill some time. My best friend was currently busy these past weeks as well since she recently scored a job as a fashion intern. Her dream was finally coming true, and I couldn't be more happier for her.

Before I knew it, the two of us went our separate ways because it was almost time. Just like I promised, I wanted to make sure that I was the first person Bryce would see.

And, what would be better than showing up with a cup of hazelnut coffee?

Exiting out of a nearby café, I was happily heading to my car until my phone started ringing in my bag. Thinking that it would be Bryce, I immediately searched through my purse and pressed the answer button without taking notice of the caller ID.

But, it wasn't Bryce's voice.

It was Mason.

The words he was saying on the other line weren't making any sense. Sure, I could hear him, but none of it was registering in my mind.

Eventually, reality was hitting hard on me. I gasped in shock, dropping the cup of hazelnut coffee. The drink splattered all over the concrete ground which some of the hot liquid landed on the bottom of my jeans and shoes. People passing by me were eying me with confused faces, wondering what was the matter with me. I didn't care at the moment.

Without even thinking, I had to go back to my family. I needed to see it for myself.

My hands were shaking as I controlled the steering wheel.

That twisted, uneasy feeling was residing in my stomach, hoping that it wasn't true. My younger brother sounded so scared and serious which I couldn't recall ever happened. The stoplights seemed to be playing a joke with me by turning red with every chance it got.

Could this go any faster?

Aggravated, I pressed on the gas pedal to rush over to the market.

This couldn't be happening. It just couldn't.

When I was getting close, my heart was racing in a negative matter. My mind was only set on this very thing, and it terrified me. Parking my car, I ran towards our market and stopped when I reached a reasonable distance.

It was all true. My family were standing outside together, and I caught their saddened expressions.

My stomach dropped ten floors, seeing our very market not belonging to us anymore.

All our hard work went down the drain through my very eyes. The bittersweet memories of that one summer flew before me. So many questions were stirring up inside of me that very moment.

Stepping closer to the scene, two faces I had never seen were talking to my family.

Our market was closed down and covered with a sign I couldn't read from afar. When they seemed to notice my presence, everyone turned around. My dad looked ever so serious as he was comforting my mom. She was holding back the tears in her hazel eyes. Mason looked completely in disbelief as his face pleaded for me to do something because he was helpless right now.

Approaching the businessmen, my voice shook.

"What's going on, sir?"

The one with salt and pepper hair combed back and a thick mustache replied sternly, "This building has been outbought by Mrs. Monica Valentino."

My head suddenly throbbed at the name, and I questioned, "Excuse me? That can't be. We—We paid every month, we didn't do anything wrong. I— what do you mean?"

"Ms. Lockhart, you heard correctly. We must have everything evacuated immediately for Phenix Empire to begin their next project."

My lips dropped into a frown.

"This is wrong. You can't do that!"

"You are dealing with the Valentino family," the other man noted as he span our market keys between his fingers.

Disbelief was all that I felt for a few minutes. However, anger soon resided in me because this market meant so much to my family and me.

No one — not even Monica Valentino — could take that from us.

Even with all the money in the world, there was no possible way that I would let her get away with this.

Clenching my fists together, I stated bitterly, "If this is her sick way of getting me to talk to her, then so be it."

Disregarding my parents' shouts to come back as I ran back to my car, I needed to settle something that I should have done a long time ago.

"Why'd you do it?!"

I came barging in Monica Valentino's clean office without thinking properly.

Usually, I wouldn't dare to treat someone's parent with such disrespect, but I was tired of being scared. I was tired of letting Monica Valentino step over me.

Even if she was the mother of Bryce, bringing my family between our situation was the last straw. I thought that she didn't have that resentment towards me anymore, but I guess I was wrong. Monica Valentino was standing by her desk, definitely surprised. Her face fell from my lack of manners and disgust soon occupied her striking face.

Those cold brown eyes grew into thin slits as she spat, "Who allowed you to come to my office? Let alone, barge in like you own the place?"

Letting courage support me, I took several steps closer to her and demanded, "Tell me why'd you do it."

Monica Valentino folded her arms and retaliated, "I don't need to tell you anything, Maisie Lockhart. I don't have to tell you anything, remember that."

This wasn't my usual self. I was boiling inside. Not because of the way she treated me. I didn't care if she treated me like this because I could live and deal with it.

What made my blood curdle was the fact she decided to hurt my family and take away one of the most important things to us. What did my family do to deserve this? They didn't do anything wrong. So many things I wanted to yell out because I had enough.

Tightening my fists into a ball, I cried out, "Why do you keep doing this to me? Why did you have to bring my family into this?"

Her presence was strong as she angled her face higher, making her feel superior to me. Bryce's mother moved away from her desk, taking a few steps towards me. Her heels clanked against the hardwood floors, making my body shiver with anxiety. Her dark brown eyes continued to stab right through me.

Her voice were as sharp as knives as she replied, "I told you many times to leave my family alone, but you never listen. Do you?"

My voice came out weaker than intended.

"Because I have a relationship with Bryce, is that it? You didn't have to drag my family and take our market away! You don't know how hard we worked for that!"

The tears were trying to push themselves out of my eyes, but I resisted. I didn't want to appear any weaker. Monica Valentino shook her head, keeping that cold appearance.

"I don't want my son to be with you. Having you in our lives will ruin all the hard work we worked for."

Gulping down hard, I bit my lower lip before responding, "But, we're happy together. Why can't —"

She interrupted, "I don't care. Do you understand? I have given you many chances to walk away from Bryce, but you didn't take any of those chances. I let you two do what you want which I regret. That's not how it is supposed to be, Maisie. You are just a regular girl. You won't ever belong in our family, and I want to keep things that way."

His mother's eyes darted at me as she emphasized the last few words darkly.

You know that saying: "Sticks and stones may break your bones, but words won't hurt you"?

Why was it that her words were hurting me right now? It felt like she was mentally pounding my head, and I wasn't as strong as I thought I would be confronting her.

Not being able to find any words to reply back with, Bryce's mother went on, "If I have to resort to something like this to keep you away, I will do whatever it takes. I'll give you back the market when you decide to stop being selfish."

Monica Valentino spat out, "Do you not see that when you and my son are together, no one will be happy. Do you want your family to suffer because you are being selfish? Do you want Bryce to suffer because you are being selfish? Do you want my family to suffer because you are being selfish?"

As she throwing those harsh questions at me, I found myself falling apart. Her brown eyes flickered. She smirked once she saw my distorted expression. The way she managed to take over me was success to her.

My eyes fell to the floor, and I replied slowly, "I-I don't want that. I don't want to see anyone hurt, but please answer this."

"Hurry up because you're wasting my time," she demanded quickly.

Picking up my head, I looked directly at her in the eyes.

I questioned with all the confidence I had left, "What did I do for you to hate me this much?"

There was something that changed in her dark brown eyes that I couldn't understand. Monica Valentino glanced away momentarily. I noticed that she was growing uneasy especially with the way she was hesitant in finding a way to answer. After a short pause, her striking face gazed back at me.

She remarked through a glare, "It surprises me how you don't have a clue."

When she noticed my dumbfounded expression, Bryce's mother shook her head once more.

"Of course, she wouldn't tell you. She was always the good one in everyone's eyes."

Bryce's mother soon began to circle around me causing me to grow self conscious.

She claimed through a discreet tone, "You're a spit image of her, you know that? The moment I first saw you, I knew. It took everything I had to compose myself in front of everyone. Of course, my husband couldn't help but notice too."

Once Monica Valentino returned back to face me, she scoffed lightly, "I almost didn't believe it at first, but I guess things have their way coming back, don't they? You and your family just couldn't stay away."

"W-what are you talking about?" I inquired as my eyebrows scrunched together in frustration.

Her cold brown eyes landed back at me as she hissed, "Your mother. Your mother, that's why."

My stomach twisted itself, and I was scared to even ask. However, I needed to know. I wanted to make sure these assumptions I had in my mind at the moment were true.

Clearing my throat, I asked, "How is my mother part of this?"

Bryce's mother scowled, recalling back to that time, "Just like you, your mother almost took everything away from me. I didn't let that happen though. It didn't happen in the past, and it won't happen now. Not ever."

Piece by piece, it all started to make sense:

Through it all, I heard Mom say to herself, "He looks exactly like him..."

"What did you say, Mom?" I asked, tilting my head with curiosity.

Bryce's father soon nodded his head.

After a short pause, he asked, "One more thing Maisie, is your parents doing alright? Your mother?"

Slightly confused, I tilted my head but answered anyway, "Yeah, they're doing great. Thanks for asking. Can I ask why?"

Those dark blue eyes lit up, and he let out a soft chuckle.

"Oh no, it's just we knew each other at one point of our lives. That's good to hear. I'm very glad."

"Yes, it's true. We were friends when we were younger," Mom stammered into a sentence.

Scrubbing the dishes clean, she sighed.

"I wasn't pretending, honey. He isn't the same person he was long ago."

Once she turned the faucet off, it left the kitchen to silence.

Suddenly, a smile grew on her face, and Mom replied, "Sweetie, that was back then. I worry about him sometimes too but I know he's doing great."

"Monica, how could you?"

We broke off the cold glances and turned our attention towards the office doors.

It was Mom.

I didn't know why I felt like I was about to explode that very moment. Was it because of all the frustration and exhaustion building up inside of me? Or was it because I found out the truth this way even though the answers were already there?

Curtis and Monica Valentino, and my mom were all connected in the past.

And somehow, someway, Bryce and I got stuck together.

Chapter 30

"**G**et out."

Those two words were the first things Bryce's mother hissed at my mom the moment she stepped foot into her office.

Not believing this was all happening, my eyes couldn't help but widen seeing Mom act like this. I always saw Mom as the gentle, motherly type of person. Right now, Mom had such a harsh tint in her hazel eyes. The entire look in her face was so grave.

The question that came to mind was how exactly did these two know each other?

My heart raced uncontrollably, not wanting to see my mom get in this conversation. Mom didn't budge from Monica Valentino's warning and continued to move closer towards her. Immediately, I held onto my mom's arm to keep her right by my distance. I gave her a pleading look, insisting not to do anything.

In return, Mom expressed an apology through her eyes. However, Mom's hazel eyes soon darted right back at Bryce's mother.

She asked once more, "How could you, Monica? Even up until now?"

Keeping that cold atmosphere, Bryce's mother folded her arms. Her eyes were narrowing sharply at Mom in response.

"Doesn't this bring back memories, Elianna?"

Mom's eyes flickered slightly until she ignored the remark and questioned with persistence, "I don't consider those memories, Monica. I don't understand why you have to act like this. Why?"

Monica Valentino cringed as she revealed her inner emotions.

"You never stop, do you? Just because I was the one who ended up with Curtis, you always managed to show up in my life again. Why don't you just leave me alone? You and your daughter need to leave my family alone!"

"Don't you care about Bryce's behalf? He cares about my daughter. My daughter cares about your son! Why can't you see that?" Mom retorted back, trying to etch it in her brain.

Bryce's mother shook her head vigorously and screamed out, "I know what's best for my son! Leave my office right now! Don't ever show your faces again!"

Feeling completely hopeless as the two were brawling with one another, I had to stop this from getting any worse. Before I could motion Mom out of the office, I completely froze, seeing the pair who rushed through the office doors.

It was Bryce's father, Curtis.

And, Bryce himself.

The two had the most perplexed expressions as their blue eyes widened in shock, absorbing the whole commotion.

Bryce.

A rush of guilt ran past me, knowing that I broke our promise. I was supposed to be the first person Bryce saw when he got back from the airport. Bryce's icy blue eyes were stuck on mine momentarily before pulling his attention to his mother — they were expressing sorrow and guilt. How I wished I could stop time this very moment so I could hug him after so long.

Having his presence here relaxed me in some ways. Even if right now, there were so many complications.

Curtis Valentino seemed to have done a double take, catching sight of Mom beside me.

His lips slightly pursed as he whispered out, "Elianna?"

Bryce questioned, his eyebrows scrunching in confusion, "What's... going on?"

When Bryce's father couldn't answer, Bryce shifted his eyes earnestly, searching for an answer in mine. I gradually glanced away, not knowing a right way of explaining it.

This was the last thing Bryce needed.

A horrible welcome back committee.

Mom's eyes soon clouded up as she was exchanging looks with Curtis. It was the kind of expression that was hard to comprehend. Yet, it looked like their past memories flashed right before them as they reunited with one another. Everything was just so awkward at the moment. It felt like all of us were biting on our tongues to prevent an answer from escaping.

Grabbing Mom's hand, I slightly murmured, not looking at the Valentino's, "We're leaving."

"Good."

Monica Valentino's cold voice slithered through my ears.

"Monica, what did you do?" I heard Curtis question his wife before we completely exited out her office.

The atmosphere completely transitioned the moment we stepped out. When Mom and I made it out to the parking lot, I quickly composed myself when I found Mason in the driver's seat of Dad's car, windows down. He was waiting for Mom — or the both of us — and his dark brown eyes lit up once he spotted us.

When we walked over there, I asked through a whisper, "Does Mason know?"

In return, Mom shook her head, and I wanted to keep it that way.

"Your faces aren't too happy. Should I be worried?"

Mason's facial expression dropped as he poked his head further out the car window. Shaking in disagreement, I forced a smile.

"We just need a hold on a little bit longer."

Mason's nose wrinkled, observing my face closely.

"Maisie, I'm not stupid. What happened?"

"You don't have to worry, Mason."

"Well, seems to me that something's very wrong."

"Don't worry about it, Mason."

"Don't lie to me. I hate when you do that!"

Mason gave me a slight pout, his eyes yearning for the truth.

"You two, stop that please," Mom interrupted lightly.

Mason glared at me momentarily and I sighed in return, looking the opposite direction.

Mom continued, "Honey, I'm going home with Maisie. We'll talk about it together, okay?"

In reply, Mason slightly grunted before nodding his head in agreement. Once he turned on the car engine, Mason pulled away from the parking lot and went off first. When it was the two of us again, Mom fixed her attention towards me. She already caught the look in my eyes. Mom knew they were also begging for the truth.

As she pulled me into a hug, Mom apologized continuously through our embrace.

Until I heard someone say, "Maisie..."

It was my delivery boy.

Breaking off our embrace, Mom soon gave an apologetic look at Bryce and me before heading inside the passenger's seat of my car to give us our privacy. Taking a deep breath, I couldn't find any words to say to him. It felt like the world had stopped.

Everything was already too overwhelming and having Bryce here felt so unreal. Right now, it seemed like Bryce was only a figment of my imagination. Bryce reached out to hold my hand, making me shiver a bit despite the warmth he was giving off.

"Maisie, don't go. We can fix this. I can work things out."

My stomach knotted up, taking in Bryce's voice. It has been three weeks — three long weeks — and he was finally back home. Instead of a sweet reunion I dreamed about, the untold truth just had to be revealed.

How wonderful.

Gazing up at him, I gulped down hard before muttering out, "Bryce, can't you see that everyone is getting hurt?"

His jaw clenched momentarily before answering, "Nothing will happen anymore. Let me talk to my mom about this. I'll tell her to fix what she did."

Shaking my head, I pressed, "She's never going to stop Bryce! I don't know what happened between my mom and her, but I can't keep seeing my family suffer because of it."

"I don't know either! Do you think that's going to stop me from liking you?" Bryce countered back.

Stunned by his words, I felt my eyes start to tremble again. This time, I was too weak to resist the tears from falling.

Sighing, I tried to explain, "I've been trying to look past your mom so many times, Bryce, but I'm so tired of trying. The last thing I ever want is for my family to get hurt."

"If you give me a chance, let me fix it. I know how much that market means to you and your family. But, what about me? Do I mean anything to you, Daisie?"

Bryce's blue eyes were growing with a trace of frustration.

Of course Bryce did.

Nodding my head, an unwanted tear dropped from my shaking eyes.

"You do, Bryce. I don't want you to trouble yourself all the time though."

Bryce's eyes widened, and he ranted out, "You think I care about that? As long as we're together, that's all I need. You never let me or anyone help you which is driving me crazy!"

"Because I don't need any help! You don't have to worry about me from now on, Bryce. I'm sorry," I cried out through a quivering lip, pulling away from his grasp.

Truth was, not only did I want to see my family hurt, but I didn't want to see Bryce getting hurt having to deal with his mother and me if we stayed like this.

Before Bryce could stop me, I was already starting my car up. The sound of the engine roared as Bryce took a few steps back as his face fell in distraught. It was a haunting sight to take in which caused my heart to burn with guilt.

Mom flashed a disappointed expression upon me, but I tried ignoring it as I drove away from Bryce Valentino and Legends Hotel.

"Honey, you didn't have to do that."

Mom's worried tone rang on the right side of my ear as I turned the car engine off. We just arrived at the garage lane of our house.

Instead of replying back, I asked in a lifeless tone, "Mom, how do you know Monica and Curtis Valentino?"

Mom was now holding onto my hand tightly. When I glanced at her direction, Mom's hazel eyes were expressing apology.

"I told you to come back so I could tell you. I didn't want you to find out that way."

It was a little too late for that, wasn't it?

Noticing my blank expression, Mom tried to ease up the atmosphere by giving me a soft smile. It didn't work at all.

As I waited for an explanation, her voice was stern as she recalled back to that memory, "Monica and I were friends during high school. Best friends to be exact. I always admired a girl like Monica. She was always determined and self driven. We were very close during our sophomore until senior year. During our junior year, I met Curtis. It was only when senior year began, our feelings for one another grew, and we eventually started dating. Monica didn't like it though. She never supported our relationship, and I didn't want to think it was because she was jealous. During that winter break I asked her... for the complete truth."

Letting out a sigh, Mom continued, "Monica told me it's because I didn't deserve someone like Curtis. She said that I would only bring Curtis down. At the same time, Curtis was helping his parents with the company. I knew Monica was classifying me as average because of my family background compared to Curtis and his elite family."

"It broke my heart, hearing that from a person who I thought was my best friend. I thought that Monica appreciated our friendship because we got along so well. I was surprised at first how she would hang around a person like me when she was also from a great family, but her hidden colors were shown right at the moment."

"Because of that, I was scared and believed what she said. I walked away from our relationship. I didn't bother with Curtis after that. We would communicate every now and then, but until that moment Monica and him started dating. It was like our existence together vanished."

"During this period, your father was always there by my side. He told me countless times to be careful because he didn't want to see me hurt. I thought that your father saw me nothing more than just his best friend, but I realized he looked at me differently. It was more than that. With him, I knew that things will always be right. No matter what happens, your father and I would be able to make it through together."

When Mom fixed her attention back at me, she claimed in a warm voice, "You're probably going to ask if I regret leaving Curtis. I don't. I hope you remember me telling you that your father is the love of my life — that we were chasing after the wrong people at the time. In the end, I was always going to stay happy with your father."

Never did I expect this all to happen. The entire time I was listening with wide eyes. My knotted stomach seemed to have untied itself, and I couldn't help but feel sorry for my mom. She already suffered.

"Mom, why didn't you tell me this? Doesn't it hurt you to see Bryce and me together?"

Stroking the top of my hair, Mom smiled heartily in comfort.

"I'm sorry, honey. Your father and I decided not to because for the first time, we finally saw you happy with someone besides us. Your father, you know how he is, he's always the kind of person who wouldn't judge and puts in the effort to know the person first. I wanted to do that too. I was worried at first, but we both soon saw goodness in Bryce. You're asking me if I get hurt seeing you two together? Maisie, of course not. What happened in the past, happened in the past. You deserve to be with whoever it may be. That is all I wish for."

Instantly, I pulled my mom into a hug. It was an uncomfortable kind of hug since we were both sitting in the car, but this hug was what I needed after everything that happened today. Mom tightened the embrace, running her hand through my hair to comfort me.

"I don't want my past to affect your future, dear. It shouldn't. Maisie, I want you to do what makes you happy in the end," I heard Mom whisper by my ear.

Smiling faintly at her words, Mom placed her hand on my shoulder and replied back with an encouraging smile. Behind my mind, there was a voice telling me to let Bryce go because of all the pain and suffering that had been happening and would probably keep going.

Should I listen to that voice?

Once the two of us got out of the car, Mom headed towards the front door first. Locking my car with the keys, I let out an exhausted sigh before following her. What made my heels pull to a stop was when I reached the walkway to our front door and found Logan Valentino there.

Logan was speaking to Mom momentarily before the two turned around, acknowledging my presence. To be honest, I was in no mood to talk with any of the Valentino's right now.

The Valentino cleared his throat, fixing his business suit.

"Can we talk, Maisie?"

Where had I heard this before?

Even though I was slightly afraid for whatever I was about to hear, I nodded anyway. Mom gazed back at me shortly until she headed into our house, shutting the door behind her.

When we reached each other at a reasonable distance, Logan stated, "I told you to stay away from Bryce, Maisie."

I shrugged, my reply sounding more bitter than sarcastic.

"I'm not even going to bother asking why since I'm tired of getting no direct answer."

But at the moment, Logan's midnight blue eyes revealed it all.

He knew.

Logan knew this entire time and kept the truth concealed from me too.

Letting out a gasp, I almost screeched from the discovery, "You knew, didn't you?"

As I narrowed my eyes at Logan, his facial expression was starting to betray him. Disbelief was running all over me. First, Bryce's mother, and now Logan?

Shaking my head, I had to clarify, "Logan, this whole time you've been telling me to stay away from Bryce, but you pretty much left out the reason why! You lied to me! How could you do this to me?"

As Logan tried reaching out to me, I resisted by taking a few steps back, indicating that I did not want any kind of comfort or sympathy at all.

I watched as his Adam's apple bobbed up and down before answering back, "Maisie, I should have told you I knew about your mom and Aunt Monica."

"Why didn't you then?"

I felt betrayed because I never expected Logan to hide this from me. There was no answer to what seemed like forever. Scoffing lightly, I was done with everything.

Lifting my right hand up, I shook my head.

"You know what? Forget it. Just leave, Logan."

Even if Logan did try speaking up, I tuned him out. Not bothering to look back, I closed my house door.

However, the moment I shut the door, I bit my lower lip hard to stop myself from crying once again.

Chapter 31

5 6 missed calls.

That was how many phone calls I purposely didn't pick up since yesterday. They ranged from Bryce to Logan to David to Vanessa. Even though I did feel guilty for ignoring all the calls, I was too busy and focused on trying to contact a lawyer to help my family and our case the very next day.

After going through countless lawyers, none of them would follow up. They all said the same excuse that they couldn't do anything the moment I mentioned the name Valentino.

Only then did I realize how powerful of a name the Valentino's held.

It was frustrating, but the last thing I wanted to resort to was to ask Bryce for help. I didn't want Bryce to go against his own mother. Mason didn't understand that though.

Despite me telling Mason my explanation, he believed that asking Bryce would be the only way to get our market back. There was just too many things going on already.

I was Maisie Lockhart. I would be able to work it all out.

Well, that was what I had been trying to tell myself.

Sighing, I put aside the market business for a moment and collected my mind back to my family and the Valentino's. This entire day got me nowhere, and it was almost sundown.

Right now, I was standing on top of a hill somewhat close to my neighborhood, taking in the view of the city. I used to go here all the time with Mason after he woke up from his coma. Even though we'd be silent most of the time here, it was comforting. This was a spot where we could just think.

Even if getting the market back was the top priority in my head, my attention-seeking heart was secretly yearning for Bryce.

I tried to forget about it, but seeing his pained face when I left was haunting me. How could I do that to him? His mother has nothing to do with our relationship.

However, his mother's words were coming back to slap me in the face as a reminder.

"Do you not see that when you and my son are together, no one will be happy. Do you want your family to suffer because you are being selfish? Do you want Bryce to suffer because you are being selfish? And do you want my family to suffer because you are being selfish?"

And then Logan.

Anger was starting to fuel me momentarily until I started to wonder if it was because I chose Bryce. Did Logan keep it from me, knowing that I would get hurt in the end? I never thought of Logan to be that person though. Shaking my head, I was starting to regret walking away from my conversation with him. I should have listened to what Logan was about to say, but I was too upset to even think straight.

These mixed emotions were messing me up badly.

My thinking charade was interrupted when I heard someone clear their throat behind me. Feeling a shot of shock run up my spine, I slowly glanced over my shoulder.

If I had to choose between a creeper or Logan Valentino right now, I would choose the creeper.

Okay, maybe not.

"How did you find me here?" I questioned from the silence, trying to keep a blank expression.

Logan moved closer as he replied in a low murmur, "Mason."

Mason, you're killing me here.

When he approached me, Logan gazed at the scenery momentarily before throwing in a compliment, "This is a pretty nice spot you have here."

"It was nice," I hinted, biting my tongue after I said that.

Knowing that I made the atmosphere awkward, Logan sighed before stating, "Maisie, please let me explain myself. I don't want you to stay mad at me."

Expressing no emotion through a shrug, I pursed my lips, "Honestly Logan, I don't know what to feel towards you right now. Since you're here, say what you need to say."

Taking a deep breath, Logan's midnight blue eyes soon stared into mine.

"I found out about your family's past with mine the day of the presentation. When I was standing outside the hallway, I overheard Aunt Monica speaking with her secretary from the other side. They didn't know I was there, and I heard Aunt Monica saying that she couldn't take it anymore — that she couldn't keep seeing Bryce with you. I didn't know why until she told her secretary everything — about your mother and her."

It all made sense.

That was why Logan faced the other direction when I came out of the presentation doors. That was why he had such a bothered expression on his face.

"Why didn't you tell me then, Logan?" I questioned with a slight frown.

Logan ran his fingers through his dark hair and muttered, "Because I didn't know if her story was true or not. This is going to sound so stupid, but please hear me all the way."

I nodded.

Logan's gentle voice confessed as it was also covered with hurt, "I like you, Maisie. When we first met during that date, I wanted to get to know you more, but Bryce had your attention first. Didn't he? Once I heard about your mother and Aunt Monica, I thought that I would have an advantage in getting your heart. I didn't want to do something like that, so I kept it to myself and tried to win your heart the right way. Obviously, it didn't work, but Maisie, I want you to know how sorry I am."

Before I could even say anything, Logan continued, "This whole time, I thought I would be the better person for you because of that. I was wrong. I kept telling you that Bryce would hurt you, but in the end, I was the one who hurt you."

As much as I wanted to stay mad at Logan, my heart was starting to fill itself up with guilt. It was wrong of me to be mad at him. Logan shouldn't be the one to tell me the truth about our families' past. The only thing he had to be honest about was his feelings which he was yet something I couldn't reciprocate back.

I stammered into a sentence, "I'm also sorry, Logan... I shouldn't have snapped at you. It wasn't your place to tell me. And, I'm sorry not being able to return the feelings you had for me back."

Logan shook his head.

"I was being selfish, Maisie. I wasn't thinking about you or Bryce, but only myself. I regret what I did. When I found out what Aunt Monica had done, it made me realize even more how much of a selfish person I was. Maisie, you need to let Bryce help you. We're going to get your market back."

"I can't. Bryce shouldn't have to choose between me or his mother," I remarked, trying to hide my sadness.

After a moment of silence, Logan suddenly asked, "When two people are put through many obstacles and trouble, yet they manage to make it through everything no matter what — you know what they call that?"

"What?" I replied, dumbfounded.

"Fate."

Logan's blue eyes locked onto mine. A grin grew on his face as he left me speechless. He nodded his head once more.

"I'm sure that Bryce already made a choice. Don't let Bryce go, Maisie. You and I both know that you don't want to do that. I was just another obstacle, and I don't want you to worry about me. Right now, I'm just the voice to encourage you to keep fighting. Go to him, and work things out, okay?"

His words got to me.

Logan's little, silly speech about "fate" was all that was in my head — like the moment that invisible light bulb turned on above your head. Logan, no matter how many times he had left me frustrated and confused, was undeniably right. That was what made me finally see how ridiculous it was for me to leave Bryce.

"I'm never this damn emotional, but thank you Logan," I announced, attempting to lower my head to prevent him from seeing my tears.

I eventually heard Logan say through a comforting tone, "It may not be easy, Maisie, but you have us supporting you both. I-I'm really sorry again."

Sighing from exhaustion, I ran my fingers through my hair and nodded.

"Logan, I know you're sorry. And I'm sorry —"

Logan abruptly cut me off, his lips pulling into a smile, "How about you go to Bryce right now as a way to show you're sorry?"

A soft laugh escaped from Logan, causing me to break into a smile after a long day.

Going back to Legends Hotel wasn't exactly what I pictured doing after the sudden reveal in Monica Valentino's office. Even so, I needed to talk to Bryce. It was wrong of me to leave him like that. I shouldn't have walked away and yet, I did.

Shaking my head, I scolded, "You really were acting stupid, Maisie."

Preparing myself, I got out of my car and headed towards the back side entrance of the hotel. It was a shortcut to the Valentino's offices, and my gut was telling me that Bryce would be there.

Don't laugh, I guessed it was a natural instinct.

Logan was walking along my side, and he gave me an encouraging grin. I felt relaxed until my stomach flip-flopped the moment we gazed off our glances and found Monica Valentino walking out of the exit doors.

Wasn't this just wonderful timing?

Not only did my body stiffen from surprise, but so did Logan's. The two of us stopped on our shoes, and Bryce's mother only directed her cold glare towards me. She momentarily looked away from me and turned her attention to her nephew.

"Logan, what are you doing with her? You know better than that," she hissed as she angled her face up.

Why did she always degrade me like that?

As a response, Logan shook his head and corrected, "Aunt Monica, Maisie is a good friend of mine."

Monica Valentino scoffed out, "That's what they want you to think."

Her brown eyes then shifted back to me, and she frowned.

"And, what gives you the right to come back here? I thought I told you and your family to never come back."

Keeping a strong front, I answered firmly while taking a few steps closer to her, "Mrs. Valentino, I'm here to see Bryce. He's important to me and I care about him a lot."

Before she could say anything, I went on, "I may not be rich, I may not have a high education of some sort, I may not be able to ever achieve your expectations, but you need to know how much your son means to me. We both make each other happy. I can assure you that I'm not what you assume me to be. If you give me a chance, you'll see what kind of person I really am."

Could I just say how good that felt to release out?

However, the reaction I got from Bryce's mother was not what I expected.

Her face fell into disbelief before she literally started to laugh at my face. When I looked over my shoulder towards Logan, his jaw was clenching tightly from her response, but his eyes were telling me that I did the right thing.

"Do you honestly think you're that worth it?" she jeered.

Feeling a sudden pull of negativity on me, I faced Bryce's mother once again, and she was still chuckling to herself as she shook her head side to side in amusement.

Clearing my throat, I responded, "I'm not putting myself on a pedestal, Mrs. Valentino. I just want to make it clear that people like me are more than what you think."

Folding her arms, she ignored my words and stated through a scornful tone, "Well, you're not, so don't bother. If you want me to stay polite right now, I suggest you leave before I call the police."

Oh, the irony in her words.

When I didn't budge, Bryce's mother decided to hover towards me. The two of us were only a foot or so apart from each other. It was unpleasant, yet for the first time, she didn't scare me. I stayed my ground and prepared myself for whatever she was about to say. Her dark brown eyes disappeared slightly as they turned into thin slits.

Monica Valentino warned, "If you know what's better for you, Maisie Lockhart, you'll leave just like Elianna, and this time never come back."

"Mother, step away from Maisie," a familiar voice entered our grave conversation.

My heart stopped hearing that voice, knowing who it belonged to.

It was Bryce.

The look in Monica's face was a shocking sight. Her face was covered by doubt, finding out that her own son said that.

A deep scowl grew on her face, and she turned around to confront Bryce. My eyes then glanced towards Bryce, and we locked eye contact. Despite him holding a solemn expression, those glacial blue eyes were soft as we exchanged glances. Seeing him tugged my heartstrings like always.

His mother shouted, "Bryce! Are you out of your mind?"

Bryce shrugged, unaffected by his mother's ice like attitude.

"I guess you can say that, but my heart knows what it wants, Mother. It's Maisie Lockhart."

Stunned, my eyes widened once I heard Bryce's confession. A small smile crept on my lips. I watched as Monica Valentino's shoulders lifted from frustration. She turned around abruptly back to me, causing me to flinch back a little from surprise.

Her eyes grew larger and she claimed hysterically, "Look what you did! You are ruining my family!"

Bryce tried to step closer to his mother. His voice was calm as he tried to relax his delirious mother.

"Mother, stop it. The only person ruining our family is you."

I couldn't believe what I was hearing.

Just when my ears couldn't take in reality, the sounds of a nearby car tire came screeching our way.

Where was that coming from?

Glancing over to my right, I dropped everything that was happening for a moment when my eyes quickly caught sight of an uncontrollable car. A shiny, black four-seater was swerving and it was coming towards us — towards me. What felt like a car moving in slow motion was really happening all too quickly.

How to react?

Looking back at Bryce's mother, she was marching towards me, completely disregarding what was happening around her.

What was she doing?

Feeling my feet rush towards her, I heard low screams and shouts that I couldn't completely understand, but I saw my arms reaching out to get his mother out of the way. The last thing I saw was a distraught Bryce, and the surprised facial expression of the driver as it appeared like he was trying to step on the brakes.

Suddenly, it all felt too soon.

A strong force was pushed against me. It wasn't to a point where I felt myself flying, but it was a harsh impact. Feeling my head hit against the cement ground, pain was the only thing taking over.

Within a second, I was welcomed by darkness.

I guess this would be a perfect time to say that this so-called "fate" had funny ways of working out.

Chapter 32

This feeling.

It was hard to explain actually.

The last thing I saw in my mind were a bunch of daisies. They were circling around me, just swaying from side to side, with actual smiling faces in the center. Honestly, it was creeping me out a bit. That was until one daisy started speaking — yes, with moving lips and everything — telling me that it was time to wake up.

I wouldn't have it any other way.

My eyes fluttered open slightly, being greeted by a bright light. The light wasn't coming from the ceiling. The source was coming from the right side of me. It was sunshine, seeping through the window.

I was alive.

Blinking several times, I stared at the ceiling for a moment until someone hovered over me. Wincing slightly from surprise, I had to make sure that I wasn't seeing things.

Carly?

Except Carly looked older and much taller. I was sure that the little girl hasn't grown that tall. It has only been a month or so. Hasn't it?

Squinting my eyes, the Carly I was looking at gasped happily, knowing that I was awake. She grinned ear to ear, almost waiting for me to say something.

"Carly, is that you?" I answered weakly, my focus was gradually getting better.

Older Carly gave me a chirpy reply, "You're finally awake! You've been sleeping forever!"

Gulping down, I asked through a shiver, "How long?"

"For ten years! Can't you see? I'm a lot older now," Carly announced, nodding her head as her locks of brown hair followed her movements.

Wait a second.

Ten years!

Losing my cool, I tried to get up from my sleeping position.

I shouted from panic, "Oh my god, it's been ten years? Have I aged? I'm thirty years old right now!"

Frantically looking around the perimeter, I was on a hospital bed in a private room. The older Carly was the only one here. My eyes shook from bewilderment when I found a cast on my left leg.

The accident.

Everything replayed right back to that moment. Bryce, his mother, Logan, the car — everything. My mind was starting to get all dizzy. This couldn't be happening. Another dream, that must be it. As I took deep breaths, I gazed back at Carly who was standing there joyfully with her hands behind her back.

I pointed at her, still shaking.

"This is a dream, right?"

Carly shook her head.

Here I was, so close to jumping out of the bed and run off to see what has become of the world until a little voice popped out.

"Okay, I think we should stop now before Lockhart here loses her mind, Candace."

At that instance, a little girl rose from the left side of my bed, making me scream. The little girl was Carly — still a nine year old, still adorable as ever. Clamping my mouth shut, my widened eyes then looked back Older Carly.

It was Candace Reynolds this whole time?

Shaking my head once more, I started to laugh a little hysterically.

"Wow, I completely lost it."

The real Carly reassured me, "We shouldn't have tricked you, Maisie. But you're still sane. I hope. I'm still Carly and that's Candace. She dyed her hair back to brown when we got back home. We heard about what happened to you, and I had to fly back to see if you're okay! You've been sleeping for three days. Welcome back!"

Okay, now that made more sense.

Still woozy from this surprised awakening, I tried to relax my racing heart that was beating out of control for no reason.

The now brown-haired Candace then giggled out, "Don't worry, you're still looking good. I'm going to tell everyone you're finally awake!"

The elder sister rushed out of the door, slamming it shut leaving Carly and me alone.

There was a part of me that wanted to start crying from being tricked by the Reynolds' sisters like that. I really believed that I had been sleeping for ten years. I didn't want to be thirty just yet! When I sat there as I recollected everything that happened, Carly soon jumped up to pull me into a hug. Breaking into a smile, I returned the embrace.

Carly rejoiced, "I was so worried about you! How are you feeling? Do you remember anything?"

The good thing was, I actually did remember.

When I nodded my head, I sighed.

"I can't believe you guys tricked me like that. And I feel okay, just a little shaken up."

Carly gave me a satisfying smile before hugging me tightly once more. I missed this little girl more than ever.

Questions started to pop out in the back of my mind. Where was my family? What happened after the accident? Was anyone else hurt? What happened to the Valentino's? And, where in the world was Bryce?

My questions were soon answered when the door swung back open.

In came all these familiar faces — my parents, Mason, Vanessa, David, Logan, Candace, the doctor, and lastly, Bryce.

All of them expressed happy — okay, happy was an understatement — complete brightened up faces once they saw me completely conscious. I was smiling as well, but at the same time, was holding a confused expression still. The first ones to approach my side was my parents.

My parents both had tears welling up in their eyes. Mom and Pops hugged me gently, and I felt Mom stroking my hair as she whispered happy blessings. I heard Pops sniffling which caused me to bite my lower lip. I never wanted to see my parents worry or cry for me like this.

After our hug, Mom and Pops both told me how much they missed me and how happy they were to see me awake. I couldn't have asked for better parents. Holding onto their hands momentarily, I was soon greeted by Mason, Vanessa and David.

Mason cried out, "Maisie! I swear, you were superman in your past life or something! I miss you!"

Letting out a soft chuckle from his actions, I couldn't even reply back because Mason decided to hug the life out of me. Suddenly, I felt him retrieving back from Vanessa's tug.

Vanessa warned playfully, "Mason, let your sister breath! She just woke up."

Mason pouted, but no one really fell for his little puppy face. I held in a giggle as he muttered some nonsense under his breath. Vanessa and David both huddled around me, smiling brightly at the sight of me.

David claimed through his grinning, "You gave us quite a scare, Maisie."

Vanessa's green eyes were widening as she exclaimed out all her worry, "Not even! I seriously had a heart attack, Maisie! Don't scare me like that, okay?"

As I nodded my head, Vanessa wiped the tears from her eyes and hugged me lightly.

She whimpered, "I don't know what I'll do if I don't have Maisie Lockhart in my life."

Did I ever mention how much I love my best friend?

As the three stepped back, Logan soon approached my side.

His dark midnight blue eyes glowed from the sunlight as he beamed, "Welcome back, Maisie. You feeling okay?"

Giving him a smile back, I nodded my head once more. He reached out his hand, causing me to flinch back slightly until I realized that he was touching something wrapped around my head.

Why didn't I notice this before?

Logan stated, "Your head doing fine?"

Reaching up, a bandage had been wrapped a few times around my head, leaving me a little confused. That was until I remembered hitting my head against the ground before passing out. I thought a broken leg was already bad. As I replied with a reassuring smile, Logan gave me a slight nod before making a pathway for someone.

That someone, my friends, was my delivery boy.

My heart was beating quicker, seeing the sight of Bryce.

He was covered up by everyone that I was worried he was gone. Bryce took several steps closer to me, and for a moment, it felt like it was only the two of us. Bryce reached for my hand as a sweet smile grew on his face. Bryce's soothing voice calmed me down as his captivating sky blue eyes laid upon me.

"I'm so happy to see you awake. I've miss you so much."

I cried.

Should I be ashamed?

Right now, I didn't care.

Happy tears fell from my eyes, and I nodded my head in agreement.

"I've missed you too, Bryce. I've missed all of you — I'm so happy that you're all here with me."

"I'm sorry to barge in, but may I have a moment with Ms. Lockhart?" The doctor claimed through the happy atmosphere.

He gave Bryce and I an apologetic smile before taking a step closer.

Bryce and I locked gazes once more before he eventually let go of my hand to give complete way for my doctor. However, I didn't want him to let go. Come to think of it, I never properly gave Bryce a welcome back since he returned from his business trip.

The doctor gave me a wide grin.

"Hello Ms. Lockhart, I'm Doctor York. It's definitely good to see that you're awake. How are you feeling right now?"

"Is it okay to be feeling no pain at all? I feel great actually," I replied honestly.

Dr. York laughed in amusement and pointed out, "It's the medication that's preventing you to feel complete pain or maybe seeing a special someone?"

A few chuckles scattered throughout the room causing me to flush out red from the doctor's tease.

Dr. York then questioned, "Do you remember what happened to you, Ms. Lockhart?"

Pondering briefly, the same flashbacks appeared again. It caused me to cringe slightly as I remembered Bryce's mother and the car that hit me.

Wait, was Bryce's mother okay. What about the driver?

Nodding my head, I answered, "I do. The accident — I pushed Mrs. Valentino away from the out of control car. Doctor, is Mrs. Valentino all right? How about the driver?"

Dr. York explained, "Good, looks like your memory is still in tact. Mrs. Valentino is perfectly fine because of you actually. She had a very light injury since her knees scraped against the concrete. The driver is okay as well. The airbag deployed in time, only giving him a mild injury as well. I'm sure you're wondering what happened to you, correct?"

I nodded.

"I hate to say, but you do have a broken leg, Ms. Lockhart. Your cast will have to stay on for at least 5-6 months depending on the progress of your fractured bone. For now, you'll be using a wheelchair or crutches, but don't worry. In due time, you'll be able to walk on two feet."

"You have several bruising on your arms, but that will also heal in due time as well. The bandage on your head was caused by your head hitting against the concrete. The injury on your forehead is not that severe. You did lose blood but not to a point where it was a massive amount," Dr. York stated while he was going through the check up, even showing me an x-ray of my leg.

After scribbling a few notes on his clip board, Dr. York nodded with a satisfying smile.

He encouraged, "Other than that, you seem to be responding well. Your vital signs are good, and your road to recovery is starting off well. You do need to stay in the hospital for a few more days so we know for sure that you'll be okay to release."

After thanking Dr. York for everything, he nodded, "I'll be making my rounds then. Ms. Lockhart, welcome back. I wish you the very best. If you need anything, feel free to contact the nurse. I will be coming back for another check up."

Everyone in the room gave their thanks to the doctor before he waved a small goodbye and exited out the door.

Soon, everyone gathered around my bedside.

Mason was the first to speak as he beamed, "Maisie, did you see all the flowers in your room? Look, you're famous!"

A little surprised, my eyes fully glanced around the room, and he was right. My room was showered with varieties of flowers that occupied pretty vases. I spotted several cards that said get well soon, but my eyes were immediately stuck on the vase of daisies.

My heartstrings were tugged, knowing who those were from.

Carly then remarked through a tiny frown, "What kind of question is that?"

Everyone, including my parents, all laughed at Carly's stale remark. Mason folded his arms as he grunted.

Once I caught up with everyone, Vanessa coughed out a hint, "I think it's time for some lunch, don't you think?"

Mason's brown eyes widened, in the middle of telling me how the market was doing, and whined, "What? I'm not hungry, I want to talk to Maisie!"

As a reply, little Carly kicked Mason's shin and pulled Mason down so she can whisper something in his ear. Mason's widened eyes grew even larger until he nodded. Candace, who I still couldn't believe tricked me into thinking she was the older version of Carly, giggled.

"Mason, you are too adorable!"

Mason stopped his whining and cleared his throat. His eyes shifted slightly towards me, and I remembered how Mason never really liked Candace because of everything she did to me. I gave him a slight shrug, and a tint of red soon revealed upon Mason's cheeks.

Before I knew it, everyone was walking out of the doors, waving goodbye.

I gasped, "Hold on, where are you all going?"

"You don't want me here?" A voice answered.

It was Bryce.

Settling my attention on him, I smiled bashfully as he chuckled to his entertainment. Bryce pulled up a chair towards my side and held onto my hand. For a moment, the two of us just stared at each other.

The kind of staring that didn't bother me at all.

He finally broke the silence, "I'm sorry for everything, Daisie. I'm sorry I couldn't save you from getting hurt."

"You shouldn't be sorry, Bryce. I shouldn't have walked away from everything. I was just so upset," I confessed.

Bryce shook his head and insisted, "You have every right to be upset though. My mother — I don't understand what she was thinking! You don't have to worry anymore, she won't bother you and your family anymore. I hate how this had to happen to you, Daisie. I swear, I will never forgive my mother for what she did to you and your family."

As he was talking, Bryce's icy blue eyes were growing colder by the second.

I replied to ease up his tension, "No, Bryce. I don't want you to do that to your mother. It's okay, trust me."

His eyes widened in disbelief.

"After everything? She never really was that much of a mother to begin with, but that doesn't matter right now. You don't know how much you worried me."

Lightening up the mood, I gave him a smirk.

"Oh, I worried you, huh?"

A small laugh escaped from his lips momentarily until we both laughed together.

Bryce stated more clearly, "I'm serious. Don't ever do something like that again, Daisie."

"Trust me, I don't want to."

I gave him a heartfelt smile. In the back of my mind, I wanted Bryce to be okay with his mother. Even though he was by my side right now, I didn't want him to leave his mother alone.

Bryce then questioned out of the blue, "You mind if I write on your cast?"

A little surprised, I raised an eyebrow as I inquired, "You don't think that's too elementary school?"

"Not when Bryce Valentino does it."

He winked through a confident statement.

And like always, only the delivery boy could pull that off.

Letting out a laugh, I nodded my head as I told him to go for it. Soon, Bryce pulled out a black sharpie from his pocket — did he keep that on him all the time? — and wrote whatever message he was writing.

Seeing a satisfied grin stretch upon his lips, Bryce took a step back once he finished to admire his work.

Bryce smirked.

"I think this one is my favorite."

I rolled my eyes playfully and stifled a laugh.

"Because it's the only one, right?"

Without a reply, Bryce soon assisted me up so I would be able to see what he wrote.

My eyes widened reading what his neat handwriting scribbled:

Delivery Boy loves Daisie

Gradually looking back at him, Bryce clarified with that charming grin on his face, "It's my favorite because it's the complete truth. I love you, Maisie."

Completely stunned for a moment, I had to make sure I heard right. It was like my emotions got the best of me once again. Why did I have to wake up being so emotional? Holding back the tears in my eyes, I smiled brightly as I nodded my head happily.

"I love you too, Bryce."

Bryce then motioned closer as he hugged me sweetly.

Hugging him back, I whispered, "I never got to say this, but welcome back."

"For the both of us," Bryce added.

Our eyes gradually met with one another, and I knew. Bryce's lips eventually met mine, causing my heartstrings to be tugged madly.

How my heart fluttered in every possible direction.

A real kiss from Bryce Valentino. The kiss felt too perfect, and I was literally melting as our lips touched. Happiness was all that was flashing my way at this very moment.

There was something wrong in Bryce's words that night during our stay on Valentino Island.

I was always happy since then because being with my delivery boy was all that I needed to completely feel this way.

Chapter 33

Ever since I woke up, I was slowly getting some movement back in my body. The nurses would kindly assist me, and I'd wheelchair out the hospital to get some fresh air outside. Dr. York told me that I'd be learning how to walk with crutches soon. However, the pain was starting to take effect. Sometimes, I'd get shots of pain coming from my leg or my head. After a little medication though, it would gradually disappear.

Four days after my awakening, I wasn't expecting this particular visitor.

Sitting in the wheelchair, I was taking in the pleasant scenery of the hospital's courtyard. Since it was still August, the summer heat was still present, but it wasn't as hot as it was during June or July.

I just didn't like being stuck in bed all the time.

"Hey Lockhart, someone is here to see you."

Looking over my shoulder, I already knew that was Harold.

Harold was one of the registered nurses I met here. Harold called me by my last name, but I didn't mind because hearing "Ms. Lockhart" was getting a little tiring. He was three year older than me, but despite him sounding blunt, Harold was really kind hearted towards the patients and was passionate for his job.

However, my stomach twisted when my eyes caught sight of the person standing next to him.

It was Bryce's mother.

She was in her fashionable business clothing. Her expression was stern, and I stared blankly at her for a second before giving them a small smile. Even though I still had mixed emotions towards Monica Valentino, it felt good that I was alive and breathing.

And, so was she.

Harold jokingly saluted me before walking off to another patient, leaving me with Mrs. Valentino. She walked towards me, and for the first time, her cold facial expression softened. Or, maybe my eyes were just playing jokes on me. Being polite, I motioned her to sit in the bench across from me so we'd reach each other at eye level. She listened and took the seat as I gulped down, wondering what she was going to say.

"I see you're doing better, Maisie," she started the conversation, her voice sounding light.

I gave her a quick nod.

"It's not as bad as yesterday, but I'm getting use to it. I heard you got hurt too. Ae you okay?"

Bryce's mother stared at me momentarily which caused all sorts of thoughts to run through my head. That was until she let out a sigh.

"How is it that after everything, you still care about my behalf? That you took the stand to save me and not yourself?"

I replied sincerely, "Because... I'm not the type of person who would want to see anyone hurt. Whatever was happening at the time shouldn't affect my decision to keep you safe."

Taking in my words, she nodded her head and stated, "Right when that happened, it felt so unreal that I was capable of hurting someone like that —"

"The accident wasn't your fault, Mrs. Valentino," I reminded.

Monica Valentino shook her head and insisted, "I'm still the one to blame. I let my history and jealously affect both you and Bryce's future. When I saw you there, completely helpless, I couldn't look at myself the same way. Bryce was always telling me how great of a person you are, Maisie. How you were able to start your family business by yourself, how you managed to help Legends Garden from being torn down... and to be honest, I guess I just couldn't accept it."

I questioned in a low murmur, "Couldn't accept what?"

Her brown eyes stared into mine as she revealed, "That Elianna was able to raise her children so successfully. That even though I have all of this, I was still not satisfied with myself because in my eyes, my old friend still beat me. It's immature of me, isn't it? What I'm trying to say is that I take full responsibility for everything, Maisie. I know I have no right to present myself to you like this after all that I've done."

Inhaling deeply, I soon answered, "Even so Mrs. Valentino, I'm glad you did come though."

It was true.

To have this conversation with Bryce's mother right now was reliving. I would rather have this talk then go on my life leaving things unsaid. When Bryce's mother heard me say that, her eyes widened in disbelief.

After a short pause, she let out a soft chuckle.

"You remind me so much of your mother, you know that? It's great you got that from her. Even though I really don't deserve your forgiveness, I came here to apologize to you, Maisie. I truly am sorry. I even bought so many people into this stupid dispute of mine. All my words and actions I've said and done to you and your family is something I regret."

Realizing the genuine tone through Monica Valentino's words, I could already feel the guilt she was going through. A part of me couldn't help but hold onto that anger I felt, but I knew I needed to let go.

Pops always told me that everyone deserved a clean slate if I saw that they deserved it. I believed that Monica Valentino deserved a fresh start.

We all did.

"Mrs. Valentino, I think we should start over," I eventually proposed.

Bryce's mother soon nodded her head in agreement, and a sudden smile grew on her lips. It shocked me greatly because she had such a beautiful smile. This was the first time Bryce's mother actually smiled at me. I probably looked like a fool as I gaped from surprise. Changing my expression within a second, I eventually grinned back.

Monica Valentino's eyes lit up as she stated, "Thank you, Maisie. For giving me a chance."

"It's going to take time, but I'm sure this is what's best for us," I said through a smile while the wind gently passed by, making several strands of our hair move along with it.

After a moment of silence, Bryce's mother began talking again, causing me to look back at her. There was a shy grin appearing upon her lips as her strong brown eyes gazed at me.

"This is probably late to say, but I really do admire a person like you, Maisie. I admit, I hold onto my pride too much. However, holding onto my pride isn't taking me anywhere. It ruined my relationship with my own son and my family. I guess I was too blind by proving myself because you just reminded me of your mother."

Tilting my head to the side, I pointed out, "Thank you, Mrs. Valentino. I feel like you're not giving yourself enough credit though."

Sighing, she continued on, "Of course when it comes to business, I'm on top of my game. When it comes to life and people, I tend to forget about my loved ones. That's something that you and your family naturally succeed in."

I then encouraged, "Bryce once told me how much he wants you to be there. Even though he may seem cold towards you, I know Bryce loves you too... just a little patching up is all that needs to be done."

Studying my face slightly, Monica Valentino soon nodded her head.

"Thank you, Maisie. I'll work on bringing my family closer. There's one more thing I have to say."

When I insisted her to go on, Bryce's mother smiled once again.

"I was wrong to tell you to stay away from Bryce. No matter how many times I tried to deny it in the past, I could see that you changed my son for the better. You've given him more love than I have ever given him. I won't be the one to say what either of you should do. In fact, I would love for Bryce to introduce you to me as his girlfriend."

Wait a second, I hope I heard right.

Blinking my eyes from doubt, I clarified again, "You're accepting us, you mean?"

Monica Valentino's dark brown eyes curved in amusement, seeing my surprised expression. She nodded.

"Yes, I would love that."

The two of us shared genuine laughter and smiles after that. I never thought a moment like this would come.

To a new beginning.

"Congratulations to the married couple!" Everyone screamed and shouted with joy.

Bryce held my hand tightly and grinned that warm, loving smile at me. Smiling back in return, everyone reunited with Zack and Kelsey in celebration for their November wedding.

It had been three months since the incident.

All of us was rejoicing with the newly weds at the reception. The wedding was held in one of the other hotels Phoenix Empire owned, Valkyrie Heights. Legends Hotel was still under construction — where the wedding was originally supposed to be at — but slowly and surely, the garden was reaching completion.

I sighed happily as I took in the joyous atmosphere that was happening all around me.

Spotting Vanessa and David, the two were dancing together in the dance floor with Zack and Kelsey next to them. Little Carly was chasing after a group of kids while Candace was busy talking to her friend. This friend of hers was a boy whom we believed the two are sharing a huge interest with one another. Logan was occupied by a large group of boys and girls. Bryce pointed out that they were cousins and close friends of theirs. The Valentino's parents were all gathered around the table, talking with the tear-filled parents of Zack and Kelsey.

Zack and Kelsey's wedding was absolutely gorgeous. I did cry a bit from happiness. Their reception was just as pretty filled with tons of people attending. The outdoor ceremony was decorated with paper lanterns and icicle lights that streamed down and created an inviting mood. Their music selection ranged from classic, soothing wedding sounds to danceable tunes. The theme colors, sea-foam green and crème, were scattered all over from the tables to decorations, making everything so classy.

And their food — let's just say — I couldn't get enough of their wide selection.

"Hey you two! Having fun?"

Kelsey was all smiles this whole day, but I couldn't blame her.

Standing beside her was Zack, who threw a proud grin at Bryce and me. The two were simply adorable together. I had to point out how stunning Kelsey was in her white wedding dress. It was all custom made. She appeared like a princess with its poof-like bottom and timeless design on the top.

Nodding my head, I beamed, "The wedding is so beautiful. Everything's been great. Congratulations you two!"

Zack grinned and reminded, "Feel free to get some more food. Oh Maisie, I really wish you were able to dance. You know, you two should show us those dancing abilities."

We all broke into laughter after.

Unfortunately, I still had my cast on which was covered by everyone's signatures. It was like a high school yearbook all over again. Even though wearing a cute dress for this special occasion was nice, it couldn't hide the fact there was this humongous thing around my leg.

After composing myself, I pointed out, "No, it's probably a good thing. The dance floor and I don't get along very well."

Kelsey chuckled, reaching out to pinch my cheeks.

"Aren't you the cutest thing? We're going to make our rounds now, thanks again for coming!"

Once the two left to accompany the rest of their guests, Bryce turned his attention to me. He looked so handsome in that suit of his with his black hair styled nicely. Bryce even decided to match his tie with the color of my teal dress.

He smirked.

"I don't know what they're talking about. Let's dance, Daisie. We can show them."

Placing a hand on my hip, I raised an eyebrow and giggled lightly.

"Show them what? Bryce, my dancing will look like wobbling if you ask me."

"I think a wobbling Daisie would be an interesting sight to see," Bryce teased gently, carefully pulling me closer to him.

Growing red in the cheeks, I tried to appear unaffected and countered, "Right. It's just another excuse for you to laugh at me, huh?"

Shaking his head, Bryce corrected, "Of course not. Think whatever you want, but I say you're beautiful. Cast or no cast."

"And I say, you are... so full of mush."

Hiding a smile, I couldn't help these heartstrings that were being tugged madly.

"If I'm so full of mush, why are you redder than a firetruck right now?" Bryce joked.

"Because…" I tried to think of a good excuse, "it's really hot right now."

Yeah, that didn't really work out.

Bryce tapped his chin as his glacial blue eyes roamed around the area before stating, "Okay, two things. It's November, Daisie, so it's pretty cold right now and two, are you only feeling that way because I'm here?"

Scoffing a laugh, I huffed, "Never mind, you're so full of yourself."

Bryce Valentino was never going to change, but I loved it.

He smirked again.

"I can tell you're lying. Anyway, dancing is overrated at weddings. Let's go to courtyard. I'm sure you'll like the koi pond we have there."

Nodding along, Bryce assisted me towards the hotel's breathtaking courtyard.

For a while, I thought Legends Hotel was the best hotel I had ever seen, but Valkyrie Heights was trailing right behind it. It had more a nature theme. Legends deemed a modern, up to date style. I had always loved nature, and Valkyrie Heights was the perfect place to feel like you were venturing out a beautiful landscape.

My eyes widened.

"This… is a koi pond? More like a koi lake!"

I was not over exaggerating.

After Bryce closed the iron gate behind us, a vast water pond occupied my eyes. It was the size of a two — maybe more — large swimming pools with a stone made gazebo smacked right in the middle. A fountain of Greek figures were to the right of it.

Moving closer, there were a bunch of koi fish swimming around the clear waters. Several stone steps were placed throughout the pond to reach the gazebo. As much as I wanted to hop the stone path way, that would be too much of a challenge with a cast on.

Bryce chuckled.

"My grandfather is known for creating things with a grand scale. Do you like it?"

Nodding my head, I beamed, "It's gorgeous. Your hotels are amazing."

"Valentino, remember?"

Bryce winked.

I stuck my tongue out and joked, "Does over confidence run in the family or only for you?"

He played a hurt face and countered teasingly, "This kind of persona is natural and attracts people like you."

Once again, Bryce got me again. Feeling defeat, I was now the one trying to fake an angry expression. It wasn't held long as soon as Bryce grabbed onto my hand tightly.

Bryce smiled warmly.

"I'm joking. Did I ever tell you that I seem to have an attraction to a Daisie's persona?"

I bit my lower lip before fighting into a smile.

"That's real cute, delivery boy."

We both shared another laugh together as we admired the scenery before us.

After a moment of silence, I hesitantly bought up, "Your... mom was trying to talk to your earlier."

"Yeah, and like the other times, I chose to ignore her," Bryce answered, his eyes falling to the floor.

I watched as Bryce's jaw clenched. When he did this, it signaled that he didn't want to talk about it. Through the past three months, Bryce had been giving his mother the cold shoulder. After the talk with Mrs. Valentino, she was trying to build their broken relationship, but Bryce wasn't really responding back so well.

Smiling lightly, I waited until he gazed right back to me.

Reaching up to fix a lost strand in Bryce's hair, I mentioned, "She's trying, Bryce. Give her a chance, yeah?"

Bryce didn't say anything for a while until I continued to press about the matter.

I added in an encouraging tone, "Bryce, she wants to be the mother you've been wanting. Don't you think it would be better now than never?"

He shrugged.

"If she expects everyone to forgive her for all that she's done, she's crazy."

"I'm not saying you have to forgive her immediately, Bryce. Of course, it's going to take time. Just try, how about that?"

Bryce momentarily glanced off to the koi pond to recollect his thoughts. I knew that behind those resisting blue eyes, he wanted to forgive his mother. He wanted to give her that chance. A smile grew on my face once I saw Bryce nod his head twice in agreement.

Bryce pulled his attention back at me and grinned.

"I'll try," Bryce then added, "thanks Daisie."

Confused, I questioned, "For what?"

All of a sudden, there was in shift in Bryce's tone. He wasn't that teasing, confident delivery boy at the moment.

His sky blue eyes stared sincerely in mine as he revealed, "You changed me, you know? You... opened my eyes."

"Well, I did take you to the optometry, remember?" I joked gently, even if this was a serious moment.

Memories of the first time Bryce and I encountered each another flashed before me. My heart was fluttering at his words. To hear that directly from Bryce made me feel so happy.

He let out a short laugh before restating again, "No, seriously. Ever since you entered my life, a lot of things happened and changed for the better. Thank you. I'm happy to have you here, I hope you know that."

"Bryce..."

"Are you happy to be with me?" Bryce asked, his warm hand intertwined with me.

To be honest, I think happy would be an understatement — it was more than that.

The kind of feeling I had when I was with Bryce had no match with a simple word like "happy". Everything became more complete when Bryce was by my side.

"I've always been, Bryce," I joyfully reminded as Bryce's face lit up at the same time.

Bryce's soothing voice ran through my ear.

"I love you, Maisie Lockhart."

The way my delivery boy's face would turn a slight tint of red would always amuse me and make me smile every time. My heartstrings would never stop being tugged whenever Bryce said those words to me.

"And I love you, Bryce Valentino."

Bryce soon leaned in to kiss me gently, and I returned the sweet kiss. Every time we kissed, it always felt so perfect. It was like we were stuck in the moment. This wasn't "attraction" anymore, it was reality. We worked hard to reach this point — to reach complete bliss — and every step of the way was completely worth it.

"Hey lovebirds! You don't want to miss the cake, do you?"

Bryce and I broke off from the kiss and searched for that voice.

It was David.

Vanessa was by his side with a huge smile occupying her face. Bryce looked at me, and I looked back at him. We exchanged glances momentarily, smiling at one another.

"Well, it isn't a wedding without Bryce and Maisie there, right?" Bryce joked as he cupped his hands.

We all laughed before Bryce and I walked back together to join the rest.

I remember Logan Valentino telling me these words: "When two people are put through many obstacles and trouble yet they manage to make it through everything no matter what... you know what they call that?"

Fate.

From what I experience, fate did happen — in many kinds of ways.

Fate bought Bryce Valentino and me together.

I would always be Bryce's Daisie, and Bryce would always be my delivery boy.

Epilogue

Two years had passed.

A lot happened since then.

After Zack and Kelsey's wedding, everything seemed to be going uphill and stayed consistent when it reached the top. Bryce did as he promised and decided to put in the effort to work out the relationship he had with his mother. Their current family bond was growing stronger and closer. Whenever I saw Bryce with his parents, they all appear more brighter and filled with genuine smiles.

My family stayed the same throughout these past two years. Lockhart's Pantry was ours forever, and business was treating us well. Mom and Pops were still happier than ever — mostly because I wasn't their single daughter anymore. They joked about that part, but I think they were serious. Also, I felt relaxed, seeing how Mom and Bryce's mother were gradually repairing their broken friendship.

And Mason? He definitely grew up. My brother got accepted into the university he wanted, and he was going the right direction for medical school. Mason even decided to minor in music, and his band was gaining even more recognition from the public. I couldn't be more proud of him. There was also news that Mason was seeing this girl — but he wouldn't tell me anything, yet.

Vanessa and David were still together. No questions on that. The two were simply passionately in love! I never lost my close friendship with my best friend, and I never planned to. We would even double date when we had the time.

Right now, Vanessa was working on her very own fashion line through her partnership with Phoenix Empire. Everyone loved the uniforms Vanessa personally designed for the Valentino's hotels. I didn't blame them — it made me wish I was still working there. Just to wear the cute outfits, of course.

With Logan, we became very good friends. Not like we weren't good friends to begin with, but there was now a strong trust we held with one another. Last time I talked to Logan, he told me about this girl he met. This girl, in particular, gave him the "attraction". And when that attraction occurred, there were only three words I could say to that: go for it.

Candace Reynolds was no longer a model. She did it occasionally, but what got everyone's attention was how this pretty girl had a natural talent at golf. She was preparing to play professional according to the email Carly last sent me. Remember the boy who went with Candace at Zack and Kelsey's wedding? Turned out the two officially started dating a week after the wedding — not like I didn't see that one coming.

Concerning Carly, we talked every now and then because I loved to hear how she was doing, whether it was email or over the phone. She became a little sister to me. During Carly's 10th birthday, she had us all fly to Europe to celebrate. The trip was simply magnificent. It felt like that was a birthday gift for me. Carly said that she would be coming back to see everyone with Candace before this summer came to an end. I was definitely looking forward to another reunion with everyone.

Wearing a mint-colored summer dress this fine afternoon, I was waiting outside Legends Garden near the wishing well.

The wishing well was even better than what I pictured now that it was bought to life. Bryce even added in a small garden of daisies next to it as a surprise for me. I tried my best to hold my emotions, but Bryce always managed to surprise me all the time. Since the wishing well was my design, I received various compliments from many guests and employees, saying how the wishing well added charm to the garden and the hotel.

The feeling of accomplishment and happiness would always occupy me when I was here. Just like what we hoped for, it attracted more people to come and appreciate the beautiful garden as a whole.

Holding two cups of hazelnut coffee, I briefly glanced down at my exposed feet and let out a small smile. Having a cast on for half a year was a weird adjustment, but it was even more bizarre having it taken off. When I got my cast off last February, it was like I was reborn again. I nearly danced around the doctor's office.

I would never forget the look on Bryce's face when he watched me acting ridiculous.

"Daisie!"

A smile grew on my face because I already knew who called.

Following Bryce's voice, I found him walking towards me in that stylish business suit of his. Looked like Bryce finished his meeting earlier than he said. Ever since last year, we both work together for

Phoenix Empire. Bryce's mother had been helping me get adjusted into the company, and everything was working well so far.

Bryce grinned brightly as those icy blue eyes practically glowed from the sunlight. When he reached a reasonable distance, he instantly planted a kiss on my cheek which caused all sorts of butterflies to flutter around my stomach.

"Sorry to keep you waiting," he tried to explain, but I immediately cut him off by shaking my head.

I insisted, "Don't worry about it. Here, you look tired."

Smiling, I handed him the coffee cup, and Bryce's face expressed joy. Taking the cup, he winked.

"Tired? When I'm with you, you always wash my tiredness away."

A laugh escaped from me, yet I felt myself turning red in the cheeks.

"Bryce, you know that doesn't work on me."

Bryce smirked as he teased, "Here we go again."

He knew that I was always in denial. These heartstrings of mine would never stop being tugged. Bryce glanced off momentarily at the wishing well beside us.

He pointed out, "Come to think of it, I've never seen you make a wish since this was finished. You're not going to?"

I grinned, shaking my head once again.

"Nope."

Slightly confused, Bryce raised his eyebrows and asked, "Daisie, it's your own idea. Why don't you try it?"

Fighting the smile growing on my face, I replied honestly, "Because I don't need to wish for anything else. My wish was granted the moment we were together."

As soon as I said that, I immediately noticed the heartfelt look appearing on Bryce's face. I, Maisie Lockhart, was also able to tug heartstrings as well.

Bryce smiled, trying to cover that tint of red growing on his cheeks.

"I'm the one who was supposed to say that."

"Too bad, I beat you," I joked before we soon laughed together.

Taking a sip of my coffee, I soon remembered that Bryce called me to meet him here for a reason. Looking back at him, I was about to ask why until he stopped me. Bryce's words seemed cryptic right now.

"I think there's one more wish that needs to be granted. For you... and for me."

Growing curious, I placed the cup away from my lips and tilted my head.

"One more?"

All sorts of thoughts and questions were swirling around my head.

Bryce grinned.

"Close your eyes."

Even though I couldn't read Bryce's current facial expression, I followed his words anyway. My heart started to race as I wondered what Bryce was planning to do.

All of a sudden, I heard Bryce clear his throat.

"Excuse me Ms. Maisie Lockhart, I have a delivery for you."

Thinking this was my cue to finally open my eyes, my heart nearly stopped beating at the sight.

I found my boyfriend — my delivery boy — Bryce Valentino on one of his knees.

This "delivery" was a small, velvet box that contained a beautiful ring sitting on top of his palm.

Taking this all in, I nearly collapsed. For a moment, I stood there, thinking this was just another dream of mine. My heart started to jump in all directions. It felt like it was going to force itself out anytime soon.

The diamond ring winked in the sunlight. My eyes slowly made their way towards my delivery boy. Bryce showcased that sweet smile I loved.

"Maisie Lockhart, will you marry me?"

My eyes blinked several times. I had to make sure this was real.

My delivery boy was proposing to me!

Feeling my mouth drop, I already knew that I was becoming excited.

"Bryce, you want me to — is this — Bryce, this is — oh my gosh, what is the matter with me?" I tried to compose myself until I exclaimed out with glee, "Yes! Yes! Of course I will!"

A wide grin grew upon Bryce's lips, and he stood up fully before taking the ring out of the box. I literally gasped, not believing this was all happening. Right now. Right here.

Gently taking my hand, Bryce slid the gorgeous ring through my ring finger. It was a perfect fit, and no words could describe how beautiful it looked. Completely overwhelmed, I was seriously fighting back the tears in my eyes — out of pure happiness. Gazing at the ring and then back at Bryce, I couldn't stop myself from smiling.

And yes, the tears streamed down my cheeks anyway.

"Daisie, try not to spill your cup of coffee on me," Bryce teased, trying to get my state of mind back to reality.

When my only response was a giggle, Bryce lightly added, "I know we're still young, and we can wait to get officially married, Maisie. But, I already know I want to be with you my whole life."

"Of course, I understand that. But Bryce, I want to be with you my whole life too," I claimed sincerely.

Bryce soon reached out to wipe the tears away from my face. Usually, I never thought this would ever happen to me. I probably sounded like those girls in the fairy tales, but this — it was much better than that.

Bryce nodded his head, pleased, as he kissed me on the forehead. "I love you."

"I love you," I returned happily.

Soon after, we shared an unforgettable kiss, knowing that we would share the rest of our lives together. As we broke away from our kiss, I immediately hugged Bryce only to be lifted up by him. He literally carried me and twirled me around. The two of us laughed together from happiness.

I shouted, almost losing grip of my cup, "Bryce! The coffee!"

Bryce shrugged before letting out a rejoice, "A little stain isn't going to hurt me. We're going to get married!"

Being in his arms, I kissed my delivery boy once more before shouting the same thing. Whatever was happening around us didn't matter right now.

At this moment, it was only Bryce and me. And, I would always treasure it.

Through the twists and turns of events that led to this day to when my delivery boy managed to take my heart away, that was what made our story. From the time Bryce would call me "Daisie" to when I would classify him as the "delivery boy", that was what made us who we are. And to the moments when our heartstrings were tugged endlessly just by being with each other, that was what made our hearts beat as one.

I was just a girl who didn't believe in "love at first sight".

I still believed it.

Because true love never happened in an instance.

It grew, just like a daisy, but eventually gave you warmth, just like a cup of hazelnut coffee.